MURDER
WEARS A
RED HAT

MARY MITCHELL SAVIDGE

PublishAmerica
Baltimore

This is a work of fiction. Names, characters, and events are products of the author's imagination. Any resemblance to actual events or persons living or dead is purely coincidental.

First printing

At the specific preference of the author, PublishAmerica allowed this work to remain exactly as the author intended, verbatim, without editorial input.

ISBN: 1-4137-8867-X
PUBLISHED BY PUBLISHAMERICA, LLLP
www.publishamerica.com
Baltimore

Printed in the United States of America

To Marjorie Phillips Mitchell
my mother
from whom I inherited the ability to write,

To Lucille Fletcher
the author of *Sorry Wrong Number*
who put pencil and paper into my nine-year-old hands
and suggested that I might like to write,

To Tom Deans
my teacher
who told me that I could write,

And to Dalton Savidge
my husband
who has always supported me in my need to write,

This book is lovingly dedicated.

Chapter One

The first thing you should know about Helen Oberheim's Red Hat Society is that it was definitely not the first Red Hat Society to be organized in Snyder County! Oh, she and her sidekick Dottie Swank may have officially registered their club and arranged for a write up, complete with a colored picture of the two of them all decked out in fancy purple clothes, wearing wide red hats, that appeared in the Community section of our local newspaper. But that was months, no at least a year, after we had started our Red Hat Society!

And so what if we didn't bother to register ours? That is supposed to be the beauty of a Red Hat Society. You don't have to officially do anything to form one, or belong to one. All you have to do is be fifty years old, or older, and wear a red hat and purple clothes when the group goes out to lunch or tea. That's why Harriet and Sybil and Jaye and, sometimes Sally, and I enjoy ours so much.

I'm Sukie Davis. My real name is Susannah, and I was named

for my great grandmother, grandmother, great aunt and several cousins, all of whom were named Susannah and called Sukie. It's a "family thing," and I'm constantly asked, by the new people I meet, about the origins of my name. As a child, I remember being thoroughly embarrassed when people asked me to explain my name. Now, I've recited it so many times I just run through the explanation as if it were a script. It has become a litany for me.

I'm wife to Preston Davis, better known as Bud, mother of two grown daughters Maggie and Anne, grandmother to four of the most bright and beautiful grandchildren ever born, and a former English teacher of many years. If my friends and I went in for that sort of thing (we definitely don't), I guess I could be considered the president of our Red Hat Society, or the Queen Mother as the president is called. I did start it, but I'm not a typical joiner. I have never been one; neither have my friends. Maybe that's one reason why we all get along so well. We don't like being tied down to prescribed meetings and behaviors.

Face it, for many years I didn't have time to do much of anything but write lesson plans, attend faculty meetings, prepare meals, wash Brownie or girls' field hockey uniforms, and attend class plays (when I wasn't directing them). My life, up until our daughters went off to college and, actually, until I retired, has always been circumscribed by family and professional boundaries.

*   *   *

Helen Oberheim, on the other hand, always relishes organizing things. She is a charter member of our Martin's Field Garden Club, and she was the one who organized the town's Civic Committee. She also spearheaded the Susquehanna Valley's Gourmet Club, which was a lot of fun. Bud and I had been members for two seasons, until it fizzled out.

Unfortunately, Martin's Field and its environs, tiny Snyder

County, located in the still basically rural center of Pennsylvania, are definitely not a hotbed of gourmets eagerly awaiting their next opportunity to sample expensive wine and food. Oh, plenty of people who live here drink, at the local Fire Company, bars and restaurants, but very few of them can tell a Pinot Noir or a Chardonnay from Chateau Screwtop wine. The locals eat, too. But more about that later.

Now, beer is another subject. Snyder County's good old boys can tell you the name of a brew by a single sniff or sip. This is considered high etiquette in some quarters, around here. And, perhaps, I am not being totally fair. The county was settled by German immigrant farmers in the latter half of the Eighteenth Century. I'm sure they brought their love of beer with them. It has certainly flourished, here, ever since.

But, to get back to our Red Hat Society and how it started. I suppose the seeds were sown years ago, before I even turned fifty, when I first read the poem "Warning" by Jenny Joseph. I'm sixty, now, and have read it many times since then. I have also had the good sense to retire from teaching, after being an English teacher in the Martin's Field High School for thirty years. But the first time I ever read the poem was when a friend of mine, also a teacher, gave me a copy of it for my birthday.

I loved the essence of the verses from the moment I read the first two lines, which warned the world that when the author grew old she would wear purple clothing and a red hat.

How delicious! The words reminded me of my own mother, recently deceased at the time I first read those lines. Mama had been a survivor. Of the Spanish Influenza in 1918, when she was a child, of drinking bathtub gin and going to speakeasies when she was a flapper, and of being the wife of a career Naval officer during WWII. She had loved the color purple and had owned a huge, red, lacquered straw hat from the 1940s, which I had worn and my daughters after me, while playing dress-up as children.

There is a picture on the bottom shelf of the bookcase in our living room, of Mama and me, taken in 1943, in the back yard of the Gemberling Building, located on Market Street, in Martin's Field. That's where Mama and I waited out WWII, while Daddy served, overseas, as gunnery officer on the battleship U.S.S. Massachusetts. In the picture I am wearing a little dress with a Peter Pan collar and my hair is all wispy. It didn't turn curly, like it is now, until I was about two and a half. Mama is kneeling beside me, in the grass, and she has on her red, lacquered straw hat and is smiling, bravely, out from under the wide brim, into the eye of someone's Kodak box camera.

Thinking of Mama, whenever I read the poem, still warms my heart and brings tears to my eyes.

Last year my friend Brenda, who is also a teacher and who lives in New Jersey, where Bud and I own a beach house, showed me a newspaper article from Southern Jersey that featured a Red Hat Society. Apparently the Societies had been proliferating in that state ever since a California woman named Sue Ellen Cooper had founded the first chapter, dedicated to middle-aged and older women having fun. I thought belonging to such a club would be great fun. And I guess that's when the idea for starting a Red Hat Society began to occur to me.

As soon as I returned from the Jersey shore I contacted my closest Martin's Field friends: Harriet Shinskie, Sybil Heim Curtis, Jaye Wolfe Harper, and Sally Mahan Thomas. All of them had been teachers, at one time or another, in the Martin's Field Area School District. When I think about it, most of my female friends, everywhere, have been teachers at one time or another. It was the most readily available vocation for college educated women of my generation. In the 1960s a bright faced young woman, clutching a college diploma in her hand, could choose teaching, nursing, secretarial work or housewifery and motherhood as her career. A lot of us chose teaching.

Sharing the same profession is what had first brought the five of us together. Sybil, Jaye, and I had known each other from our school days. Jaye and I had attended the same elementary school, and Sybil had been a year ahead of us at Martin's Field

Area High School. We'd lost track of each other when we graduated and attended different colleges, but had reunited when we began teaching in our hometown school district. This hadn't happened at exactly the same time for all of us. Sybil, Jaye and I had been involved in early, disastrous first marriages and had lived in the suburbs of large cities before we began our careers in education.

Along the way, the three of us and Sally, too, had married a second time. I guess hope and optimism spring eternally in the female breast because even after their second marriages had failed miserably my three friends continued, and continue to this day, to search for the right partner.

They've tried on-line dating, speed dating, blind dates, even hopeless flings with married men. No one's soulmate has surfaced, so far, which is both depressing and frustrating because Sybil, Jaye, and Sally are very attractive, very intelligent, very witty women. Of course, they are ladies *of a certain age* and most of the men we know are looking for younger, trophy dates. Disgusting! My guess is that many of today's men see themselves as Harrison Fords or Clint Eastwoods. Talk about having delusions!

Harriet and Sally had come to Martin's Field from more distant parts of Pennsylvania. Harriet was from Shenandoah, in the not too far away coal regions, and Sally had been part of a large Catholic family in Altoona. Harriet has never been married. She's been engaged three times but has just never made it to the altar. We may have come from different backgrounds and had different experiences, but, once we all met, in the early '70s, we discovered that we shared mutual interests, not the least of which were good food, parties, attractive men, and literature.

Once I had shown Brenda's newspaper article to them, all four of my friends thought starting a Red Hat Society would be a hoot.

"I especially like the thought of going out to lunch or tea!"

9

Harriet exclaimed when I'd finished outlining the idea. We were all sitting on my sun porch, in the still warm, late afternoon sunlight of an early September day, and we had just finished gobbling down my freshly made banana bread, in a lady-like fashion, of course. Now we were finishing up our iced tea.

Harriet is also retired from teaching, and she's getting a little chubby. I'm a tad chubby, myself, since, now that I'm home more I have time to cook Bud's favorite meals and bake cakes and pies. My cooking had been pretty much been limited to "open, heat, and serve" while I was teaching. Who had the time or energy to rush home and produce a five-course dinner, after facing down surly adolescents and trying to teach them how to write the five-paragraph composition all day? Not I! I'm making up for it now, and my waistline shows it.

Sybil and Sally left education, years ago, to pursue other careers, and Jaye is fast approaching the point of no return that teachers reach when they "burn out" but still have to put in years of service until they can qualify for retirement. She constantly has dark circles under her bright blue eyes and lines across her forehead, as Harriet and I had before we retired.

"The Victorian Lady is serving high tea next Wednesday," Sally chimed in, "I got a flyer in the mail, and the menu is to die for! What's more, I won't be leaving for Chicago until next Thursday, so I can go with you if we decide we want to start this society thing and wear red hats."

Sally works for a publishing company that sends her all over the country, selling books and programs to school districts. As a result, it is often difficult to include her in our get-togethers. It is usually even difficult to talk with her, as opposed to her answering machine, when anyone calls her.

"Let's do it!" Sybil thumped my butler's tray coffee table with her hand as she spoke. "But first we need the hats," she reminded us, and we all agreed.

So off the five of us went to search through closets at home, thrift and antique shops, and the local department stores until each of us found just the right red hat. Mama's red straw hat had fallen to pieces years ago, so I had to go fairly far afield to find my just right red hat.

After two days of searching, I finally unearthed a 1930s era red cloche that sported a huge, gold lamé bow in an antique shop two towns away from Martin's field. The bow had been perky, at one time, I was sure. But by the time I found the hat the lamé of its bow was going gray and the bow, itself, was so limp that it hung down to my neck.

After I bought it I removed the bow and refurbished my new vintage red hat with a bow I fashioned from red tulle. It cost substantially more than I had planned to pay, but I fell totally in love with it the minute I saw it!

I also found, in one of the many catalogues I receive weekly in the mail, purple t-shirts that were perfect for us to wear to tea. The shirts had been created obviously with Red Hat Society members in mind and sported the logo of a wide brimmed red hat.

I picked up the phone and ordered five of them the minute I saw them, paying the extra postage to have them "delivered within three working days."

"They're adorable, but how are we going to wear them to high tea at a classy restaurant like The Victorian Lady without looking absurd?" asked Sybil, the most fashion conscious of us, once she'd seen the shirts. "Our hats are dressy. Hell, just wearing hats in this day and age is a fashion statement! There's no way the shirts are going to look right."

We were gathered on my sun porch, again, in the late afternoon, this time nibbling brownies made from my Aunt Abigail's family recipe, and exhibiting our red hats. Sybil had found what my mother and aunts had always referred to as a *whimsy* from the 1960s. It consisted of a wreath of tiny red flowers that had once perched proudly atop a beehive hairdo, and was surrounded with a once stiff red veil. Harriet had contacted her mother, made a quick trip home, and now possessed a wide-brimmed red felt hat that sported a huge rhinestone pin. It was also from the '60s.

Jaye had purchased her hat from the Boscov's Department Store in the local mall; one of the few stores left in our area that still sells hats. It was a red straw pillbox with a jaunty spray of cherries on one side that bobbled when she turned her head. Sally's hat made us all laugh, which didn't seem to bother her in the least. It was tall, made of what appeared to be red taffeta draped over a hat form that was almost cone-shaped. It had a tiny brim, into which was tucked a huge, sweeping black feather, and it was the most unusual hat I'd ever seen, outside of the 1940s movie version of "The Women."

"You look like that character in the children's book The *Something-or-other Number of Hats of Bartholomew Cubbins*! You know. The one by Dr. Suess," I'd laughed so hard as I told her this that I almost choked on a brownie crumb. The old habit teachers and former teachers have of fortifying themselves with goodies, in the late afternoon, dies hard, believe me.

The Bartholomew Cubbins book had been a favorite of mine when I attended elementary school, and I had bought and read the book to my children and grandchildren numerous times as they were growing up. Sally's hat did, indeed, resemble the hats featured in Dr.Seuss' book.

"If the crown wasn't so high and it were green instead of red, you'd sort of look like Robin Hood," Harriet added, absentmindedly fingering the huge, flashy pin on her own hat as she spoke. "Every time I put my hat on I feel like Lillian Russell, wearing a gift given to me by Diamond Jim Brady."

"You wish!" Jaye crowed. "Hey, we could all use a Diamond Jim right about now. All except Sukie, of course. Bud is a Diamond Jim in the Rough."

I smiled a little as Jaye spoke. I'm the only one of my friends whose second marriage is intact. Heck, I'm the only one of the group who is married, period, and I am married to a very understanding, very generous man who just happens to be nine years younger than I am. When Bud and I met, dated, and married, in the early Seventies, our relationship had been somewhat of a scandal in Martin's Field.

Today, after twenty-nine years, we are still married and still happy. When we *plighted our troth*, in June of 1972, everyone, except our good friends, had given our chances of making our marriage work six months, at the most. Funny how all the *nay sayers* have long forgotten the discrepancy in our ages. Small towns work that way. What someone does is big news for a day, maybe a week, and then interest shifts to what someone else has done more recently. I guess it is how we locals keep ourselves amused, since Martin's Field has so little in the way of social life or distractions.

The only movie theater the town had enjoyed shut down twenty-five years ago. Even the farmers don't come into town on Saturday nights to sell their produce and shop as they had when I was a girl. The downtown district of Martin's Field keeps shrinking as the years go by. Solid family stores like the hardware and dry goods stores, the A& P and drug store have been replaced by gift shops and up-scale furniture stores. These are frequented by travelers driving through town as much as they are by the locals.

Sally said nothing. She was conspicuously quiet. She has a live-in boyfriend, Rodney, who is an enigma to the rest of us. He seems to have come out of nowhere, to have no past, no visible means of support, and he doesn't fit in with our group, in any way. Bud, who is always kind to a fault and gives everyone the benefit of the doubt, summed Rodney up in a terse comment, after we had left a dinner party Sally had thrown at the beginning of the summer.

"I suspect he's a burned out hippie."

I shared Bud's summing up of Rodney with my other Red Hat friends, all except Sally, of course. None of us wants to hurt her feelings by making unkind comments about the first boyfriend she's had, in years who has lasted for more than six months. We all agree, however, that Rodney, with his short bleached hair, red and blue star tattoo on the back of his neck, and rambling attempts at conversation, fits the burned out former hippie profile. But he makes Sally happy, and that is all that is important. None of us has to live with him and his eccentricities.

I turned the conversation back to the matter at hand and away from men, which is where most of my friends' conversations usually meander, by suggesting, "Let's wear red turtlenecks under the t-shirts. It will make them look more elegant."

This answered Sybil's question concerning the propriety of our wearing the purple t-shirts. I'm usually good at solving my own fashion problems by dressing in layers. As the old saying goes, it *covers a multitude of sins* caused by my love of food. Heck, we all love food. But, somehow, Jaye, Sally and Sybil manage to stay slim. Sometimes I just hate their metabolisms. Never them. Just their damned metabolisms. I think I was born without one!

"Makes sense to me," Sybil agreed. "I have a turtleneck just the right shade of red to match my hat."

"Don't we look great?" Jaye exulted as we all sat around evaluating each other's choices in chapeaux. "I haven't worn a hat in years!"

"Good Lord! I look exactly like my mother getting ready to leave for eleven o'clock mass," Sally moaned. She had risen and was gazing into a mirror that hung on the sun porch wall.

I'd already made a reservation for high tea, at 4:30 P.M. the following Wednesday, at our favorite, extremely upscale for our area, restaurant The Victorian Lady, run by our friends Phil and Mary Gajda. The Victorian Lady is located in Lewisburg, about twelve miles north of here. Such an establishment would never flourish in Martin's Field where most diners rate the excellence of their meals by the quantity of food served on their plates, not the quality of the food. Covering the huge portions of meat or potatoes served in any Martin's Field restaurant with one of the yummy sauces Phil uses in his cuisine would be considered high treason! Sybil refers to most of our local restaurants as "The Scoop and Shovels."

Phil Gajda is a master chef, a graduate of the Culinary Institute of America. Every dish he prepares is a gastronome's delight. When Bud and I go to dinner at the Victorian Lady we always enjoy poring over the menu to see what new dishes Phil has prepared, even though Bud always orders the beef tournedos or a similar beef dish. He is so predictable, and we go there so often, that the waitresses, all of whom we know by name, usually just ask him what appetizer and drink he wants to order. If I were wealthy, and money was no object, and if Bud didn't dote on my roast chicken dinners and blueberry pie, I'd hire Phil as our personal chef. What heaven to have him cook all our meals!

And so, on Wednesday, we all put on slacks, wore red turtlenecks under our purple shirts, donned our red hats and ventured forth to the first meeting of the, to our knowledge, only Red Hat Society in Snyder County. Believe me, the last thing on any of our minds was registering the club, initiating members, or pledging a ritual. WE were ready to eat!

Upon reaching the restaurant we kissed Mary Gajda, who was acting as hostess, on her beautiful pink cheek, sat down at our table and immersed ourselves in yummy finger sandwiches, scones and cup upon cup of delicious tea! All of us gossiped and laughed in the pure joy of being in each other's company. What an auspicious first meeting of the society we had formed to celebrate ourselves…vibrant, fun-loving, middle aged women.

And how we laughed and scoffed at the other Red Hat Society when we read about it, months later, in the paper. By that time we'd worn our hats and purple shirts and been to tea and lunch a half dozen times. And we felt that only we knew what a Red Hat Society was supposed to be about. I remember saying to myself, "What nonsense, Helen Oberheim, you arriviste (remember, I'd been an English teacher with a penchant for vocabulary study). You and your members with your formal pledge taken by everyone and your junior satellite club of members younger than fifty who have to wear lavender clothing and pink hats! What complete nonsense!"

How ridiculous and uptight that other Red Hat Society seemed to us.

Little did we know what truly ridiculous scenarios were about to present themselves to two of us, and how thankful we'd soon be for one of those other, properly registered, Red Hat Societies located in a totally different part of the country.

Chapter Two

If you live in Central Pennsylvania and are male, even if you are not an alumnus of the University, Penn State Football Season is a sacred, almost mystical time of year for you. A time of rising early on Saturday mornings in the extreme heat of early September, or the clear, invigorating chill of October, or the bone rattling cold of November. A time of packing the car or van or truck, in a prescribed, almost ritualistic manner, with articles of food and clothing appropriate to the mystical, solemn yet electrically charged and greatly anticipated event about to take place. The devotion to and importance of a home Penn State football game is handed down from father to son, father to son, for generations.

The same devotion to Penn State football can be observed in the wives and girl friends of the Central Pennsylvania males, although for them it is probably an acquired taste. For each of them, as it was for me, this taste was probably acquired over the space of some time, years, in fact. Years during which they have attended the games with their men and prepared the tailgate feasts for them and their friends that are traditionally held before each game. In the beginning each woman probably saw the tailgate preparation and execution as her main function at a game. Then, suddenly, one day she discovered that she knew all the players' names and their positions. She discovered that she knew the meaning of the *yellow hankies* that the officials threw on the field. If she was like me, she experienced a sports epiphany and was ushered into the mystical realm where her husband or boyfriend already dwelt on game day!

Partying in the parking lots that surround Beaver Stadium is a big part of Penn State football game tradition. So is the consumption of thermoses of Bloody Marys, cases of beer, dozens of sandwiches, bags of potato chips and pans of brownies that are set out upon portable picnic tables. These tables are set up behind the tailgates of station wagons and vans or the beds of trucks parked side by side in narrow spaces marked with numbers, for season ticket holders, or in fields of lush green grass, for those who attend only occasionally. Some fans arrive in huge RV's, haul out gas grills and prepare delicious smelling meals made up of many courses. Others pull up in tiny sports cars and bring out large paper tubs of commercially prepared fried chicken. In most cases, however, every vehicle, no matter what its size, is decorated with huge blue and white paw prints, Penn State Lion logos, and even various stuffed Nittany (read mountain) lions, in honor of the team's mascot.

For the space of an afternoon, a new community is created among the closely parked vehicles. Fans who never met before share food, stories of the glories experienced at past games, and the hopes of bowl games to come. Small shrieking children race about with tiny blue and white paw prints painted on their cheeks. Older children toss footballs to each other in hastily organized games. No one pays much attention to where the balls land. Between the vans, in someone's potato salad, against the metal doors of the Port-a-Potties. Camaraderie is King, and everyone asks, "If God didn't love Penn State why did he make the sky blue and white?"

Bud and I have had season tickets for the home Penn State games since 1980 when Maggie matriculated there as a freshman. During her senior year in high school we had all held our breaths. Maggie, usually so level headed, so reasonable, had tossed reason out the window and applied to Penn State and Penn State, only. She'd ignored the pleas of her parents, teachers, and guidance counselors to apply, also, to back-up colleges and universities, on the off chance that she would not be accepted at her one and only choice of schools. I, myself, was amazed by her actions. I'd never imagined that Maggie would be happy at a large university. All through high school she'd been *a big fish in a little pond*.

Our firstborn daughter (the first thing Bud had done when he and I married was to adopt Maggie and Anne, ten and seven at the time, children of my first, disastrous marriage) had upped the stakes even more by insisting that she attend Penn State's Main Campus for all four years of her post high school education. In the '80s this was somewhat of an anomaly. Most students attended a Commonwealth Campus of the University for their first two years and transferred to the Main Campus in State College, Pennsylvania for their junior and senior years. Not Maggie. For her it was all four years on Main Campus, or nothing.

All arguments with her, to the contrary, fell upon deaf ears.

"Penn State has exactly what I want," she had told Bud and me. "They offer a degree in Communications that is all laid out. You know exactly what courses to take. Every other school I've looked at says 'make up your own schedule of courses for Communication. Choose what you think you need.' I don't like that. I don't trust it!"

I could see her point. I understood that Maggie was being driven by the need she'd always had for security. Penn State's well-organized Communication Course offered her that security.

So Maggie applied solely to Penn State with a preference for Main campus duly noted on her application. She was in the top ten percent of her high school graduating class, a class officer, editor and chief of the yearbook, secretary of the band, a member of The National Honor Society, and she had taken all the Advanced Placement English classes that our high school offered. But, supposedly, this would not help her much. We had been told that Penn State processed applicants solely by computer. There wasn't even any personal interview. With 35,000 students how could there be? The University relied heavily upon SAT scores. Maggie's scores had been respectable but not outstanding. We all sat back and waited. I crossed my fingers and prayed ardently, every night.

In January the confirmation came. Maggie and all her friends who had applied to Penn State received their envelopes on the same day. I, who hadn't slept in weeks, and had suffered indigestion intense enough to fell a rhinoceros, waited with baited breath as she opened her letter.

"I'm in!" she screamed and threw her arms around my neck, "I'm in and on Main Campus, too!"

We danced around the kitchen laughing and, on my part, crying in happiness and relief. All my painful doubts about her going to Penn State melted away. She'd taken a gigantic risk, for the first time in her very careful life, and it had paid off.

Anne, when she came home from Girls' Basketball practice, was impressed, as only a younger sister who considers herself a jock can be. "Way to go!" she exclaimed, "They have great sports facilities. I've only seen the hockey and softball fields, but they rock!"

Bud, of course, was quietly ecstatic, when he heard the news upon arriving home from work. Never a man to give himself over to a great show of any emotion, he held Maggie tightly for a moment and congratulated her. Only I could tell by the way his eyes shone just how happy and relieved he was that she had been accepted to his favorite school.

Turning from the women in his life, gathered in the kitchen, he whipped a piece of blue paper out of his briefcase and asked, "Do you know what this is? I've had it for months. Ever since you applied to Penn State, Maggie."

We all looked at his beaming face, waiting expectantly.

"It's a form to apply for Penn State season tickets. Football!" His voice was jubilant as he waved the blue paper in our faces. "This way your mother won't get too homesick for you. We can see you when we come up to the games," he quickly justified.

I smiled. I'd known that Bud wanted season tickets for the home Penn State games for years. Ever since we'd met we had attended one or two games a year. We'd watched the south end zone of Beaver Stadium change from a completely open space with a gorgeous view of the mountains surrounding State College, to an area filled with aluminum bleachers, to a built in student section.

Little did we know, on that January day, that in the years to come we would see Penn State drop the teams it traditionally played as an Independent and join The Big Ten. We would see the entire stadium raised by twenty-five rows of seats, or more. We would behold, in awe, two end sections arise over our heads, like the decks of giant aircraft carriers, raising Beaver Stadium's capacity to well over a hundred thousand spectators. A new era in our lives had begun. Maggie's four years at Penn State Main Campus and our lifetime of Penn State football.

"Let's all go to the Penn State/Northwestern game next Saturday and make a gourmet tailgate to have before the game," I suggested to The Red Hat Society, as we sat before a roaring fire at Sybil's house.

It was the third week of September and the weather had turned unseasonably cold. In our part of the state we can usually count on temperatures in the 70s or high 60s well into the middle of October. This year, for some unknown El Nino or La Nina reason, overnight the temperature had sunk into the low 50s

21

and a chill wind had blown for several days. Not our usual September weather at all.

"Too cold!" Jaye objected clutching her mug of extra rich hot chocolate finished off with a dab of Ameretto flavored whipped cream on the top. We were all indulging, trying to chase away the chill of the afternoon.

"It is supposed to be in the high 60s, maybe even seventy, by Saturday. Bud can easily get all the tickets we need, and Penn State is favored to beat Northwestern by ten points," I quickly rattled off in defense of my plan. "Besides, think of the fun it would be to eat really great food and, for you guys, to check out all the cute men tailgating around us."

"Umm, count me out," Sally wiped whipped cream off her upper lip, as she spoke, and burrowed down even further into the pile of pillows upon which she and Harriet reclined. "Rod and I are spending the weekend at Eagles Mere. We're staying at the Lodge overlooking the lake. Tres romantic!"

In response to this news, the rest of us all gave each other a look that clearly read, "And you're paying the bill." In the time that we had known him, Rodney had never held a job that any of us knew about. He seemed to enjoy playing the role of "house boyfriend" while Sally worked hard and made good money to support both of them. While there was nothing wrong with this arrangement, as long as Sally didn't mind it, the rest of us, her friends, worried that Rodney was taking advantage of her.

"I don't have any plans," Sybil spoke up quickly to cover the momentary silence brought on by Sally's announcement. "I agree with Sukie. It's high time The Red Hats dined al fresco. I'd love to go. Who knows, I might even watch the game!"

Sybil had been a cheerleader in high school, so she really might understand the game better than the rest of us. She might even have real interest in it; she'd watched enough football in her younger years. At least she was showing some enthusiasm for my idea.

"How late will be get back?" Harriet asked. "I have to drive to

Shenandoah to take Mom and Aunt Maddy to church on Sunday morning."

Retired, Harriet lived alone, except for her beloved cat Fred, but she drove the twenty-five miles to the coal regions, where most of her family lived, to take her mother and assorted aunts to mass every Sunday. They were all in their eighties, lived alone, also, and Harriet felt responsible for them. Perhaps this feeling of responsibility was an underlying reason why she had been engaged three times but had never married. If it was, I doubt that Harriet was even aware of it. And if she was, she certainly never talked about it.

"It's a twelve thirty kickoff so we'll have you home by five that evening," I reassured her.

"Okay, if it's going to warm up," Jaye relented. "What should we make for the tailgate? And I certainly hope you don't think for a minute that we're going to wear our purple shirts and red hats to the game!"

"No, no, no," I assured them. "This is not a formal meeting of the Red Hats, not that we're very formal to start with. You know everyone wears blue and white to a Penn State game. This is just a chance to have fun."

"And eat!" Harriet added gleefully.

Everyone thought, quietly, and drank hot chocolate for a minute.

"I'll make my spinach balls and mushroom puffs for appetizers," Jaye offered. She reached for the chocolate pot and refilled her mug, as she spoke. "I'll bake them right before we leave, and they should stay hot in my Pyrex carrier until we get to the game."

"And I'll make Chicken Parisienne for the main dish, since it was my idea," I added.

"I'll take care of dessert," Sybil mused. "Do we want chocolate cheesecake or Black Forest cake?" She was our pastry expert.

"Chocolate cheesecake!" we all shouted together. It was her

specialty.

"With lots of whipped cream," Harriet added, "And since I don't cook I'll bring rolls and butter and mints and anything else we need."

"Well, you know I never unpack the picnic basket during Penn State season so we have plenty of plates and silverware and cups. And Bud will make his famous Bloody Marys. So, I guess we just need a couple bottles of wine, and some soda, and we're all set," I leaned back and smiled at the prospect of the good food and drink that would be spread out on our folding picnic table.

We'd be sitting under the little maple tree that grew beside our numbered parking place, in the South End Zone parking lot at Beaver Stadium. It promised to be a very good Saturday, especially if the temperature rose and the sun shone in a blue sky, as it had on so many football Saturdays in the past.

"We're taking who to the Northwestern game!" Bud queried when I filled him in on our plans, that evening at dinner. I'd been very careful to prepare a meal of fried chicken from my own closely guarded recipe (I'd shared it with Maggie and Anne, but they're family so that doesn't count). Anytime I have news that could be upsetting in any way to my husband I make it a rule to pave the way with one of his favorite meals, especially one that features chicken. His meat of choice.

After twenty-nine years, I often joke with friends and new acquaintances that I don't have a marriage I have *Let's Make A Deal*. I express a wish, like could Bud please clean out the garage, or there is a gorgeous gold bracelet in the Ross Simon catalogue that I'd love to have for Christmas and Bud will good naturedly respond, "How many chickens is it worth?"

This means how many chicken dinners, usually roasted with all the trimmings or deep fried, am I willing to trade for whatever it is that I want. It may sound strange but I think every married (read long married) couple has its own bartering system, whether it is voiced aloud or tacitly understood. Bud's and mine just happens to be chickens.

My friends have learned about this, over the years, of course. Sometimes, when we are out shopping and I linger in front of the window of a jewelry store or remark about a cruise advertised at the travel agency at the mall they will laugh and ask, "How many chickens will that cost?"

It may sound strange, but it works for my husband and me. Bud and I banter back and forth, usually laughing, until we reach a quota of chicken dinners that we both know I couldn't possibly prepare and Bud couldn't eat in ten years or more. Then, in due time, I receive whatever it is I have requested, and I prepare chicken dinners until Bud "cries uncle" and requests beef or pork, for a while.

I have found, over the years, however, that it doesn't hurt to ease into a sticky situation or speed a process along by preparing the chicken dinner first and then making the request.

"The Red Hats, Darling," I replied smiling brightly, "You know. Jaye and Sybil and Harriet. Sally can't go. She and Rod are spending the weekend at Eagles Mere."

"Huh!" my husband retorted in disgust. I couldn't tell whether he was responding to my news about Sally and Rod, for whom he had little respect, or the thought of taking four women to one of his precious Penn State games. Bud takes his football very, very seriously.

However, not wanting to make things more difficult, in case they were going to become so, nor go on the defensive, when I might not have to, I smiled brightly, again, served Bud another crisp brown drumstick, and answered, "The girls are just going to love the tailgate and the game. You'll be their hero for taking them, and everyone is going to bring food. I'm making the chicken with artichokes that you like, and Sybil is baking a chocolate cheesecake." I thought it best to leave out Jaye's spinach balls and mushroom puffs since Bud, like most men, isn't particularly into appetizers.

"Think of poor Sally stuck at Eagles Mere with Rod, when she could be at Penn State, with us, "I wheedled, adding a big helping of scalloped potatoes and another drumstick to Bud's plate.

"You know she'll have a ball," Bud replied dryly. He's known my friends for many years and, although he is cordial to them for my sake and because he genuinely likes most of them, he has few illusions about any of them. "She's always in hog heaven when there is a man involved."

I made no protest about his summation of Sally's character. He was right. She does seem to need a man in her life to make her happy. Whereas my other single friends have weathered a marriage or two and come out declaring they would never marry or live with a man again, Sally leaps at every opportunity to have a meaningful relationship with a member of the opposite sex. The problem is that very few of her relationships turn out to be meaningful. In the past, some of them have warranted Bud's scorn. Even the Red Hats, her best friends, have had to admit they've been doozies. Somehow, however, I think this relationship of hers with Rod just might be the right one. He certainly seems to idolize her, and has never shown anything but kindness to the rest of us.

Saturday dawned clear and warm. The sun shone in a cerulean sky.

Bud and I were up by seven, dressed in our "lucky" blue slacks and white shirts bearing Penn State logos. We had our part of the tailgate efficiently packed into our Dodge Caravan. My Chicken Parisienne casserole, succulent pieces of chicken breast swimming in a cream sauce redolent of leeks and artichoke hearts, was carefully resting in the carrier that held a heatpack, which had been microwaved ahead of time to keep it hot. The rest of our provisions consisted of three bottles of Chardonnay chilling in the ice chest, a gallon thermos jug of Bloody Marys and one of ice water, a dozen chilled bottles of cola, my grandmother's roomy old market basket filled to overflowing with paper plates, plastic glasses and silverware, and a bag of Milky Way candy bars, which Bud loves, thrown in for good measure.

There is no on-street parking on La Dawn Lane where we live (it's a very narrow, dead end street leading, at the end, to the community swimming pool) and our ninety degree angle driveway is not conducive to parking. So we'd agreed ahead of time that Bud and I would pick up the rest of the group that morning. Backing out of the driveway we made the rounds and picked up the Red Hats, as we had begun to refer to ourselves. First, we stopped at Jaye's apartment near the high school, added her spinach balls and mushroom puffs in their heated casserole container, and helped her take her seat in our van.

Next, we turned onto one of the older streets of Martin's Field, where Sybil lives in the house that has been in her family for at least three generations. She was ready and waiting on the porch, and Bud lovingly received the high domed cake carrier containing her chocolate cheesecake that she handed to him. She took her place next to Jaye, and Bud secured the cheesecake next to the picnic basket.

Harriet was the last of the Red Hats to join us. She lives in a very small house about a mile outside of Martin's Field, in what must have started out to be a development of single family homes. The builder had run out of money after constructing just three small houses, and Harriet was able to buy one of them for a song. She and her bag of rolls, mints and potato chips were quickly stowed in the back of the Caravan, and we were on our way.

The fastest way to get to State College from Martin's Field is to drive "up the hill and down the hill until you get to Kratzerville" as the old rhyme in our county goes. By the time one has recited the rhyme, however, one has passed through Kratzerville, which consists of about two dozen houses and a general store.

From there the road twists and turns until the traveler reaches a scene reminiscent of all the serene and lovely English villages ever seen, up close and personal or on a PBS travel documentary. At New Berlin, a hamlet just a little larger than Kratzerville, a high bridge crosses a low creek with verdant banks. Here weeping willow trees trail their branches in the water and flocks of birds gather in all seasons. Weathered brick buildings with white cupolas can be seen farther up the northern bank and houses dating back to the early 1800s nestle between the brightly painted Victorian homes, not very British village looking but charming, nevertheless, that line the wide main street.

The Penn State bound caravan of vehicles begins in earnest at Mifflinburg where we pick up Route 45, sometimes known as the Purple Heart Highway. Traffic on a home Penn State game Saturday is usually bumper to bumper on this two-lane road. Today was no different from any other game day.

We progressed, sometimes slowly, sometimes at a more rapid pace, if Bud was able to pass the cars ahead of us without eliciting too many screams of terror from the women in his van. Some of these were mock protests. All the Red Hats know that Bud is a safe, if somewhat fast, driver. However, some of our passengers really do cling to the arms of their seats, their eyes large with fear. I, of course, am used to Bud's driving, even though I have seen him reduce full-grown men in the back seats to mounds of quaking jelly when he decides it is time to pass the car ahead of him on Route 45 on a jammed-up game day.

After a drive of a little over an hour, through the ever rising terrain of some of the last Pennsylvania countryside still dotted with small dairy farms, we reached the summit of the trip at Hairy John's State Park (named for a real mountain man who once inhabited that prime wooded hunting area). Our ears were popping all the way up the mountain so I began tapping the cooler of Bloody Marys at my feet and handing plastic glasses of Bud's famous drink over my shoulder to my friends. We crawled past serene Woodward, inched our way through the traffic jam at Milheim, and before too long turned onto the State

College bypass. This fast moving four-lane highway whisked us past the tiny hamlets of Oak Hall and Lemont, until we could see Beaver Stadium rising before us in the distance.

This was a good thing. My friends had run out of old college drinking songs and gossip by the time we passed all the fans parking in the fields surrounding the stadium and pulled into our own numbered parking place in one of the macadam lots surrounding the huge edifice. We tumbled out of the van, eager to stretch our legs, set up the tailgate, start eating and continue drinking.

It was a gorgeous day. Not too warm, not too cool. The sky was blue; the sun shone optimistically. Bud roamed from tailgate to tailgate greeting old friends and colleagues, sharing a beer, discussing players' injuries. My friends and I lolled in the folding directors' chairs that Bud and I always took to the games. We filled our Penn State Blue paper and plastic plates time and time again from the delicacies spread out upon our folding picnic table. Drank the rest of Bud's excellent Bloody Marys and opened the chilled wine.

"This is heaven!" Harriet sighed as she reached for yet another spinach ball. She and the rest of the Red Hats were letting their eyes wander over the assortment of male fans dressed in blue and white, who strolled past our parking spot. Sometimes the women's eyes met as they shook their heads positively. More often than not, maybe as a result of the wine and Bloody Marys they'd consumed, they giggled like teenagers and rolled their eyes in amusement at the sight of grown men wearing hats shaped like mountain lions or shirts bearing risqué slogans.

I sighed too. It was such a mellow day. I was in the bosom of my best friends, eating scrumptious food under a perfect canopy of blue. What could be better? What could dare to spoil things?

I never should have asked. I never should have tempted fate.

Chapter Three

When the envelope arrived in the mail, on a Monday morning in October, I barely glanced at it. Bud and I received so much junk mail, especially I, that my first impulse was to toss it into the kitchen trash. Besides, I was in a hurry to leave the house and join Harriet for an Early Bird sale at the mall.

I continued hastily sorting the large pile of envelopes and catalogues that I had just brought into the kitchen from the mailbox at the foot of our property. That day there was so much mail that it had been bound together by a rubber band. Monday was always a big catalogue day, and all of them were mine, so they went into my pile on the kitchen table. I relegated the ubiquitous envelope to the bottom of the unsorted mail.

Most of the bills, except for those generated by my charge cards, went into Bud's pile. His pile also received the brochures from golf resorts, notices of local blood drives, the agenda for the next school board meeting, and the Moose and Elk magazines.

There were notices of sales at Boscov's and The Bon Ton. They both contained coupons, and since I was already on my way to shop with Harriet, I could take advantage of saving more money at both stores. I quickly slapped them onto my pile.

People magazine was late, again, arriving on Monday instead of Saturday, and I snatched it up because I actually recognized the actress on the cover. She was older than was the Hollywood starlet of sixteen or seventeen who usually graced the magazine's cover and, despite plastic surgery and liposuction, her face had vastly more character than those other actresses' faces, and she was carrying a few extra pounds. The article about her promised a more interesting than usual read.

When I saw the envelope for the second time it really almost joined the unsolicited credit card offers and advertisements for space in frozen food lockers that I routinely toss into the trash. It was addressed to Mrs. Susannah H. Davis, which is not my legal name and it was, therefore, a giveaway, I figured, that it was junk mail. Then, I read the return address and logo neatly printed in green ink onto the upper left-hand corner:

Office of the Tribunal
Archdiocese of Harrisburg
1034 Limestone Pike
Harrisburg, PA 17100.

What on earth? Seeing the envelope took me suddenly back to the days, more than thirty years ago, when I'd been married, unhappily, to my first husband and living in a suburb of Philadelphia. I had converted to Catholicism several months into the marriage, when I was pregnant with our first child Maggie. Years later, after the birth of Anne, we lived on the street behind Our Lady of Sorrows Catholic Church in Strafford, to which we belonged. In those days I was a stay-at-home mother, as were all the women of my age who I knew, and I seemed to always be collecting for Catholic Charities, or a church fundraiser of some sort. Each time I ended up collecting the request for me to do so had arrived in an envelope similar to the one I held in my hands.

If that's what this was, a plea for me to collect money for the Catholic Church, again, boy, did they have the wrong person! My first marriage, to Larry O'Brian, had been the result of a whirlwind summer romance at the New Jersey Shore, where he'd been a lifeguard and I'd been a waitress. The romance should have ended in September, when he returned to St. Stephen's College and I to Bucknell University. Unfortunately, at ages twenty and twenty-one we'd been sure that we were truly in love, and we'd eloped that November.

Our marriage in a Lutheran parsonage in Frederick, MD was quickly followed by Larry's being excommunicated from the Catholic Church and expelled from his Catholic college. Both his parents and my mother had been furious with us, but made the best of our foolish choice. The O'Brians had insisted that we remarry in the Catholic Church, and we had complied. The Catholic Church had been mollified and Larry was able to go back to school. I'd finished the first semester of my junior year at Bucknell and then joined Larry, in Hampton, PA while he finished his senior year.

At the time, I'd felt wrapped in a warm cocoon of first love. Why did I need to worry about finishing my college education? I'd found the man of my dreams, or so I thought at the time. He would protect me and support me, always. He said so. No wife of his would ever have to work, Larry had often bragged.

Foolish, overly romantic me! I soon discovered, first hand, that the only way one truly learns anything is the hard way. And my way with Larry was destined to be very hard, indeed.

I didn't even want to think about the unhappy seven years that had followed that rash elopement! The births of Maggie and Anne were the only positive things I could claim from that first, miserable marriage. Larry O'Brian had cheated on me with every woman he'd met during the time we were married. As a husband, he had humiliated me beyond any wife's endurance. He'd broken my heart but I had stayed in the marriage, telling myself that I was doing it for my children. I didn't want Maggie and Anne to grow up without their father. However, when he refused to hold a job or support his family in any way, I was forced to face the fact that if the girls were to have any kind of normal life, with the hope of things such as orthodontia and a college education in the future, I'd have to leave Larry and find a way to provide those things on my own.

I'd called my mother, who was a widow, and begged her to allow me to come home, bringing the girls with me. Then I borrowed money from the local bank and finished the last two years of my college degree in English at Martin University located at the edge of town. I'd met Bud, who was a year behind me there, in the process.

And, now, the Catholic Church was sending me a letter asking for my services? Didn't they know that the first thing I'd done when I left Larry and moved back to Martin's Field was to renew my membership in the Lutheran Church and bring up my daughters as Lutherans? Apparently not.

I tore open the envelope and pulled out the letter it contained, ready to have a good laugh at the expense of the ignorance displayed by the Catholic Church. Instead, what I read made me sick in my stomach and forced me to sit down on the kitchen chair closest to me.

The letterhead on the heavy bond paper bore the same shield and crown logo as had the envelope and the words THE TRIBUNAL, DIOCESE OF HARRISBURG in huge, what seemed to me, mile high, green letters. The ominous look of the letterhead and the weight of the words it bore made me gasp for breath. I felt as if all the air was being sucked out of my lungs. I dropped the letter on the table.

Scenes of the Spanish Inquisition from long ago read history books flashed in front of my eyes. I felt the unsettling pangs of fear a child experiences when called to the principal's office, indeed the same fear a teacher often feels, even if unfounded, when so summoned.

My stomach grew increasingly queasy, and I began to perspire. This was no mistaken plea for my help in collecting money for The Catholic Church. This was something more serious and far, far more threatening.

When I could breathe again, and my head had cleared a bit, I picked up the letter and forced myself to read further.

O'BRIAN-PURCELL 201-43
(Archdiocese of Charleston)
October 2, 2001
MRS SUSANNAH H. DAVIS
10 LA DAWN LANE
MARTIN'S FIELD PA 17301

Dear MRS DAVIS:

The Tribunal of the Roman Catholic Archdiocese of Charleston has been asked by Lawrence J. O'Brian to consider the possible ecclesiastical nullity of your marriage to him. Chiefly, these reasons focus on the intentions and the freedom of the parties at the time of the marriage, their attitudes toward marriage, and psychological factors such as maturity; judgement and personality traits which could have affected the ability to form a stable and permanent relationship.

I stopped reading closely after the first two sentences of the first paragraph, and skimmed the rest of the letter. It was difficult to comprehend the entire meaning of this ecclesiastic-babble. However, there were sentences in the next three paragraphs that jumped out at me.

A "declaration of nullity" means that a former union cannot be considered valid and binding in accord with the teachings of the Gospel and of the Church: therefore, it is not an obstacle to either party's marrying in the Catholic Church at this time.

Since you reside outside the Archdiocese of Charleston and the marriage did not take place there, church law directs that a case such as this be considered by the Tribunal of the place where you live. The Tribunal of the Diocese whereby Lawrence J. O'Brian lives may also consider the case with the permission of the Tribunal of your diocese.

If I do not hear from you within two weeks of the date of this letter, it will be presumed that you do not object to the case being considered by the Archdiocese of Charleston.

Sincerely yours,

Rev. Xavier R. Bednardcek J.C.L.

Rev. Xaviar R. Bednardcek J.C.L.
Adjutant Judicial Vicar

There was an additional sheet of paper included in the envelope. It bore the name of the Secretary to the Tribunal of the Archdiocese of Harrisburg and a telephone number at which she could be reached. It also stated that if the respondent (which I assumed was Mrs. Susannah Davis) chose to contest the granting of an annulment, he/she had to appear in person before the Tribunal, and the amount of distance that needed to be traveled was not an acceptable excuse for not appearing. Also it noted that contesting an annulment could cost from $500.00 to $2,000.00.

Oh, it was all very cut and dry. Never mind the threats it implied. I began to feel even queasier than before.

Good God! Realization began to set in. This letter was a document from Larry, via the church, requesting an annulment of our second marriage, which had taken place in a small Catholic Church in Northumberland, PA, across the Susquehanna River from Martin's Field. The marriage had taken place forty years ago and the church was no longer in existence! It had been consolidated with another small Catholic Church several years ago when congregations shrank, the number of priests to serve parishes had dwindled, and it had no longer been economically prudent for the Archdiocese to maintain small churches.

For heaven's sake, the marriage was no longer in existence! Larry and I had been divorced a year after I'd returned home. A small smile attempted to curl about my lips. This request for an annulment was so ridiculous, so silly, So Larry! Again, I was tempted to toss the letter in the trash and simply ignore the situation. But, unbidden, old memories began to surface.

Larry had driven to Las Vegas, almost a year after I'd left him, and obtained a Nevada divorce. At that time, he and the girlfriend who would become the second Mrs. O'Brian were living over a drycleaner's shop in Center City Philadelphia.

He and I had lost the house in Rosemont where we'd lived with the girls for three years. We'd purchased it, using as a down payment the small inheritance I'd received from my grandmother when I turned twenty-one. The small, two story colonial had been situated in a lovely neighborhood of young married couples, and the girls had enjoyed the companionship of built-in playmates their ages. All the young families had similar backgrounds and about the same amount of income. I'd quickly bonded with the other wives and we'd held children's birthday parties in our back yards and taken turns hosting frugal dinner parties on Saturday nights. We'd become an extended family for each other, offering child care services, showers for expected new babies, casseroles and sympathy in times of trouble.

By the time we lost the house, there'd been a lien on it due to long-accumulated, unpaid bills. Larry had proved to be a compulsive gambler and an alcoholic, who squandered his bi-weekly paycheck before he ever reached home. My heart was broken when we'd had to sell the house to satisfy our debts. I'd cried my eyes dry as I bid farewell to the women who had been like my sisters and the cozy house where I'd nested with my daughters. This had happened about a year before I'd left Larry and returned to Martin's Field.

Larry didn't want to be married to me or to take responsibility for supporting Maggie and Anne. At the same time, I don't think he could believe that I had left him. In a grand gesture, probably prompted by the girlfriend with whom he was living at the time, he had driven to Nevada to legally shed me because he was determined to get a divorce, and I had refused to give him one in Pennsylvania.

Under Pennsylvania law, in that long ago time, the amount of child support that Maggie and Anne would have received from a divorce was pathetic. Of course, that was a moot point. He was sending us no support money at all. My mother was supporting us, more or less. I picked up a few dollars tutoring public school students while I was a full time student, myself, at Martin University, but it was certainly not enough to provide for the three of us.

I hadn't met Bud, yet, and so, stubbornly, I was in no hurry to end my miserable marriage just to accommodate Larry. He, on the other hand, was in a lather to marry his girlfriend, who was just as young and misguided as I had been when I married him. Oh, well. She hadn't been the second Mrs. O'Brian for very long. A third one had followed quickly upon the heels of number two.

What the hell was Larry up to now? Why was he seeking an annulment? He'd been married and divorced twice, after our divorce, and was now living with wife number four in South Carolina. Why try to eradicate our union, which had taken place so long ago? It had already ended, legally, in divorce. Why dredge up all the rancor that had existed between the two of us during our marriage and the Nevada divorce? Why rehash it?

In the twenty-nine years that Bud and I had been happily married I hadn't thought often about Larry. Unless I'd heard about him from one of the O'Brian family members, he hadn't entered my mind for years at a time. This was absolutely ludicrous! It was unfair to force me to remember things that had happened in the painful past!

Any amusement I had felt over the ridiculousness of the situation had fled. I was getting angrier by the minute. Not only was Larry's attempt to secure an annulment at this late date unfair to me it was heinously unfair to Maggie and Anne.

If Larry and I had never been married then our daughters would be illegitimate in the eyes of the Catholic Church and, probably, the O'Brian family. Maggie lived near Larry's family and saw her grandmother O'Brian and some of her eighteen cousins regularly. This was a cruel and selfish act on Larry's part.

But, wait a second. The letter said our marriage could be considered invalid by the Catholic Church because of "certain attitudes toward marriage and psychological factors such as maturity." Larry was sixty-one years old, had never done an honest thing in his life, and believed all the lies he constantly told himself and others. It seemed highly unlikely but could he be planning to admit that he had been immature and psychologically unfit for marriage when he married me? Could he be planning to take the blame for the failure of our marriage in order to secure an annulment?

How out of character for him. He'd never accepted responsibility for anything in the years I'd known him. This was puzzling.

On the other hand, I didn't see any way he could blame me. I'd never done anything to warrant blame. I'd married him in good faith. I'd been a good and faithful wife to him and a loving mother to our children. I'd even taken instruction and converted to Catholicism to make him happy. Everyone who had known us, back then, had been quite aware of my efforts to make the marriage a success.

What happens when two people divorce is that one ex-partner usually keeps all the former couple's friends. At least this was true back in the 60s when Larry and I divorced. Today it may be different. Today the friends may feel free to choose an ex-spouse with whom to ally themselves without paying any attention to that spouse's behavior. Maybe they stay friendly with both, although I doubt it. In the case of Larry and me, I'd kept all our friends, even the ones who had originally been his. I think they felt that Larry had treated me badly and their sympathy lay with the girls and me.

I pondered the situation, again. The thought that Larry might be willing to accept the responsibility for his acts, even to obtain an annulment, proved to be a fleeting one. It was, indeed, out of character for Larry. It would always be out of character for him. No, that wasn't it.

At this late date, what was the purpose of this four-paragraph letter written in ecclesiastical-speak? Larry was, to my knowledge, happily married to his former high school sweetheart, who was such a pathetic case that she'd actually sought him out, paid for his third divorce and taken him to live with her.

I hadn't considered what sort of marriage ceremony theirs had been. Probably a civil one, as had been his second and third. I really didn't think that he was considering another divorce and remarriage. This wife, number four, had money and could afford to support a feckless man averse to working, which is what Larry had always been.

One thing I did know! I'd gotten past the desire to laugh the whole thing off. And I no longer felt any fear or queasiness. I decided that what I felt was real fury. Molten anger that my ex-husband had the gall to serve me with this letter, cause his daughters and me pain so that he could have what he wanted. Now that I'd decided that, I just had to quell the rage inside me long enough to be able to think straight.

Hm-m-m-m. I was supposed to contact the Harrisburg Tribunal within two weeks of the date on the letter. I looked at it, again. The letter was dated October second. Today was the tenth. This Tribunal person, or group of persons, I wasn't completely sure what the term meant, was certainly not allowing me much time to mull over this situation and respond. If I was going to respond.

There in lay the rub. Did I want to respond? Was this whole hideous situation worth responding to, no matter how angry I had become? It certainly might cost a lot of money and effort to object to an annulment. I'd have to talk it over with Bud, of course, but my curiosity was piqued. What the hell was really going on, here?

Rising from my chair, I stuffed the letter into my purse, which always hung from the back of a kitchen chair, and grabbed a jacket from the coat closet in the living room. I couldn't wait to meet Harriet and share the contents of the Tribunal's letter with her. It would be interesting to get the take of a devout Catholic, such as she, on the subject.

I found that my hands were shaking on the steering wheel as I drove to the Susquehanna Mall only a few miles north of Martin's Field. I remembered how my hands had shaken, similarly, on a long ago summer day when I'd been notified that Anne and her friends, the entire girls' basketball team from Martin's Field Area High School, had been in a car accident.

I'd rushed out of the house and driven the a mile or so to reach the site of the accident, tears of fear pouring down my face as I drove. On that drive not only had my hands shaken on the wheel but I'd found myself praying out loud as I drove.

When I'd reached my daughter, I'd found Anne and her friends to be fine, although the vehicles in which they'd been traveling were demolished. My first sight of the girls was chilling, however. They were all lying in the grass of the field beside the road where the accident had happened, waiting for ambulances to take them to the hospital to check out their conditions.

Sinking down beside Anne, I'd hugged her and then run my hands all over her body, from head to toe, as I had when I'd first held her, as a newborn, in my arms. Only then was I satisfied that, except for her bleeding knees, the result of hitting the dashboard of the car upon impact, she was fine. Only then did I stop shaking. I wished my hands on the steering wheel would stop shaking now.

Since I had been the only parent present at the accident site, once I'd checked Anne over I'd left her sitting on the curb and gone from girl to girl until I'd ascertained that none of them was badly hurt. Kerri Shambach the tall blonde center on the girls' basketball team had sustained a broken collar bone and had to sit out the first two games of the season, once school resumed that September, but the whole incident had turned out so much better than I had feared.

Today the pit of my stomach felt very much as it had that day. This wasn't a good sign, I decided. I was way too upset over this bolt-from-the-blue letter!

Harriet was sitting on a bench in front of The Bon Ton waiting for me, as we'd arranged. Sun was streaming down on her from the skylight high above her head and the potted ficus tree next to her bench looked extremely healthy. She smiled and got up as I approached her, but her smile died quickly when she saw my face.

"What's wrong?" she asked reaching out quickly to take my arm.

"You won't believe what I just got in the mail!" I gasped, sinking onto the bench she'd just vacated. "I can't believe it, myself."

"Sukie, what's happened? You're white as a sheet. Tell me," Harriet shook my arm gently as she sat down beside me.

And, so, I took a deep breath and told her.

Chapter Four

"This is nuts!" Sybil sputtered as she paced back and forth in front of us. "Who does Larry think he is? Henry the Eighth?"

"I can't believe he'd really do this," Jaye slapped the annulment letter, which she'd been reading, against her leg, which was crossed over the other, as she sat in the armchair facing me.

It was later the same afternoon and The Red Hats were gathered at Sybil's house, in her living room. The high ceilinged, old-fashioned parlor doubled as a library, computer room and, sometimes, spare bedroom for her. The Heim house, as it was always referred to by the citizens of Martin's Field, was large and many of the rooms now stood empty. When we'd been growing up, Sybil Heim's house had been a hub of activity. Not only had the Heim family been a busy group of individuals but, also, Mrs. Heim had welcomed Sybil's friends as if they were her own. I'd been one of those friends and had spent a lot of time there, after school and in the summer.

Now Sybil lived alone in the house. Her parents were dead,

and her brother, a doctor was married and lived in Boston. Her younger sister, the free spirit of the family, had died in Haight-Ashbury in the '70s from a drug overdose. Sybil used only three or four of the house's many rooms, and she seemed to like it that way. She was comfortable.

"What I can't understand is why you even care?" Sally tossed her comment at me seemingly offhandedly, not meeting my eyes as she spoke. She sat cross-legged on the floor, paging through a magazine "It's not like either you or Maggie or Anne are Catholic."

I swallowed hard and met the eyes of my friends as they all turned toward me to gauge my reaction. I was sitting, squeezed between Jaye and Harriet, on the small sofa that was the largest piece of furniture in Sybil's living room. I felt numb, despite the warmth of indignation exuded by my friends, who had hastily gathered to hear about the letter. Harriet, who held my hand tightly, had called everyone from the mall on her cell phone and made arrangements for us to gather as soon as the school day ended for Jaye.

"I...I'm just furious that after all this time," as I gathered my thoughts and spoke, a sob rattled in my throat. I forced back tears of anger. "I'm just so damned mad that after all this time," I began again, "After all this time, and all his other marriages, he'd want to hurt the girls by doing this to them...making them illegitimate!" At this point I broke down, completely, and let loose the tears that had burned behind my eyes since I'd left my own house, earlier in the day.

"Bullshit!" Sally cried, grabbing the letter away from Jaye. She'd already read it once. Everyone had. "It says, right here, at the end of the last paragraph, that "the annulment does not affect the status of any existing children of the union'."

It did? That morning, when I'd read the letter, I'd been so upset by the time I'd gotten to the end of it that I'd overlooked that sentence completely.

"Oh, yeah?" Harriet shot back at her. Harriet was a Catholic in good standing, while she considered Sally to be one who had fallen away from The Church. So I wasn't sure whether Harriet's anger was directed at the Catholic Church or Sally when she added, cryptically, "Well, the Church can't have its cake and eat it too! Either the marriage existed or it didn't. Either Maggie and Anne are illegitimate, or they're not! If there wasn't any marriage how can there be any legitimate children?"

I had a feeling that besides registering the pain that Harriet felt over what she perceived as an injustice being perpetrated upon me by her beloved church this comment of hers was a pointed reference to the fact that neither of Sally's marriages had taken place in the Catholic Church.

Sally and her first husband had eloped to Maryland when they were in college, where they had been married by a Justice of the Peace. Her second marriage had also taken place outside the state, but none of us had been invited so, although we'd seen pictures of the small, outdoor wedding in New York, we had no idea what sort of clergy, if any, had officiated. For some reason this stung Harriet.

"I suppose you consider Jack to be illegitimate, too," Sally had laid the letter aside and returned to the magazine she'd been perusing. Her voice didn't seem to register any concern over Harriet's comments, as she referred to her only child, the son born of her first marriage. Jack was a very talented young man, an artist, who lived in Los Angeles and seemed to have weathered what most people would have considered a very unorthodox childhood. We all agreed that being brought up by Sally, for many years on her own between marriages, had been a rocky experience for him. But it didn't seem to have done him any harm. He was both happy and successful.

"Oh, cut it out, you two!" Jaye interposed. "This problem is Sukie's. She has to decide what to do; how to respond to this annulment letter."

"The first thing you have to do is call the Archdiocese of Harrisburg and find out where you stand," Sybil asserted logically. "Larry may live in South Carolina but this letter was sent to you from Harrisburg. Just call the telephone number listed in the letterhead. I think it's the same one that's in the cover letter, too, and ask how much it will cost you to fight the annulment, if that's what you want to do. With the Catholic Church it's always about money. Remember when Jennifer Rice wanted to annul her first marriage and the Church told her it would cost her two thousand dollars?"

She was alluding to a younger teacher we all knew who had wanted to marry her second husband in the Catholic Church and couldn't afford to pay for the annulment of her first marriage. Jennifer had ended up holding her second wedding in the Methodist Church to which her second husband belonged. Today she and he appeared to be very happy Methodists.

"I don't know if I want to fight this annulment," I sniffed, attempting to dry my eyes with a tissue Harriet had kindly fished out of her purse. "I don't know if Larry's worth it."

"Larry isn't worth spit, but you won't know if the annulment is worth fighting until you find out how much it's going to cost you if you do," Sybil commented dryly, ending her pacing and sinking into a chair.

"All right," I agreed, meekly. "I'll call the Harrisburg Archdiocese when I get home."

"Oh no you won't!" Jaye instructed me in her most authoritative teaching voice. "You'll call that number right now while we're all here to give you moral support. If you go home you may wimp out and just ignore the whole thing."

"Maybe that's what Sukie wants to do. Did you ever think of that? Maybe ignoring the whole thing is the best thing she could do," Sally raised her head and and her voice, seeming to become involved in the situation for the first time.

"Point of interest," Sybil added, speaking in an even tone and directly to me. "Does Bud know anything about this, yet?"

Again all eyes turned to me.

"No-o-o," I admitted. "I didn't want to call him at work. You know how he hates to be bothered at the office, and," my voice wavered again, "I don't know how he'll react to my being as upset I am by it."

"Come on, Honey," Sybil continued in a much softer voice. "Tell us the rest of it. The real reason you told us first about the letter, and Bud doesn't know anything, yet."

Everyone in the room, except Harriet, had experienced a bad first marriage. Sally and Sybil had experienced two. Among us we had survived six divorces. We all knew every sad and sordid detail of each other's relationships. So, the four women whose eyes now rested upon me were experts, of a sort. And they were waiting for me to *come clean*, to *spill the beans*. To search my soul and tell us all the truth that lay beneath the anguish I felt right now.

"Bud adopted Maggie and Anne, so no matter what their shithead-of-a-biological-father does they can never be illegiti- mate. They may be hurt by his actions, hurt for you, but they don't consider him to be their father. Bud is the only father they recognize. Look how they both refused to invite Larry to their weddings, or tell him when they had their babies. Come on, Girl, 'fess up," Jaye also spoke softly as she turned, took my other hand, squeezed it, and looked me squarely in the eye.

"I guess," I began in an almost inaudible voice. "I guess if the Catholic Church annuls the marriage, even though it ended in divorce thirty-some years ago, it will seem like all the pain I suffered, all the bad things I went through in my marriage to Larry were for nothing. Like he gets away Scot free, like he always did. Like I don't get any credit for being brave and putting up with all the crap I put up with. Like he wins, again. Like all that time when I couldn't get him to pay child support. Like the time he gave me the crab lice he'd picked up from some woman, and I found one in Annie's hair…she was only two! And he claimed that he hadn't given them to me, that I'd given them to him." I seemed to be free-associating, not making much sense. I pulled both my hands away from the comforting grasps of my friends, covered my eyes with them, lowered my head, and began to sob and wail uncontrollably. The sounds I made were those of a trapped and hopeless animal.

How long had the rage and indignation that I had just let out been festering inside me? The intensity of letting it all out frightened me. I was shaking. At the same time, the catharsis felt good. It felt wonderful! The tears and sobbing seemed to be washing away a hurt I'd carried with me for a long, long time.

The Red Hats all sat very still. In the golden rays of October sunset that streamed through the windows, they seemed to be frozen, like ants preserved in amber. They stared at me, quietly.

At last I stopped sobbing and, raising my head, attempted to mop up my eyes with my soggy piece of tissue. This seemed almost like a signal that released them from inertia.

"Oh, Honey!" Jaye was hugging me. At the same time Sybil and Sally rushed to me, to pat and soothe me. Harriet began to fish for another tissue because she had, quietly, also begun to cry.

"I thought," I continued when everything had settled down, everyone was reseated, and I had voice enough to speak again, "I guess I thought for such a long time that I was some kind of hero," ever the English teacher I corrected myself, "heroine, I mean. Saving the girls and myself from Larry. Leaving him way back in the '60s when nobody did that kind of thing. It became part of my identity. Like a badge I wore. *I'm a horrible-marriage and divorce survivor, and I came out on top.* I feel like if the Catholic Church wipes out my marriage to Larry all of what I think of as heroism, on my part, gets wiped out, too."

"Sukie!" Harriet turned and nearly shouted at me. "You're all heroines," her arm swept the room," You've all survived bad marriages and divorces. You've all raised children from those marriages. The Red Hats have all come out on top!" This meant a lot coming from Harriet, who had never married, never had a child, and never talked about it.

"And you're married to Bud, now. Happily married. You've

47

been married almost thirty years. Why should what the Catholic Church and its stinking annulment, or anything about Larry matter to you?" Sally asked sincerely, her eyes resting on me. She was no longer on the defensive. Harriet's testimonial seemed to have smoothed away any acrimony that had existed between the two old friends.

"I don't know," I admitted softly. "I just know that it does, and I feel so disloyal to Bud. It's killing me. How can I tell him about the letter and how I feel about it? The last thing I ever want to do is hurt him, and I know it will." I was on the verge of tears, again.

"Don't tell him," Sally leaned forward as she spoke. "Throw that damned letter away and don't ever tell him about it, or how it made you feel!"

"Yes," Jaye found her voice. "I agree with Sally. Throw the letter away. If you don't respond, the Tribunal will just go ahead and grant the annulment, and you don't ever have to get involved or tell Bud anything about it!"

Ah...In retrospect, what sage advice my friends offered me that day. And how many times in the future, as things developed, would I wish I had taken that advice?

Chapter Five

I sat on the couch in the dusk of my own living room, waiting for Bud to come home. Spread out on my lap, and beside me on the cushions, were family picture albums. Pages and pages of little girls with smiling faces and their happy parents: Maggie, Anne, Bud and I.

As I turned the pages, there were pictures of Maggie and Anne dying Easter eggs, opening Christmas presents, grinning as they made ready to dive into the community pool at the end of LaDawn Lane. Pictures of the four of us at Disney World, taken by helpful strangers. The four of us in front of Buckingham Palace on our first trip to London.

So many of the pictures I'd taken and had admonished Bud not to put his fingers up behind the girls' heads, aping rabbit ears. A favorite trick of his that made the girls squeal with laughter. I began to feel weepy again.

This was a family, these four people. This was a testimony to a happy life. What was I doing even thinking about letting Larry and the Charleston Archdiocese into the lives of the people I loved the most? This little charmed circle.

I opened one of the more recent albums and pictures of my four grandchildren brought a smile to my trembling lips. The first picture was of Philip, the oldest, Maggie's son, in his crib nine years ago, gazing up at a Winnie the Pooh mobile. Philip his second summer on the beach in front of our shore home, in his first bathing suit that looked like a balloon with a swelling wet diaper under it. Could that picture really have been taken seven years ago?

Ian, Anne's son, when he was a year old, looking like a blonde Buddha, as he sat on her lap and started into the camera with his huge, pale blue eyes. Ian holding the tails of a black and a yellow Labrador Retriever, one in each hand, on the day that he had pulled himself to his feet for the first time. Hard to believe he was eight, now. Hannah and Abbey, our beloved first granddogs, whose tails he held were old ladies, now. Anne and Greg had given us adorable *grandpuppies* long before they had become the parents of Ian and Livvy.

Little Susie, Maggie and Dan's daughter, named for me and for all the past Harris women. She was the artist of the family, and the first picture I found of her was one in which she had smeared herself and the wall beside her with the contents of her diaper. She looked so proud of herself in that picture! Today she drew pictures that showed real artistic promise, and was a seven-year-old gymnast.

Livvy was the youngest of the crew. She appeared to be a figure right out of a Gainsborough portrait, with a mop of dark ringlets around her cherubic face. In reality, though, she was as tough as naugahide. Nothing could make her cry. She'd set her little jaw and make a crusade out of not letting you see that she was upset. She was also brilliant, having taught herself to read when she was three and a half.

I called them my *little people*, a phrase my mother had coined when referring to her grandchildren Maggie and Anne. They were my heart, as Bud was. I found my greatest delight in their company. Things they unwittingly said were all the more hilarious because they didn't realize how funny they were. And made me laugh more heartily than anything else I'd ever heard. Each summer the four of them came to stay with us for two weeks. Two weeks during which the older ones took swimming lessons at the community pool, and we all played games together and sang silly songs. I told them stories about their mothers when they were little, remembering how much I'd loved hearing stories from my Grandmother Purcell, when I was young, about when my father had been a little boy.

But Granny Sukie could only play and sing, tell stories and referee their games for so long. Bud was their savior at the end of many a long summer day when my nerves had frayed. He'd open the door from the garage to find them lined up with their arms held out to him in supplication. Then he pull off his tie, drop the newspaper he'd hoped to read and scoop up as many of them into his arms as he could carry and take the four of them out to the van. He'd whisk them off to the indoor Mc Donald's playground or the arcade at the mall, where they'd busy themselves with the endless tokens Bud provided for them, while I had a short respite and cooked dinner for us all.

In the evening we'd often take them up to Shikellamy Lookout, a state park with a scenic overview of the Susquehanna River and the point where its main and west branches met. How they loved the scenic panorama view at sunset. And how I loved to watch them, bathed in rosy light, their faces pressed up against the chain link fence, as they gazed intently down at the river.

I'd tell them stories of how settlers in the early days had poled their way down the Susquehanna on rafts to the safety of the now defunct Fort Augusta. And tales of the renegade white man Simon Girty with his red skinned band of marauders who had shot down upon them from the heights where we stood.

I heard the garage door going up automatically, which signaled Bud's imminent arrival. As if on cue, the lamp by the couch and the blue and white florescent Penn State logo light in the bay window behind the couch switched on. Both were on a timer. My king had returned to his castle.

"Hi," Bud entered from the garage into the dining room and dropped his keys onto the credenza covered with silver that had, mostly, been my mother's. "What are you doing?" He noticed the albums covering the couch and coffee table.

"Oh, just looking at pictures," I rose from my seat and came toward him, smiling. We kissed fleetingly as I continued past him on my way to the kitchen,

"Sukie, something's wrong. What is it?" he stopped me.

"How can you tell?" I tried to answer brightly, not looking at him directly.

"We've been married way too long for me not to be able to tell. Your voice. The way you're moving. Tell me what's wrong." Bud dropped his newspaper onto a chair, reached out and held me to him.

"Oh, Bud," I wrapped my arms around his familiar, comforting warmth. There had only ever been two people in the entire world who could convince me that everything would be all right just by hugging me and telling me so. My mother and Bud.

After a moment's embrace and a warm, lingering kiss, I produced the Tribunal's letter. I sat with Bud at the kitchen table while he read it, watching his face, studying his reaction. He read the letter slowly, a muscle in his jaw working as he did. Finally, he put it down on the table.

"So?" he asked quietly. "What do you want to do?"

"I want it to all go away!" I spoke sharply, waving my hands. I'm a hand-speaker. Tie my hands behind me and I'd be hard pressed to talk. "I want that letter and Larry to just disappear!"

"That's not likely to happen," Bud smiled a little at my so typically, impractical-but-it-makes-sense-to-Sukie answer. "Do you want to contest the annulment?"

"I don't know," I admitted. "I don't think so. It could cost a lot of money to do that."

"Yes, it could," Bud leaned back in his chair as he spoke, "But you're the only one who can decide if it's what you want to do. Will it make you feel better to do it? Is it what you want to do?"

I looked at him supplicatingly, "You know how bad I am at making decisions. I don't want to be the one to decide. I don't want to have anything to do with it or him. You know how I feel!" I was waving my hands again as I spoke.

Bud reached over and, catching my hands held them in his, as he looked into my eyes. "I can't decide this for you, Sukie. It's up to you. What do you want to do? I'll support you in anything you decide. You know that." He hesitated for a few seconds and then continued, "Larry hurt you badly, but that was a long time ago."

"I know," I answered in a voice so soft it was almost inaudible. I didn't seem to be able to raise my head.

Tears welled up in my eyes. Darling Bud. I was so lucky to have met and married him. What should I answer? What was fair to him and to myself? What DID I want to do?

As I hesitated, Bud spoke again, "I think you should call this Tribunal secretary's number and find out what this is all about. I think you need all the facts before you make a decision."

"That's what Jaye said," I raised my eyes and my voice as I spoke. "But she said I'd probably wimp out and wouldn't call. Sally said maybe I shouldn't." I realized, in a flash, as the words left my mouth, that once I'd said them Bud would know that I'd discussed the letter with The Red Hats before I told him about it.

Bud raised his eyebrows but his voice didn't change. "If you make the call do it because you want to, not because Jaye or I think you should."

"But you both do think I should," I answered him in a small voice.

"I do," Bud rose from the table and walked into the living room, picking up his newspaper as he went.

I stayed sitting at the kitchen table. I felt miserable. Had I hurt

Bud by being indecisive about what I wanted to do? By telling my friends about the letter before I told him? My head ached from crying. I was determined not to cry any more. I hadn't cried this much since my mother had died.

Finally, I got up and went to the stove. Opening the oven, I dished up the chicken caccitore that I'd whipped up earlier, before I'd sat down with the picture albums. Going into the living room I bent over Bud as he sat on the couch reading the newspaper amid open albums.

"I love you more than life, itself," I murmured, as I kissed him. "I'll call the Tribunal's office tomorrow morning. Now come to dinner. I made chicken"

Chapter Six

One of my least favorite things to do, in the whole world, is make telephone calls to strangers. Unless I'm calling my daughters or friends I don't really relish making telephone calls at all. I'd far rather sit down at the computer and dash off an e-mail, or settle myself into the recliner and compose a written note on tasteful, heavy vellum notepaper. Stationery and address labels are a weakness of mine. I love to pour through catalogues featuring samples of both. I'll always choose the written word over the spoken one, any time.

Therefore, the following day, it took me several hours of agonizing over what to say and whether I really wanted to make the call Bud and my friends had suggested I make, before I could dial the telephone number listed in the cover letter. Just the term Tribunal gave me an ominous feeling. The thought of calling the Office of the Tribunal of Harrisburg made me literally sick in my stomach.

I sat at the kitchen table, drinking cup after cup of tea and re-reading the Tribunal's letter, until I couldn't stand the suspense any longer. Finally I dialed.

When I reached the correct office it was through one of those automated receptionist's voices that instructs you to: "Dial one if you know your party's four digit extension number. Dial two if you are ordering supplies. Dial three, etc. etc." I always find them to be more trouble than they are helpful; especially if what I need is not on the menu.

This time, as usual, the drill did not include the information I needed, and the disembodied voice instructed me to "stay on the line and an operator will assist you." Why companies, businesses, even archdioceses don't just have an operator to handle callers instead of subjecting them to useless recorded messages is beyond me. I must be missing the whole point of the exercise.

When I finally reached the secretary to the Tribunal and told her why I was calling she was less than helpful.

"Yes the letter came from our office but we aren't actually handling the situation. It's just a formality," she instructed me in a singsong voice.

"But I don't understand the letter in the first place," I told her in what I considered to be a very reasonable voice. After all. Thirty years of teaching had given me the skills to handle people who are not interested in the subject at hand or who are not *the brightest crayons in the box*, to start with. "Mr. O'Brian and I were married in a Catholic Church and we had two children. The marriage was legal and consummated. How can the validity of it be in question now?"

"Well," I could tell by the sound of her voice that the secretary was chewing gum as she spoke with me. Again, something a teacher of many years can pick up on even through miles of telephone cable. "Maybe you celebrated the wrong anniversary. It says here," I could hear ruffling pages, "that you were married in a civil ceremony first."

"We were not!" I was quick to correct her. "We were married in the parsonage of a Lutheran Church in Maryland."

"Oh, well. The letter from the Archdiocese of Charleston says it was a civil ceremony," the singsong voice went on.

"It was not! I was there!" I could not control my exasperation. I purely hate telephone calls with strangers.

"If you celebrated the anniversary of your first marriage and not the one in the Catholic Church that would make it invalid," Miss Chewing Gum went on as if my interjection with the correct information had never happened.

This was ridiculous. I was getting nowhere at all with this Space Cadet.

"Let me speak with a member of the Tribunal," I told her curtly in my best mean-teacher voice.

"There's only one Tribunal. There aren't any members. It's father Flynn," she informed me. Now I really felt stupid, as well as angry. I'd taken the term Tribunal literally to mean a committee of priests who decided whatever petitions, etc. that came before them. I was nonplussed. The Tribunal was one person? Father Flynn? This was news to me, the vocabulary teacher.

"Well, then, let me speak with Father Flynn," I tried to calm down as I spoke.

"Oh, he's much too busy to talk with you," the Space Cadet assured me. "I answer all the questions from callers."

She answered all the questions? Boy was Father Flynn in trouble!

In total frustration, without saying goodbye, I hung the receiver up with a bang.

The telephone call had been an exercise in futility but it had energized me. Who to call now? The Tribunal of Charleston, if I could get through to him? A local Catholic priest? The one who had married Larry and me had left years ago, before the Northumberland church had closed, and I didn't know the priest at St. Catherine's, Martin's Field's Catholic Church. I did know that Harriet was not fond of him, even thought she only attended St. Catherine's sporadically.

I called Harriet.

When I'd finished giving her a synopsis of my call to the Tribunal of Harrisburg I finished emphatically with," I'm so frustrated I'm ready to chew nails!"

"I have a better idea," she assured me.

"What?"

"Chocolate!" Harriet and I really are on the same wavelength.

"When and where?"

"Now at the Victorian Lady. My treat. We'll have a Spoil Your Dinner Party."

"You're on!" I agreed. "I'll meet you there."

Chapter Seven

An hour later I felt calm and collected, as Harriet and I tucked into some serious chocolate desserts in the beautifully decorated environs of my favorite restaurant. How could anyone feel upset while sitting back in the comfort of a chair fitted out with a padded brocade head rest, seated at a table formally set with a dainty floral centerpiece and bone china, and with plates filled with chocolate ganache tarts and warm chocolate chip bread pudding slathered in hot chocolate sauce and whipped cream in front of them? My anger and frustration melted away as soon as I had my first bite of ganache.

Mary Gajda bustled into the room carrying a plum colored plaid teapot filled with fragrant spiced tea. "Where are your red hats?" she cried after she'd kissed Harriet and me on the cheek and begun to pour the heavenly tea into our cups.

"Oh. This isn't a meeting of the Red Hat Society," Harriet assured her. "Sukie and I just needed a chocolate and tea fix really badly."

"Well, you've come to the right place," Mary put the teapot

down on a doily in the corner of our table. "And Marilla has just put the finishing touches on a batch of triple chocolate cookies. I'll bring some out as soon as they are cool enough." Marilla is the pastry chef at the Victorian Lady and she creates magic in her part of the kitchen.

We thanked Mary, who left us to our chocolate feast. As we began sampling the desserts in earnest, we made soft little murmuring sounds after each bite.

"This is the life," I sighed, leaning back in my chair and gazing around the room at its striped wallpaper, paisley border, and crown molding. "If only chocolate could solve all my problems."

"Like making a decision whether to respond to Larry's stupid annulment letter?" Harriet's voice was muffled by the fact that her mouth was full of bread pudding.

"Yeah. I truly don't know what to do. Or what I want to do," I admitted.

"Oh, I think you know what you want to do," Harriet commented without looking at me as she spoke. "It's just a matter of deciding whether you want to put up with all the crap that goes along with telling the Catholic Church what a jerk Larry is."

"He's a jerk, all right," I agreed. As I listened to my self, I realized that I was actually giggling. Between the tea I'd drunk at home, the tea I was having now, and all the chocolate in the desserts we were consuming my caffeine level must have been sky-high.

"Well?"

"I think I'll do what I always do when it comes to making decisions," I informed Harriet of what I may have known deep down, all along. "I just won't do anything. I'll wait to see what Larry or the Catholic Church's next moves are. After all, how do they know that I even received that letter?"

"Um-m-m," my friend murmured. I couldn't tell whether Harriet was agreeing with me, acknowledging the truth in my statement of how I avoid making decisions, or simply verbalizing her enjoyment of the triple chocolate cookies Mary had delivered to our table one of which now filled her mouth.

It didn't matter. I'd made the decision not to make a decision. As usual, having done that I felt much better. Of course, it may have been the after effects of the chocolate.

As Harriet and I left the Victorian Lady were heard the din of many voices raised in conversation and laughter. Mary wasn't anywhere around to question so as our curiosity got the best of us we crept along the main hall of the restaurant to see where and from whom the noise was coming. We'd been seated in the dainty front parlor of the house to the right of the main hall. The noise was emanating from the main dining room that ran the length of the old home's left side.

Peeking around the corner of a set of antique pocket doors, Harriet and I beheld Helen Oberheim's Red Hat Society. They were seated at six parallel tables and were all dressed in purple outfits and red hats. Their junior auxiliary, decked out in lavender and wearing pink hats, was seated at two tables behind the official members. Everyone was stuffing their mouths with finger sandwiches, drinking tea, and having what appeared to be a very merry time. Harriet and I drew back as if we'd had cold water thrown in our faces.

Helen Oberheim's crass Red Hat Society was meeting in our own dear Victorian Lady! I felt violated. Of course, they could meet and revel in their official, registered, Red Hat doctrines anywhere they pleased. But in *our* restaurant! On our turf! It was a sacrilege that pushed any other concerns I had right out of my mind.

I nudged Harriet, who had been peering over my shoulder, and indicated with movement of my head in the direction of the front door that we should leave quickly and quietly. Stealthily, we were turning to go when we heard an unmistakable voice call out to us.

"Sukie, Harriet! Yoo-hoo, Girls." It was Dottie Swank. Her

voice was octaves higher than that of anyone I knew in Martin's Field. It was impossible to ignore her call.

Harriet and I froze, feeling like two small children caught peering into the living room after bedtime, when their parents have banished them upstairs to bed. Peering back around the door there was no mistaking Dottie, up out of her seat and headed in our direction. She accosted us as we tried to quickly back down the hall.

"Where are you two going? Why don't you come in and join us?" She grasped both our arms, ending out retreat.

"We, uh, have to get home," I began, lamely.

"It's getting late," Harriet quickly pointed out.

Dottie ignored our excuses and prattled on, "I understand you girls have a small Red Hat Society. It doesn't make sense to have two in our area. Why don't you and your friends just join ours? We have so much fun! Come on in and say hello to Helen. We're planning a big picnic for next summer at Knoebel's Grove. You'll love it!"

I honestly couldn't tell whether Dottie was trying to be kind or condescending. She and I had gone to school together and, years later, seen each other every day in the Martin's Field High School where I'd taught and she'd been the secretary in charge of the administrator's office. Sometimes during those years, before we'd both retired, she'd seemed so efficient. Everyone in the school knew that she, not the principal, totally ran the office. At other times she'd seemed quite vague. Probably the result of being overworked.

All I wanted to do at that minute was escape.

"Thanks but no thanks," I smiled grimly in her face, pulled myself away from her grasp, and drawing Harriet, half stumbling behind me, fled back down the hall and out the front door of the Victorian Lady.

"We have more than one hundred members!" Dottie called after us, causing us to practically break into a full run.

"What a narrow escape," I gasped as Harriet and I leaned

against the huge oak tree that grew in the restaurant's front yard. "Join their Red Hat Society, indeed!"

"I think she meant well," Harriet pointed out as she pulled herself together, "But I could never even consider merging our Red Hats with theirs. Yuck, what a thought!"

We looked at each other and suddenly began to giggle like schoolgirls. It was probably a reaction caused by our escape from a stressful and somewhat ludicrous situation on top of all the chocolate and tea we'd consumed, but whatever it was we clung to the tree laughing until tears ran down our faces.

"I really do have to get home," Harriet hiccuped after each word as she let go of the tree and made her way toward the parking lot. She does that sometimes, hiccups, when she laughs, or cries, or becomes agitated.

"Me, too," I agreed, wiping tears from my eyes and following her.

By the time I arrived home I'd calmed down enough from our confrontation with Dottie Swank and its aftermath to be able to make two telephone calls before Bud arrived home from work. I needed to call my daughters; Maggie at the Philadelphia Art Museum where she was Director of Foundation Relations, and Anne who was a vice president at The American Surgical Association in Baltimore. I always enjoyed making calls to the girls, and despite what had happened earlier in the day this was true now. The news I had for them was not pleasant but since I already knew, or thought I knew, what their reactions would be I wasn't nervous. Seating myself in the kitchen, I picked up the telephone receiver and took a deep breath.

In both cases, I know my daughters' secretaries very well and had no trouble getting through to them quickly, even though they are both very busy women when they are at work. Bud and I have three-way calling as a feature of our phone service. It comes in very handy when Maggie, Anne and I have to make a decision such as in which outlets we'll spend a day shopping together before Christmas. Or what each of us is taking to the

New Jersey beach house for the Memorial Day or Labor Day weekends when our family gathers there.

I employed the three-way calling service now, so I could tell the girls about the letter at the same time.

"Hi, Mum," they chorused in reply to my greeting.

Ever the one to get right to the point Anne asked, "What's up?"

"Well, I've had a letter from your biological father, sort of," I began.

"What do you mean 'sort of"?" Maggie inquired cautiously.

"The letter is actually from the Catholic Church. Are you ready for this? Larry wants to annul our Catholic marriage after almost forty years," I told them all in a rush, wanting to lay the news before them and hear their reactions.

"Annul your marriage. Now? Why?" Maggie demanded suspiciously. She had a vested interest in all things involving her biological father since she was in limited contact with his family.

She'd always been especially close to one of her O'Brian cousins, her cousin J.P. who was only a week older than she, and who had introduced her to his next door neighbor when all three of them had been twenty-one. The neighbor had been Dan, who nine years later had become Maggie's husband.

Of the three of us she was the only one to have met Larry's fourth wife in person. Come to think of it, she had met his third wife, too. Anne and I had been spared that indignity. When Maggie had first moved to the Philadelphia suburbs the girls' O'Brian Grandmother had insisted upon her going to lunch with Sarah, wife number three and Kelly Ann, Larry's child by that marriage. My girls' half-sister. They also had a half-brother by Larry's second marriage. That wife had been named Stephanie. The girls and I had met him when he was a baby but none of us has seen him in the last twenty-some years.

For a while it had been a joke in our family that Larry only married women whose names started with the letter "S." If one can fine humor in that fact. Until he married Martha, his wives had been named Susannah, Stephanie and Sarah. Not one of us had been Catholic. I was Lutheran, Stephanie had been a Methodist and Sarah was a Quaker Activist. Larry hadn't seemed to care. He was just never very interested in religion when I knew him. His or anyone else's.

"I don't have a clue why he wants an annulment," I admitted, although this was not completely true. I was beginning to have an idea of what was behind it all. I just hadn't voiced it yet.

"Maybe his fourth wife, Saint Martie, who is so devout you can smell incense when she passes gas, is pushing for it," Anne added, wryly. "You don't think he wants to get married again?" she added.

"That's it!" I cried, grateful to Anne for putting the two subjects together. She'd voiced the suspicion that had been growing at the back of my mind. It made sense. "He must want to marry Martie in the Catholic Church. Or, rather, Martie must want it. Larry was always so lukewarm about being a Catholic. I bet this is her doing!"

"You could be right," Maggie hedged. "But do you have to be so vulgar about it, Annie?" She admonished her sister.

"Why? Because I said she passed incense instead of gas?" Anne laughed.

My two girls have always been as different as it is possible to be and still be devoted sisters. Maggie is very proper and upright, while Anne is laid back. Most of the values Maggie lives by would never even occur to Anne to be important. As their mother, I consider myself to be very lucky. From my daughters I have always had two diverse opinions on any subject to choose from, two comfortable but diametrically different life-styles to observe.

"What are you going to do about it?" Anne asked, practically.

"What I usually do," I answered wryly. "Nothing for the present. The letter I got says it could cost a lot of money to contest the annulment and it very strongly suggests that I need to go to South Carolina to present my case if I want to contest it."

"That's nuts!" Anne continued. "He wants an annulment so you have to put out money if you want to stop him? It's not worth it, Mum. He's not worth it."

"The thing that worries me the most," I was getting into deep water, here, "is the fact that some people could interpret an annulment as Larry and the Church's declaration that you girls are illegitimate."

There, I'd said it. Now, what would be their reaction?

"No, oh no! No one would ever think that!" Maggie protested. "You and he have been divorced forever, and Bud adopted us, legally. Larry isn't our father anymore. He hasn't been for a long time!"

I couldn't tell if she was upset by my suggestion or just speaking vehemently.

"I think I know how you feel, Mum," Anne spoke very deliberately. "You feel like if The Great Pumpkin gets what he wants from the Catholic Church he wins and you get hurt again."

I half smiled at Anne's reference to Larry as The Great Pumpkin. This was the childhood name the girls had used when speaking of him. The Great Pumpkin was a character from the comic strip "Peanuts" created by Charles Schulz. In the cartoon Charlie Brown and his friends wait in the pumpkin patch every Halloween for The Great Pumpkin to show up, but he never does.

Since, after the divorce, Larry had rarely shown up for the visitations with the girls that he'd been granted in our decree; it hadn't taken Maggie's very creative seven-year-old mind long to come up with the nickname. Anne had loved the moniker, as only a four-year-old could, and The Great Pumpkin Larry had remained until the girls became teenagers and began to refer to him as Larry or The Sperm Donor.

"Yes," I sighed deeply, so relieved to know that Anne understood the situation. "That's exactly how I feel."

"Oh, Mum," Maggie sympathized, "You can't let this harebrained scheme of his make you feel that way. You can't take it personally."

"How else can I take it?" I whispered, finding myself near tears. I'd never told the girls all the things I'd gone through in my marriage to Larry. I hadn't wanted to predispose them to feel the disgust and anger toward him that I felt. "Just how am I supposed to feel?"

I'd have given anything in the world, at that moment and later, to have had the answer to that question!

Chapter Eight

Most people would probably not expect Central Pennsylvania to be particularly prone to hurricanes. Hurricanes and hurricane damage are usually associated, by those people who follow weather and natural disasters, with states located on or near the Atlantic Coast and south of the Mason Dixon Line. Those who follow hurricanes for a living also know that the states that ring the Gulf of Mexico are hurricane magnets.

Therefore, it is interesting to note that the Susquehanna River Valley, which is located squarely in the center of the state of Pennsylvania and which is a good five hours drive and hundreds of miles from any seacoast, has attracted at least six large hurricanes that I can remember during the time that I have lived here. And probably more hurricanes/tropical storms that I don't remember. Even though the Weather Bureau has stopped tagging these storms with purely female names, the hurricanes that have hit Central Pennsylvania and created the most destruction have all been female.

In the 1950s two hurricanes that occurred within a week of

each other, Hurricane Carol and Hurricane Diane, ripped up the Susquehanna River Valley and all but devastated the Pocono Mountain region, north of us. That week my mother had been showing my brother and me the places where she had worked summers when she was in college. We had left Buttermilk Falls just a day before it flooded and several people were drowned. Over the years, other "Ladies" followed a path inland, culminating with Hurricane Agnes in 1972.

Our family will never forget that one! It hit the June day after Bud and I were married and had started off on a honeymoon to Nova Scotia. Agnes stalled over the river valley for several days, caused massive flooding for miles, and cut us off from Martin's Field for a week. Bud and I tried to enjoy our wedding trip, but we both worried constantly about Maggie and Anne's safety, although they were in the custody of both our mothers. When we returned home it was to find two very excited little girls and towns along the river that were shadows of their former selves.

Now, in the middle of October, which is the tail end of hurricane season, our newspapers and the television weather reports were filled with dire warnings of what was supposed to be the last storm of a more prolific than normal season: Hurricane Marcus. He was projected to make landfall on the outer banks of North Carolina, and his predicted course was almost a straight line up through Virginia, Maryland, Central Pennsylvania, and Western New York, into Canada. It was a scant assurance that by the time he reached us he was expected to be downgraded to a Tropical Storm, with winds well below 70 miles per hour. The greater problem would lie in the amount of rain he dropped upon us.

It had been an unusually wet summer in Martin's Field and the surrounding area. In the last ten years Central Pennsylvania had suffered extreme droughts almost every other year. Farmers had lost crops over and over again and, finally, their farms. Out of state guests had inquired at Maggie's June wedding, ten years ago, what had happened to our grass. It had been totally burned out two months earlier than usual.

Now, however, our soil was saturated. How much more rain could it absorb before creeks began to overflow their banks? All those creeks drained into the Susquehanna River, eventually. Would we face another major flood of the river?

"I don't know about you, Sukie," Sybil was calling me in the early afternoon of a Tuesday I'd planned to dedicate to vacuuming the house; not one of my favorite activities. I was only too glad for an excuse to turn off the machine and sit down for a chat. "But I need a change, especially before this storm that's supposed to be coming traps us in the house for who knows how long."

Looking outside at the cool, sunny day beyond my bay window, it was hard to believe that a storm was coming.

"What do you have in mind?" I asked, leaning back in the only recliner we have in the living room and stretching out my already tired legs. I don't get nearly as much exercise as I should.

"I haven't been to Williamsburg since our last trip there three years ago," Sybil lamented. "Want to go this weekend, or do you and Bud have a Penn State game?"

"I'd love to go!" the words rushed out of my mouth so fast I had to stop for a second or two to reconsider the Penn State schedule. I usually it have memorized from August until November and tucked away in the recesses of my mind. I was happy when I got a quick okay, as ran my eyes over the mental list of October weekends.

"It's an away game this week: Nebraska. It will probably be exciting, but it will be on TV. Bud is planning to make a fast trip to Avalon to hurricane-proof the beach house, bring in the deck furniture and trashcans. You know. And he'll probably have to go into work to send out crews if the storm puts a lot of customers out of power. I bet he won't mind if I go. But, what about the storm? Going south to Virginia might be risky."

"According to Bill Simpson, on Channel 16 Weather, Marcus has slowed down, for some reason, and isn't expected to reach the U.S. until Monday. And now they're saying the Weather Service isn't sure where the storm will make landfall. We could leave early on Friday and be back late Sunday afternoon," Sybil seemed to have thought this trip out ahead of time. "I still have the number for the Motel Six where we stayed in last time, and I'd love to make a dinner reservation at The King's Arms Tavern in the restored area for Saturday night."

"Are we going to Williamsburg to eat, or to shop?" I laughed at Sybil's emphatic declaration about Saturday night's dinner, although I agreed with her completely. The King's Arms Tavern has the best peanut soup and Sally Lund bread I've ever tasted, and the atmosphere carries one straight back to the Eighteenth Century.

"Both!" Sybil declared. "Do you want me to wait until you talk with Bud or should I go ahead and make the reservations?"

"Make the reservations," I told her. "I'm sure Bud won't mind if I go, but let's stay somewhere fancier than Motel Six. That was okay eight years ago when we were still struggling 'school marms'. See if there is a Hampton Inn or a Sheraton near the Pottery Factory."

The Pottery Factory is a group of mismatched buildings, some Quonset huts, built on the outskirts of Williamsburg. It is a huge eyesore, has no air-conditioning, and houses some of the best outlet bargains in the country. Sybil and I loved to shop there, although we rarely had the chance, and when a rare chance occurred we usually came home with treasures galore.

"Okay," she agreed. "I'll call information and see what I can do. I'll call you back."

While I waited for Sybil's return call I pushed the vacuum cleaner aside and wandered outside and across the front porch. Strolling down my steep driveway I again savored the perfect fall day. The leaves on the deciduous trees that lined our street were just beginning to change into their autumn colors. What a shame if a storm were to materialize and shake them so hard that it stripped the branches bare.

Reaching into the mailbox at the foot of our property I retrieved the day's mail. Rather than return to the living room and the hostile presence of the vacuum cleaner, I perused the letters and catalogues there, in the cool, refreshing afternoon breeze. This time the letter with a return address printed in ink the color of dried blood was the first thing I saw. It was much thicker than the other Archdiocese letter had been.

My heart sank and I felt instantly queasy. The annulment, the Archdiocese, the problem that I didn't want to face all rushed back to me. Avoidance wasn't going to work. This worrisome problem was not going to just go away by my ignoring it. I had been such a child, such a coward to think that it would!

I trudged back up the driveway and into the house, around the vacuum cleaner still sitting in the middle of the living room floor, and plopped back down on the recliner. All the mail except for the Archdiocese letter slipped from my hands to the floor, unnoticed.

Tearing open the envelope, I unfolded the cover letter and read:

Archdiocese of Charleston Tribunal

I skipped through the inside address and date and began to read the body of the letter.

As you already know, the Archdiocese of Charleston has been approached by Lawrence O'Brian concerning the possibility of a declaration of nullity of his marriage to you on the grounds of invalid convalidation, the petitioner. A document of questions for you to answer and return to us is enclosed. Please return this to the Archdiocese in a timely manner in order that those appointed to study the petition may have this information before them as they do so.

According to the laws of the Church, and in an effort to respect the rights of all, you are to be informed of this action, given the right to participate or be represented, and the right to voice your objection if you do not approve of those serving on the case. They are: Very Reverend T.H. Foxcroft, JCL as Presiding Judge, Reverend Peter Prudhomme as Defender of the Bond, Reverend Harry J. Blodgett, JD as your Procurator/Advocate and Mrs. Shirley Grumman as Notary.

The formal hearing will be held at our office on November 25, 2001, at 2:00 p.m. Although it is not necessary for you to be present, you are invited to attend. The hearing will be brief. If you plan to attend please contact me. Should it be necessary, I trust you would be willing to talk with a member of the tribunal staff.

With every good wish, I remain
Sincerely,

Mrs. Shirley Grumman

Mrs. Shirley Grumman
Notary

Reverend Harry J. Blodgett

I let the cover letter drop to the floor and gazed at the thick pages of the "document of questions" that had made up the heft of the envelope. There were at least fourteen pieces of paper stapled together in the left corner, and each page was covered from top to bottom with typed questions.

I read the first three or four lines of the questionnaire's first page, which consisted of queries such as:

"Is your correct name Susannah Harris Davis? Which, of course, it isn't. It's Susannah Purcell Davis.

"At what age did you marry Lawrence Joseph O'Brian?

"At what age did you become sexually active?

"How many sexual partners did you have before you married Lawrence Joseph O'Brian?

"Was Lawrence Joseph O'Brian aware of your premarital sexual experience before you married him?"

Suddenly I became incensed! What sort of prurient questions were these, and how dared the Catholic Church ask them of me? I was a woman fast approaching sixty years of age, married almost thirty years to the same man, and a grandmother of four!

I rose to my feet and screamed at the top of my lungs, tossing the questionnaire as far as I could across the living room. This was the last straw! If Larry O'Brian thought he was going to empower the Catholic Church to treat me this way, ask questions that were none of their business, consider for a minute that it was my behavior that had led up to our divorce, not his, I was going to have to take a stand! I was going to have to fight back, somehow.

This called for a meeting of my friends. A meeting to present the newest annulment development to them. To gain their support of an idea that was fast forming in the back of my mind.

Within an hour the Red Hats had responded to my semi-hysterical call to each of them. Jaye had even cut out of her last period at school, which happened to be her planning period, but even so she'd had to fake a migraine headache to escape. Sally was out of town so there was no use trying to include her. Three of my staunchest friends were gathered around me, again, on the sun porch. A plate of Famous Amos chocolate chip cookies and a freshly opened bottle of Chardonnay was all I had to offer them on such short notice.

"Now tell me if this sounds crazy," I asked of the Red Hats, when they'd finished reading the questionnaire I'd received from the Archdiocese of Charleston. I'd already told them how violated I felt by receiving the document, and I could see that they were upset and angry for me.

"Nothing could be crazier than this damned questionnaire!" Sybil, who was holding it in her hand, dashed it to the floor in disgust.

"How dare they? Such rude questions," Jaye shook her head

as she spoke.

"What do you think might sound crazy?" Harriet asked me cautiously.

"Well, Sybil and I were tentatively planning a quick trip to Williamsburg," I paused when I saw the hurt expressions on Jaye and Harriet's faces. I quickly added, "We'd have asked the two of you but we wanted to leave on Friday morning and Jaye has to teach."

I turned to Harriet, "And it's so much cheaper if motel rooms have double occupancy, and there would be three of us going if we'd asked you. Plus you'd have to be home to take your mother and aunt to church on Sunday and we wouldn't have gotten back until Sunday afternoon…" my voice trailed off.

Harriet and Jaye nodded. They both understood.

"Anyway, the Williamsburg trip is off." I announced. "I want to go to Charleston!"

Sybil looked dumbfounded.

"I want to confront Larry, face to face, and ask him what the hell he thinks he's doing!" I jumped to my feet. "I want to ask him how he thinks he can make everything that went wrong with our marriage MY fault!"

Calm down," Jaye tried to soothe me by reaching out to touch my arm. "Why don't you just call him and ask him. Why go all the way down there?"

"First of all, his number is unlisted, and, besides that, I want to look into his little, beady eyes and ask for an explanation of why he wants to torture me after all these years!" I was so upset I was almost screaming.

"He wants to torture you because, apparently, he can. And there is something you're overlooking here, Sukie," Sybil, who seemed to have finally recovered from the shock I'd given her by announcing that I wanted to change our travel plans, was speaking very evenly. "This annulment isn't about you, at all, Honey. Larry is like a child who wants what he wants. He isn't thinking about how it is affecting you. He's only thinking about

75

himself."

"Or," Harriet added, "maybe it's his wife who is pushing for the annulment, and neither of them cares how it affects you. You always said Larry wasn't very religious while he was married to you. He married two other wives after you, outside the Church. Maybe this is all Wife Number Four's idea."

"Either way, both ways, I've got to find out." I answered my friend's logic in an adamant tone. "I've got to go to Charleston and confront the bastard."

"But Charleston is so far away," Sybil objected. "Do you plan to fly? Do you know where in Charleston he lives? Do you even imagine for a minute that Bud will let you go by yourself, and what about Hurricane Marcus?"

"I'm not going alone," I fixed my eyes on Sybil. "And we're driving. It isn't all that much farther to Charleston than it is to Williamsburg. I have Larry and Martie's address. We'll find the place, and after I talk with him, or both or them, we'll come home."

"We?" Sybil asked softly, pressing her lips together as if she were a little girl dreading the answer to her question.

"Yes, WE." I answered. "I'll drive all the way, Sybby." I was so desperate to convince my friend that I reverted to the pet name she had gone by in high school. We all reverted to calling her that from time to time. Just as Jaye sometimes went by her first initial "J" and Harriet became "Har," I'd even become used to answering to "Suke," although Sukie was already a nickname.

"I swear I will. You won't have to do anything but keep me company and help read the map. Bud and I made it there in one day, driving, when we went on vacation a couple of years ago. It's a straight shot down Route 81 most of the way, from Harrisburg. Please say you'll go with me. You don't ever have to see Larry. I'll go to his house by myself"

"What about Bud? What about the storm?" Harriet insisted, panic rising in her voice.

"I'll tell Bud that we're taking an extended trip to Williamsburg to cover the extra time we're gone," I laid out my plan to my friends, speaking very slowly at first and then speeding up as each idea occurred to me. "I'll call him everyday on my cell phone. He may not even be home if he has to go in to help run the storm up here. We can stop in Williamsburg on the way back so we'll have things we bought to show that we were there. You're right, Sybby, Bud would never let me go alone, if he knew about it. But I won't be alone. I'll have you, and he never has to find out the truth about our trip. The hurricane has slowed down. If it comes ashore it will be miles and miles above South Carolina. It will be in the Outer Banks."

"How can you be so sure where Marcus will make landfall?" Sybil asked, "You know what an inexact science hurricane prediction is."

"Oh, most of them come ashore at the Outer Banks," I brushed off the question. I was on a roll, now, with my plan. It seemed to take on a life of its own as I spoke.

"You're right." Jaye spoke up. "It's a crazy idea. It's totally nuts!"

Chapter Nine

And so Sybil and I went to Charleston.

When Bud first heard about our plans to make a shopping trip to Williamsburg he voiced concern that Hurricane Marcus could change course and hit Virginia hard, instead of making landfall in North Carolina. Of course, he had no idea about our change of plans and destination. But all the information on the weather channel of the TV seemed to bear out my protestations that the storm had slowed down and would probably not hit until several days later than first predicted. Its point of landfall was still a mystery to the weather forecasters. Hurricane prediction was, indeed, an inexact science, as Sybil had pointed out. I assured my husband that we'd be safely back home before there was any need for concern.

Making surreptitious plans for the secret trip Sybil and I would be taking was also aided by Bud's distraction due to the plans and preparations he was making at the Power Company and his projected trip to the Jersey Shore to bring in our deck furniture, gas grill, and pull down all the storm windows. There was great concern that Marcus's landfall might turn out to be much closer to home than expected: New Jersey or Long Island. Sybil and I whispered over the phone as we laid out our plans and, for good or ill, we had a lot of input from the remaining Red Hats.

"What about telling Maggie and Anne your plans?" Harriet asked with great concern. "You talk with them every Sunday, and when you don't call them they'll call you, and you won't be home. Won't that make them suspicious?"

"Bud will tell them that Sybil and I are in Williamsburg," I answered very simply.

"They wouldn't approve of what you're doing, if they knew about it. Would they?" Sybil asked softly.

"No. They probably wouldn't. At least Maggie wouldn't. Anne would probably insist upon going with us," I smiled a little, ruefully, "But I don't want them to know about it. I don't want them to have the responsibility of knowing about it. This is something that I have to take care of alone. Except for you, of course," I added the last part sending a glance hastily her way.

My friends were silent for a few seconds until Jaye jumped in quickly. Always thinking of what was dearest to all of our hearts she insisted that we take plenty of food with us.

"I'm providing snacks and things you can eat while you're driving and staying in a motel. You'll have to find someplace to stay once you get there," She announced to both of us. "You never know when you'll be stuck somewhere where you can't get food. And it will save money. I'll even include some surprises."

My mouth watered. I hadn't eaten much in the last day or so. I never can eat when I'm nervous.

Harriet was laying out our itinerary. She had access to Mapquest on her computer and was searching every inch of our projected trip, plus the location of Larry's Charleston address, which I had given to her.

I had found the old Triple A TripTik that Bud and I had used five years before when we'd stopped off in Charleston on our way to Florida. The direction we'd taken, down Rte. 81, was still marked boldly in yellow magic marker, complete with arrows. Hopefully it was still up to date enough to be of use to us because, despite Harriet's pages and pages of Mapquest information, I felt more at home using a TripTik that I knew had taken me safely from point "A" to "Z" before. Even if it had been five years ago.

Sybil and I packed quickly but logically, taking clothes for weather warmer than ours in Pennsylvania, raincoats, umbrellas, and the big Penn State tailgate cooler filled with canned soda, bottled water, and any of Jaye's snacks that required refrigeration. We checked our lists with each other over the phone, and, from the tone of her voice, I could tell that Sybil was getting into the spirit of our expanded trip, despite herself.

This was good because I had begun to feel both frightened and guilty. After receiving the Catholic Church questionnaire, I was still furious enough at Larry to keep my momentum for the trip going but, despite my cavalier attitude when I had first proposed the idea to my friends, I was having a second thought or two.

What if we got there and Larry and his wife weren't home? I really knew nothing about exactly where he lived or where he worked, if he did. Harriet's computer program had pinpointed Larry's address as being in a gated community on the outskirts of Charleston but, other than directions on how to get there, I had no idea of how I was going to find it or get into the place to confront him. I was fairly certain that once my presence was known to him Larry would not simply invite me into his home.

Also, Bud was being so sweet and understanding about "our trip to Williamsburg" that the guilt of keeping our real destination and my true intentions to myself was just about killing me. It wasn't the first time I'd kept secrets from my husband. While Maggie and Anne were growing up I'd kept many of their secrets, not telling Bud details about their adolescent love lives, heartbreaks, early delving into sexuality.

I'd walked a fine line between sharing with Bud and allowing my daughters their own spaces. Sometimes my husband had found out about things I had intentionally not told him, and he'd been hurt and angry. But since our daughters were grown, married women the need to keep secrets from Bud had all but vanished. He and I had harbored no secrets from each other in years, at least none of which I was aware. It was hard, now, to keep this trip a guilty secret. To hide intentions, of which Bud would highly disapprove, from him.

In the end, as Sybil and I were ready to leave Martin's Field, at daybreak, two days after I'd proposed the trip, Bud leaned through the window on the driver's side of our Dodge Caravan and kissed me goodbye. As usual, he told me to use cash in place of my credit cards whenever possible, warned both Sybil and me to drive carefully, and insisted that I call him everyday. And we were off!

We'd also promised to call the Red Hats we'd left behind us every day.

"You won't forget," Harriet clucked at our last gathering before Sybil and I left. "We'll be on pins and needles until we know you've made it there safely and let Larry have it, face to face."

"I wish I could go with you," Jaye kept saying wistfully.

"You keep us up to date and we'll keep Sally in the loop. She should be home from her New England trip by the time you get back. You won't be more than three or four days, will you?" Harriet was acting like a mother hen sending her chicks out into the world for the first time.

"We'll call, we'll call," I had assured them both, "and you know you'll be with us every minute in spirit."

As I drove down Rtes. 11 and 15 toward Harrisburg I couldn't believe what a lovely fall day it was. The sun was rising on our left. It glinted off the deeply blue Susquehanna River, which was also to our left, and, as we sped by, created a strobelight effect as it peered through the half bare branches of the trees that grew thickly on the river's bank. I swung the sun visor on the driver's side of the windshield to the window on my left to avoid being made dizzy by the strobing effect of the light.

I was glad to be concentrating on driving. It kept my mind from going round and round over plans that would have to be made when we finally got to Charleston. Sybil was very quiet. She was already studying the TripTik and Mapquest charts of our trip.

"Let's eat something," I finally broke the silence. I had not eaten any breakfast. I'd been too nervous and busy to do so before we left home. "There's juice in the cooler and I think Jaye baked us a coffee cake as a surprise. It should be in the cake carrier that I saw her sneak into the back of the van last night. She doesn't bake as well as you do but she's awfully sweet to make the effort for us."

"Umm," Sybil agreed with me and putting down the maps she turned around to the van's middle seat where we'd conveniently stashed our supply of food. She had to lean over so far to reach everything that her voice, when she spoke, was muffled. Still, I could make out the words, *crumbs*, and *juice*.

When she turned back in her seat she was smiling triumphantly and holding two small bottles of orange juice in one hand and Jaye's cake carrier in the other. Upon opening it we did, indeed, find a very crumbly, sad looking coffeecake. Warily, Sybil broke off pieces for both of us, handed me mine, and we each took a bite. Instantly, smiles wreathed our faces. What Jaye's *surprise* lacked in beauty it more than made up for in taste.

"Don't forget that we stay on this side of the river," Sybil reminded me as we neared the turn off for the Clark's Ferry Bridge and Harrisburg. She knew that Bud and I were both accustomed to crossing the bridge and picking up the PA Turnpike, when we drove to our New Jersey beach house or

Maggie's home in the Philadelphia suburbs.

I assured her that I would stay on the West Bank of the Susquehanna, as we did when driving to Anne's home outside Baltimore. Only, instead of taking Rte. 83, on the other side of Lemoyne, I would turn onto Rte. 81 at Summerdale, long before we reached Rte. 83.

I did this and the long, fairly straight, drive to Charleston was definitely begun.

The drive down Rte. 81 is a most scenic trip. The traveler experiences miles and miles of green trees and fields. Even at this time in the late fall, with the deciduous trees changing colors, the predominant color of the landscape was emerald, due to all the rain the Mid-Atlantic states had received. Perhaps because of all this rain and the longer growing season south of our state, wildflowers still grew abundantly in the highway's wide median strip. The riotous colors, some bright, some pastel, were a delight to the eyes.

It seemed an impossibility that somewhere off the shore of the eastern United States a monster hurricane lurked. I knew we should be listening to the radio for weather updates but I avoided doing so. I felt enough stress making this trip without hearing constant reports about the whereabouts of Hurricane Marcus! Neither Sybil nor I suggested we awaken the sleeping radio, and we didn't. I put Marcus out of my mind and, apparently, so did the friend sitting next to me.

What was even more interesting to us than the eye-pleasing colors of the trip was the number of states we passed through in such quick succession. If you followed the route carefully, on the map, you found that you crossed quickly from Pennsylvania into Maryland and then, even more quickly, across a short spit of West Virginia that hooked out below the northwestern tip of Maryland. After only a few miles spent whizzing through West Virginia you then crossed into Virginia for the longest leg of the trip.

"Did you know that there is a Williamsport in Maryland?"

Sybil asked, her mind and eyes wandering from the TripTik route into the surrounding countryside, even though we'd already passed it.

There is also a Williamsport in Pennsylvania, only about fifty miles north of Martin's Field. It is an old town that grew up originally around the lumber business and now features a theater, which is visited by many really good performers on the professional concert circuit. The Red Hats love to attend concerts there, especially the ones that feature music from the 50s and 60s. I've also dragged Bud there to see dance troupes and operas, but when I do he invariably falls asleep, or asks me, "When is half-time?"

"I'll bet there are a lot of identical town names on every map, if you look hard enough," I replied checking the van's gas gauge. "I think we'll stop for gas around Roanoke. Want to get some lunch when we do?"

"Sure," Sybil answered enthusiastically, closing the TripTik and folding the map, "although I feel kind of guilty eating in a restaurant when Jaye packed all these snacks for us."

"Stop feeling guilty and break out some more of them, "I instructed. "I bet there are some chocolate covered pretzels in one of the bags. She knows they're your favorites."

When the pretzels were found and we were munching on them and enjoying the sunshine and scenery, I was in such a blissful state of mind that I was able to put both Hurricane Marcus and Larry out of my mind. I didn't even have to reassure myself that everything was gong to be all right. For the first time since I'd suggested, no insisted, that we make the trip, I believed wholeheartedly in what we were doing.

"That's exactly what Jaye's goodies are. Snacks," I reminded Sybil hours later, as I pulled into a gas station near Roanoke. "They're for when we can't find any place to get food, or for late at night in our motel. I'm starting to get really hungry. How about lunch?"

"Okay," she smiled. "What about that place over there?" and

she pointed to a rustic establishment farther down the road that just shouted *Home Cooking*.

Mrs. Taylor's Home Style Restaurant had been established in 1947, according to the sign out front, and featured food extremely reminiscent of the home cooking in our Central Pennsylvania area. I ordered tuna salad, baked beans, and macaroni and cheese with stewed tomatoes. Three of the favorite comfort foods of my childhood. Haute cuisine they may not have been but they were delicious, truly homemade, and I ate them with relish. Sybil was very good and, sticking to her latest diet, ordered only a chef's salad.

On our way to visit the ladies room and pay the bill, I spotted a shelf above the cash register stocked with jams and jellies for sale.

"I'd like a jar of blueberry preserves and one of raspberry, please," I smiled and told the elderly woman who rang up our bill. She looked old enough to be the original Mrs. Taylor, I thought.

She smiled back at me and reached up for two of the jars. "We sell a lot of these, and our pies," she told me with a lovely hint of southern drawl.

With the jars of preserves packaged in a small brown paper bag, Sybil and I returned to the van. I always make it a practice to try jams and jellies from different parts of the country when I'm traveling. I do so with the idea that if they are good I'll order more when I get home. The best blueberry preserves I ever found were in a small grocery store I'd visited in the Seattle, WA area. They'd been made in Oregon and were delicious. When I got home and we'd finished the jar, I had fully intended to write to the company to order more. I regret to this day having accidentally thrown out the jar and the address of the company that made the preserves with it.

*   *   *

Not long after Roanoke we turned off Rte 81 onto Rte 77 and, before we knew it, we were in North Carolina. The terrain which had been fairly flat in the portions of Maryland and West Virginia through which we'd passed had become noticeably more hilly in Virginia. The Blue Ridge Mountains in the distance reminded me of the time, shortly before his death, when my father had taken our family camping somewhere in these mountains. I'd been about ten years old at the time, and we were living in Arlington, Virginia. Daddy had shore duty, which was always the best time for our family. After a trip along the Skyline Drive and a visit to the Luray Caverns, we'd set up our tent right beside a stream in a Virginia State Park. I had pictures of my brother and me swimming in a lake, a very tame fawn beside us in the water, allowing us to pet it.

I forced myself to pull my eyes from the lovely mountains and concentrate on the road. I was beginning to feel the fatigue of continuous hours of driving. I knew that Sybil would offer to drive if I complained of the stiffness beginning to grip my neck and shoulders but this trip had been my idea. I'd promised to do the driving and do it I would.

North Carolina afforded us mountainous vistas, too. All throughout Virginia we'd seen numerous small farms, and the same was now true of this more southern state. The only difference was that instead of being spread out along the road like the Virginia farms the small North Carolina farms were nestled in pockets between hills or clung to the hillsides.

When we reached the other side of Charlotte we stopped at a gas station to stretch our legs and, in my case, my neck and shoulders, use the ladies room, and put more gas in the van. Sybil searched through the cooler and bags of snacks that Jaye had packed for us and came up with a box of chocolate chip cookies and two Caffeine-free Diet Cokes. There was a picnic table in a clearing not far down the road from the gas station, and I pulled in there. By this time we were both getting really tired of traveling, and a late afternoon snack and some time spent outside the van appealed to both of us.

Sybil and I climbed on top of the table and leaned back, enjoying the warm weather of a state so much farther south than our own. We popped our Coke cans and dived into the box of cookies. The late afternoon sun felt heavenly on my back and shoulders. Yellowjackets, drunk on the fermented fruit fallen from an old, gnarled apple tree nearby buzzed by our heads in uncertain circles.

"Ah," I sighed happily, flexing both my legs.

"I don't think we can put off discussing 'The Elephant in the Room' much longer," Sybil murmured as she munched cookies contentedly.

"'The Elephant in the Room'!" I exclaimed, rudely pulled back from having let my mind go blank in the sheer luxury of being out of the van and in the open air on such a lovely day.

"Yes. 'The Elephant in the Room'. What do we do when we get to Charleston, to Larry's house? What is our plan?"

"I...I don't know," I mumbled, and I didn't.

Chapter Ten

A plan was the farthest thing from both our minds when, late that night, after picking up Rte 26 in Columbia, the capitol of South Carolina, crossing over the Congaree River, and finishing the last leg of the trip, we finally arrived in North Charleston. I was exhausted, tired almost beyond the ability to think. I pulled off the highway into the first Budget Motel I found.

We were at the point where Rte 26 merged with Rte 526, which we would eventually have to take to reach Larry's gated community. Palmetto Crown Plantation was located south of the city, near Hollywood, South Carolina, according to Harriet's Map Quest information. At this point in time I didn't care if it was on the other side of the moon. All I could think of was getting out of the van and into a bed. I could barely keep my eyes open.

"I'll check us in," Sybil offered, swinging open the door on her side of the van as soon as I turned off the ignition. "You're exhausted. Rest here until I get the key, and we can drive to whichever unit they give us."

Too tired to answer her I leaned my head back against the headrest of my seat and closed my eyes. I must have dozed off because the next thing I knew she was back in the van beside me, giving me directions to room number two-thirty-five.

We reached our unit in less than two minutes and I grabbed my overnight bag, rolled out of the van, and locked it. Sybil unlocked the door to the room and, completely dressed, I climbed into the nearest bed and was asleep before the lights were turned off.

Just before I lost consciousness I could hear Sybil speaking softly on my cell phone. She was calling Bud and explaining that we'd gone shopping and out to dinner once we'd reached Williamsburg. I remember thinking could anyone have a closer, dearer friend? And then everything was mercifully dark and quiet.

We slept in the next morning. Nothing short of a Sherman tank coming through the wall could have awakened me before nine thirty, and when I opened my eyes I had no idea where I was. Light was streaming in through a gap in the drapes of the only window in the room. I could hear the low hum of highway traffic somewhere near, but it took a few seconds before I realized that I wasn't in my own bed.

I closed my eyes and when I opened them again Sybil was standing beside me.

"It's a quarter of ten," she informed me. "Shouldn't we get going?"

Grudgingly, I struggled to sit up and shoved the pillows behind my back. I pushed hair out of my eyes with one hand and forced my eyes to focus on her and the room. A nagging pain from the arthritis in my lower back reminded me that I had slept in an unfamiliar bed. It happened every time I left my cozy bed at home where the mattress was molded to my body from years of use.

"Get going where?"

"I don't know. To Larry's house? To breakfast? This was your idea. You must have something in mind."

I felt queasy in the pit of my stomach, again, and guilty. In truth, I didn't have a plan. Far from it. I wished, with all my heart, that Bud were with us. He'd know what we should do next. Cold reality hit me right between the eyes. Bud thought we were in Virginia. I'd lied to him. I'd decided to handle confronting Larry on my own, and, now that we were in Charleston, I'd better damn well come up with a plan, and fast.

"Thanks for calling Bud last night, Sybby" I told her. "I really appreciate it. I couldn't have talked to anyone. I felt like a zombie after all that driving. I'll call him tonight. And I guess we should call the Red Hats, too. I know they're probably dying of curiosity as to how our trip is going," I tried to sound calm and confident as I swung my legs over the side of the bed. "Let's find a restaurant and get some breakfast. Do you want to take the first shower or should I?"

"I will," Sybil gathered up her pretty, quilted Vera Bradley overnight bag and headed into the bathroom. "But I hope you have a plan," she called back to me.

A small shelf in the motel lobby offered a meager selection of cold cereals, Danish pastries, coffee and juices, and billed itself as a complementary "Continental Breakfast." We made our selections and sat down at one of the tiny empty tables. All four of the available tables were empty. We were obviously the last guests to take advantage of the free breakfast. The pastries were stale and the coffee left a lot to be desired, but since we were on a tight budget the food was most welcome.

"Okay, what's next?" Sybil asked as she wiped the last crumbs of Danish from the corners of her mouth.

"We pay the motel bill and try to find Palmetto Crown Plantation," I mumbled and swallowed my last sip of coffee. I felt I was being as logical as I was capable of being at that moment "I'll pay my half of the room with cash so it doesn't show up on the VISA bill when we get back home. Bud probably wouldn't notice. I usually write checks for my own VISA bills, but you never can tell."

"Good thought," Sybil answered going through the Vera Bradley wallet that matched her Vera Bradley handbag, which matched her Vera Bradley soft luggage. She is nothing if not coordinated in her choice of accessories. "I'll put my half on Master Card."

Back in the van we consulted the Charleston City map and Harriet's MapQuest documents. It appeared that if we took Rte 526 South around the circumference of the city we could connect with Rte 17, which would, eventually, take us to Rte 700. Then all we would have to do was follow the road signs for Folly Beach and Kiawah Island, turning southwest on Rte 700 before we reached either of them. Somewhere in the vicinity of Hollywood, South Carolina we should be able to ask someone for directions to Larry's gated golf community. It all looked very simple. Too simple. In my mind I began to question the validity of Harriet's MapQuest pages.

I pulled out of the motel into North Charleston traffic. It was a Tuesday but, luckily, since we'd slept so late, we'd missed the morning rush hour traffic. Even so, I had to grip the wheel and remain alert for cars and trucks weaving in and out of lanes on the highway. Sybil, still acting as navigator, barked out instructions for making turns and kept me alerted to aggressive drivers approaching us.

"Boy, I'm glad I live in a small town. This traffic is murder!" Sybil exclaimed as a huge tractor-trailer attempted to cut us off.

"That goes double for me!" I shouted back, gripping the wheel as if it were a lifeline and attempting to keep the van under control.

The situation became even more tense when we found ourselves on Rtes 221, and then 162 instead of the route suggested by the map. Apparently, as I'd suspected, getting to where we wanted to go was not going to be as simple as the map and Harriet's information had made it out to be.

We passed over the Ashley River Bridge and I remembered

that a tour guide had told Bud and me on our first trip to Charleston that, "Charleston is where the Ashley and Cooper Rivers come together to form the Atlantic Ocean." How he and I had laughed at the Charlestonian stiff-necked, southern pride that was still alive and well more than a century after the American Civil War had ended. The Charleston residents didn't even refer to the war by its historical name. To them it was "The War of Northern Aggression" or "The Unpleasantness."

Living as close to the town of Gettysburg, Pennsylvania, and its famous battlefield, as my family and I did, we were about a two-hour drive away, we had visited both often. Especially during the years that Anne had attended Gettysburg College. The American Civil War had been our nation's greatest tragedy, claiming more American lives than any other war in which our country had been involved. But I didn't know any place north of the Mason Dixon Line that romanticized it as some southern cities did. Although *Gone With the Wind* was a well-written novel, and I'd seen the movie eighteen times when I was a teenager, I, like most northerners, accepted the fact that while Scarlett O'Hara and her friends charmed us the Civil War was most certainly over.

Confused by the differences between the Route numbers suggested by Harriet's charts, the TripTik, and the actual roads upon which we found ourselves, Sybil and I stopped at a gas station for fuel and information soon after we turned off what we had thought to be Rte 17.

"Y'all's goin' in the right direction," the young man who pumped our gas assured us when we showed him the map and told him of our plight. "Seventeen turns into Two-twenty-one fer a spell around South Charleston. It messes up a lot of tourists." He was quite handsome in a Brad Pitt sort of way, if one overlooked the many tattoos visible on his muscular arms and his uneven front teeth.

"Well, we're certainly tourists," Sybil agreed with him, "and we've certainly been messed up."

We felt somewhat better about the direction in which we were going after talking with a native of the area.

"But how do we get to Hollywood?" I asked trying to make sense of the map spread out on the hood of the van. "And have you ever heard of Palmetto Crown Plantation?"

"Hollywood's jest a little speck of a town, Ma'am," he told us replacing the hose on the side of the gas pump. "Palmetty Crown's before you git there."

"How long before we get to Palmetto Crown?" Sybil asked as I paid the bill. Gasoline seemed to be about the same price in the Charleston area as it was back home but since Bud was the one who always gassed up our cars, while I paid little attention, I couldn't be sure. Bud. I was really missing him now and feeling guiltier than ever that I had not told him the truth about our trip.

"Oh, jest keep on down the road about a mile and y'all'll turn off onto Route 165. That's the road you want. Once y'all're on that ya make a dogleg at the old mill and Palmetty Crown is just a stone's throw from there on your left."

We thanked him for his help and drove off hoping we'd recognize a "dogleg" and a "stone's throw" when we came to them. The traffic and habitation along whatever route we were traveling was becoming much sparser. It was not a sunny day, such as the day before had been. The sky was overcast and the humidity was so much higher than before that the heat it produced convinced us to shed the light sweaters we'd worn from the motel earlier that morning.

Spanish moss hung from the large trees along the side of the road and their girth told us that they were very old. The remains of an old gristmill came upon us almost before we noticed it. Only a few stones and boards, plus what was left of the large wheel, now collapsed into the stream that had once turned it, were recognizable.

The "dogleg" of which the young man had spoken appeared just as suddenly as had the mill. I made a quick turn left and then right, again, onto an even more secondary road than the one we'd been on. Now there was nothing except high grass and, eventually, water along both sides of the road. We had obviously driven into a wetland area. I was very familiar with wetlands since they abounded in the New Jersey Coast area where Bud and I had our beach house. They were considered endangered in New Jersey, and everyone did their best to preserve them and the birds that inhabited the area. I wondered if they were endangered here.

It wasn't long before the grass along the left side of the road became less unruly and it was obvious that the marshy ground had been bolstered by fill. The berm appeared to be manicured in the style of most golf courses, and we saw that we were approaching a high wrought iron fence and gates. As I slowed down we discovered a gilded sign, decorated with one golden palm tree, posted on the fence. It read: Palmetto Crown Plantation. Beyond the gates, recessed slightly and in the middle of the driveway approaching it, was a small building that, no doubt, housed a security guard, probably one who stopped non-residents from entering the community. And if the turf on the berm in front of the gates was any clue the community in which Larry lived probably boasted a well kept golf course, as well.

I pulled the van over to the right side of the road, being careful not to get too close to the edge of the berm. The last thing I wanted to do was to get our vehicle stuck in the mud of the marshy wetlands.

"This is where we have a problem," I informed Sybil. "I don't know what to do. Drive up to the gate and ask for information? Take the chance of being turned away? Drive right through like we belong here and know where we're going?"

"Let's drive down the road a little farther," Sybil suggested. "Maybe there's another entrance or, at least, a break in the fence. If we can get in, even if we have to ditch the van somewhere, we might be able to find Larry's house on foot."

"Good idea," I agreed, turning the car back onto the road and proceeding south at a slow pace. "I have his street address and house number." We both scrutinized every inch of the wrought iron fence as I drove.

Several hundred yards down the road the fence ended and was replaced by a high, carefully pruned hedge. This went on for another long stretch before it disappeared into a tangle of unkempt trees and bushes. There was no other visible entrance or break in the fence or hedge until it ended at the tangle of trees and underbrush.

I pulled off the road, again, feeling frustrated. "What now?" I asked.

"Let's find someplace to park the van and see if we can get onto the property from this end," Sybil was pulling off the sandals that she wore with her capri pants and short-sleeved sweater. "I packed my Wellies in case we ran into bad rain, and I'm going to put them on, right now. We're going to try to get through that mess of bushes over there." She pointed to the wild expanse of undergrowth at the end of the manicured hedge.

"I can't just leave the van along the side of the road," I protested. "We've got to find somewhere we can get it well off the road without getting stuck in the swamp."

"The mill," Sybil reminded me as she turned and stretched out over the middle seat of the van. She was rummaging through her suitcase, pulling out rubber boots and a pair of jeans. "It was farther off the road than anything else around here. We can park there and walk back here."

"Okay. It's worth a try," I grudgingly backed the van across the road and, with two turns, had it pointed north, back in the direction from which we'd come.

Returning to the ruins of the grist mill, I found that there was, indeed, a stretch of high grass to the north of it that appeared to be dry and which backed up to an area slightly behind the broken mill wheel. Carefully, I inched the van off the road and into the high grass. I managed to settle it partially behind the mill and turned off the ignition.

Sybil struggled into her jeans and Wellies, and I searched

through my suitcase for more sturdy clothes and footwear. If we were going to tramp through briars, kudzu, and heaven knew what, in an attempt to gain entrance to Palmetto Crown Plantation without being observed, I certainly couldn't wear the light summer clothes I had on. I settled upon the pair of jeans I had brought and my New Balance athletic shoes. I sighed as I put them on. I'd cleaned them up before we'd left home, and now I was probably going to get them dirty all over again, stomping around in some wetland swamp. Oh, well. It couldn't be helped.

"It's so hot," Sybil mopped her perspiring face as we exited the car.

"It's the humidity," I reminded her, checking my watch. "Are you hungry? It's after noon and if we're going to be hiking for a while we might want to eat some of Jaye's snacks now, before we leave the car. That's what they're for, remember? To eat when we can't find any other food."

We both thought it prudent to fortify ourselves with peanut butter crackers and cokes that were still cold thanks to the two bags of ice we'd poured over them in the ice chest before we'd left the motel. When we finished, I locked the van, stowed the keys in the pocket of my jeans, and we started walking back along the "dogleg" toward Larry's gated community.

"Have you noticed that we haven't seen one vehicle on this road since we started driving on it?" I asked my friend as we walked. "Nothing's passed us. It's dead quiet, almost spooky."

"Yeah. Palmetto Crown Plantation must be a really exclusive place."

"Either that or it's so far out nobody except the people who live here drive this road. It's a weekday so maybe anyone who would be coming here is at work, somewhere."

"Did you bring the cell phone?" Sybil asked as we continued down the road toward the fence and gates of Palmetto Crown Plantation, "You've had it turned off the entire time we've been gone. No one could reach us if they wanted to, and we haven't turned on the radio or watched TV since we left home. We really ought to check on where Hurricane Marcus is."

"No. I left it in the car," I answered trying to focus on the approaching fence, "And Bud would have said something to you about the storm when you called last night if we had anything to worry about."

"He was asleep when I called, and I woke him up. He hardly said anything before I hung up. We really should call the girls," Sybil mused, continuing to wipe perspiration from her upper lip and brow. "I wish you'd brought the phone with you. We promised them we'd keep in touch. The Red Hats must be wondering, right now, what we're doing."

"I'm wondering right now what we're doing," I commented acerbically, slapping at a mosquito that was trying to land on my exposed arm. "I always keep my cell phone turned off, unless I'm expecting a call. So why try to stuff it in my pocket to bring it with us? These jeans are already too tight. Besides, we certainly wouldn't want it to go off, accidentally, while we were sneaking around here. We'll call the girls when we know something. Right now we have nothing to report except we're hot and haven't even found a way into Larry's fortress."

When Sybil and I reached the gates and recessed guardhouse of Palmetto Crown we kept our eyes averted and tried to appear as if we were two middle-aged matrons out for a daily stroll. Out of the corner of my eye I was able to discern two shapes inside the glass walls of the building.

"It must be air-conditioned in there," I whispered enviously.

The two guards did not seem concerned by our presence, and we kept on walking until we reached the area where the carefully pruned hedge, beyond the fence, ended.

"Now!" Sybil hissed sotto voce and practically dragged me off the road and into the tangled underbrush. It seemed to me that we made a great deal of noise snapping branches and trampling dried leaves beneath our feet, as we made our way off the road and into the thicket. The bushes and vines were so thick that we had to bend at the waist and use our hands and arms thrust out ahead of us to part the foliage and move forward.

We hadn't gone two hundred yards before we came to a six-foot high chain link fence that was not visible from the road.

"It figures!" Sybil, hot, sweaty, and by now scratched and covered with dead leaves and bark exclaimed. "This sucks!"

I was really angry, too. So near and yet so far away from where we needed to go!

"I'm not turning back," I informed her, "I'm going to walk along this fence until I find some way to get over it."

I started off, walking along the fence, bent over and headed, I figured, in a southeastern direction. I was hot and sweaty, too, and my arms and neck were covered with scratches and mosquito bites, but this was going to be my one opportunity to confront Larry. I was going to get in there, find him, and vent my rage, which was becoming more and more aggravated by my physical discomfort, upon him. At this point I was so angry with my ex-husband, at that moment, that I felt I could cheerfully kill him with my bare hands!

Chapter Eleven

It seemed as if Sybil and I had been inching our way through dense undergrowth along the chain link fence for at least an hour. It could not have been that long but try telling that to a not-yet-fully-post-menopausal woman. One whose already high body temperature had now risen even higher due to the heat and humidity of a place swarming with mosquitoes and populated by who-knew-what-sort of animals and reptiles. Not to mention the temperature elevation caused by extreme frustration.

Sybil and I made a lot of the thrashing noises that filled my ears as we attempted to make headway in the dense thicket in which we found ourselves, but there were other sounds that were not of our making. Unfamiliar, warbling bird calls and small, scurrying noises added to our general sense of apprehension. Something moved quickly over my right foot causing me to give a small, involuntary scream.

"Sh-h-h-h," Sybil cautioned.

I stopped moving. Not that my stopping was greatly

noticeable since we were making no measurable headway, of which to speak, through the dense undergrowth.

"Something just ran across my foot," I gasped, "What sort of animals and snakes do you think might be in here with us?"

"Sukie, don't start! Coming here was your idea. Your terrible idea. Don't talk to me about snakes," Sybil ordered. She was slightly ahead of me but it was so dark in the thicket that I could barely make her out.

"I just wondered," I answered in a voice that sounded almost like a whine. It had the same timbre as Anne's four-year-old daughter's voice did when she didn't get what she wanted. And, Lord knows, I certainly wasn't getting what I wanted! I slapped another mosquito. This one on my neck.

"It's lighter ahead," Sybil suddenly informed me. "I think I can see water!"

We came out of the underbrush suddenly and discovered that we'd reached the end of the fence. At first the light hurt my eyes which had become accustomed to gloom of the thicket.

"Ah," I moaned, as I was at last able to stand upright and massage the pain in my lower back.

My relief at being upright and back in the light and air was short lived, however, as I noticed that Sybil wasn't showing any joy in our re-emergence into the world. And I could quickly see why. The chain link fence ended in a wide expanse of what appeared to be fairly deep, brackish water.

"Oh, great," Sybil leaned against a single large tree growing on the bank of what appeared to be an inlet. "What now?"

I could see marsh grass sticking up out of the water in places and small boats were visible along the shore to our left, on the other side of the fence. Turning to my left, I pressed my nose to the chain link and could just make out several short docks jutting out along the perimeter of the water in the distance.

"We have to get around this damned fence. I think this is the back of the development. People must keep boats for fishing at the end of their properties, the ones that back up to the inlet, or bay, or whatever it is," I reasoned. "It almost reminds me of the bay in Avalon, except it smells better."

"And how do you propose that we get around the fence? Wade in the water?" Sybil asked. She was beginning to sound sarcastic, and who could blame her? I, too, was out of sorts and ready to lose my temper at any moment.

"Exactly!" I snapped back at her and, grasping the fence, I put a foot, then my whole leg into the water.

Luckily the water at its edge was only hip deep and the fence was firmly anchored in the mud and silt beneath it. I managed to slog my way through the water and around the fence's end to the other side, where I stood covered in mud and dripping wet. To my astonishment it felt good!

"Sybby, come on," I exclaimed, "The water's not deep and it feels wonderful to be cool and wet!" I ignored the fact that my once-white shoes were now coated with black muck. So much for having bothered to clean them.

Shaking her head Sybil followed my example, splashing through the water and soon standing beside me. Her Wellingtons fared far better than my athletic shoes.

"You know what? You're right! I never thought I'd be glad to be wet and muddy but it sure is better than being hot and eaten alive by bugs in the bushes." Sybil threw her arms around me and we hugged each other and laughed from sheer relief and amusement over our physical condition.

"Come on," I broke away from my friend and motioned for her to follow. "Let's find out where we are. I don't know how big this place is. We could be miles away from Larry's house or right around the corner. We have to find 65 Windsor Way."

We began to walk along the shoreline of what I had by now figured out was an inlet. It was much like the inlet that was located next to the yacht club in Avalon, the New Jersey beach town where our summer house/rental property was located. Sybil and I quickly discovered that, while our lower extremities felt cooler than before, walking in wet, muddy jeans was not a pleasant experience. It was slow going and our thighs chafed with every step we took.

"I bet we smell," Sybil commented.

"It's the tidal water," I informed her with a small laugh. "We reek of it!"

A dock, at the end of a well-landscaped yard, leading up to the back of a gracious house nestled among tall oak trees, soon appeared on our left. It was very quiet and no one seemed to be outside. I wished that the driveway and garage area of the house were visible so we stood a chance of telling whether anyone was at home but apparently both were in the front portion of the house.

"Should we risk entering the development through this property?" Sybil lowered her voice almost to a whisper.

"Why not?" I answered. "It's as good as any, and we need to find out what street we're on."

Cautiously we walked up the flagstone path leading from the dock to the back of the house. No faces appeared at any of the windows. No voices called out. We slunk around the right corner of the house, down the sloping front yard, and into a street paved with crushed oyster shells.

"So far so good," Sybil muttered as we walked swiftly past the front of the house, which featured a neo-classical pediment and faux Greek columns. There appeared to be two more houses of similar architecture farther along the street toward a corner on which stood was a small street sign, also decorated with a single golden palm tree.

Carefully trying to appear as if we belonged in the community of Palmetto Crown Plantation and casting furtive glances in both directions, up and down the street, as we moved, we reached the sign on the corner.

"We're on Hampton Court," Sybil voiced what we both read. "I wonder how close that is to Windsor Way?"

"I wish we had a map of the development," I mused regretfully continuing to look in an appraising manner up and down the street.

"Yes," Sybil's voice was again sarcastic, "that would certainly simplify things. Too bad one of us didn't think about that before we got here." I knew the "one of us" she referred to was me.

"Well, since we don't have one we'd better start walking," I squared my shoulders and began marching rapidly in the direction of a grove of cultivated trees that I could just make out in the distance.

"Wait, wait," Sybil called after me and hurried to catch up.

I strode toward the trees, taking large steps. Both to cover the distance quickly and because I wanted to avoid further chafing as my thighs rubbed together. It felt to me like the humidity in the air was increasing with every step I took if that was possible. I almost felt as if I were trying to walk through warm honey.

"Oh, look," Sybil pointed out as we approached the trees and the carefully manicured grass beneath them. "It's part of a golf course. See the flag in the hole!"

Neither Sybil nor I know much about the game my husband plays every Sunday that he possibly can. Bud is an avid, if not a scratch, player. I've been to the public course where he and his friends play but I know next to nothing about the game. I tried once to assume the stance and swing a club but I informed Bud, after I'd missed the ball completely, that I felt like a ruptured duck and could not understand why people liked such a silly game. He just laughed and gave me what I call his "There, there, little woman" look.

"I thought there'd be a golf course in here, somewhere," I assented as I swept the sixteenth hole of the Palmetto Crown Plantation with a glance.

It was a lovely green, surrounded on one side by large, graceful willow trees and on the other by a slow running stream. Willow trees always grow well in marshy areas and this close to Palmetto Crown Plantation's wetlands the trees were thriving. The only incongruous feature of the seemingly perfect landscape that lay before us was a large dead log that lay half in and half out of the stream.

Suddenly I blinked! Amazingly, the large dead log lying half out of the stream appeared to stir. Then, to my horror, it began to move slowly toward us. At first I couldn't believe my eyes. I felt like I was experiencing a dream sequence. Then I grabbed Sybil's arm and shook it frantically.

"Sybby," I squealed. "Sybby!"

"Oh my God!" my friend exclaimed. "It's an alligator. Run, Sukie! Run!"

We both whirled and ran in the opposite direction as far and as fast as our waterlogged, mud-caked, out-of-shape, sixty-year-old legs would take us. We were back on an oyster shell road, now, and in our haste had passed several of the holes on the golf course. When we stopped for breath we found that we had regained civilization in the form of more houses on another street in the development.

"Oh, Sybby!" I gasped, bent over, trying to breathe in big gulps of air. "I've, I've never been so scared in my life."

"Me, either," she gasped back. "Where did it come from? Do you suppose anyone knows it's here? Do you think there are any more of them?"

"I have no idea," I managed to regain my breath and stand up straight. "But let's not stick around the golf course to find out."

I hurried to the street corner and read the name on the sign bearing a golden palm tree. "Tudor Trace."

"Where the hell is Windsor Way?" Sybil sounded as if she was fast running out of energy. "We could wander around in here all day trying to find Larry's house and run into nothing except more swamp monsters!"

"There just doesn't seem to be anyone home in any of these houses," I agreed. "At this point, I'd chance walking up and knocking on someone's door to ask directions. Even if it blows our cover. But all the garage doors are closed, and I haven't seen or heard anything to suggest that there are people either inside or outside."

"You said this place was downright spooky," Sybil reminded me. "I think that's putting it mildly. There's no one anywhere in here. They don't need guards to keep people out. There's no one in here to guard! I'm tired. I'm sitting down."

She collapsed under a nearby oak tree and I joined her.

Every part of my body hurt, and I knew that by tomorrow muscles that I hadn't used in years were going to be stiff and sore. I leaned back against the trunk of the tree and closed my eyes.

"What time is it?" I asked my wristwatch-wearing friend.

I'd taken to not wearing a watch since I'd stopped teaching. Before that I'd have felt naked without one.

"Three o'clock," Sybil informed me wearily. "We left the van around noon, and it has taken us nearly three hours to get exactly no closer to that rat-bastard of a first husband of yours than we were before."

"Oh, we're closer, all right," I fumed picking at one of my formerly manicured and now raggedly broken fingernails. "We're so close I can almost smell him. That's what is so frustrating. He's in here somewhere, and I can't get close enough to him to put my hands around his neck and choke him!"

"What you smell is us," Sybil, somewhat restored by resting under the tree, gave a wry smile.

"Yeah. Yuck," I held my arm up to my nose, then ducked my head to smell my rapidly drying jeans. "Pee-yew! What I wouldn't give for a shower."

"We aren't going to get showers until we get out of here," Sybil pulled herself to her feet with a moan. "Everything hurts. This is worse than belonging to a gym, and at a gym all the reptiles that chase you have two legs. Now that I think about it that 'gator did bear a certain resemblance to my second husband Chuck. He was certainly a woman chaser."

Chuckling but also moaning in pain, I stood up and joined her. At least we seemed to have raised our spirits.

"This place is lousy with streets named for British royalty. Maybe that's why there is a crown in its name. So far we've run through Hampton Court, obviously name after the Palace, and the Tudors. They belonged to the same period of English history. Maybe Windsor Way is over there, someplace, with the houses of Stewart and Hanover."

"Sukie, only you would think of that," Sybil laughed out loud.

"Wouldn't it be ironic if my having been an English teacher and knowing English Royal history brought us to Larry's street?" I crowed. "He can run but he can't hide!"

Chapter Twelve

Of course it wasn't true. Larry hadn't run out on me. At least not physically. I'd taken the children and run away from him all those years ago. He might seem to be hiding from us now, in this gated community, but we were bound to find him, sooner or later. No matter how hard the search might be. Everything about my relationship with Larry had been difficult. Why should finding him, now, be any different?

Sybil and I trudged onward, over the flat, sometimes-marshy ground of Palmetto Crown Plantation. We found that if we stuck to the oyster shell streets we made better progress. To my glee we did pass streets named Hanover Row and Mountbattan Mews. Still, we didn't see or hear a living soul, and while our muddy legs were drying and it was becoming less uncomfortable to walk, the humidity of the area really seemed to be rising and adding to our overall discomfort.

"I felt a drop of rain," Sybil informed me, "Just now. On my nose."

"Oh, great!" I grimaced. "All we need is to get caught in a

thunderstorm with no where to take shelter."

"How about over there?" I looked in the direction my friend was pointing and saw, at the end of a wide oyster shell drive, a low building with a wide veranda and high brick steps leading up to it. Its architecture appeared vastly different from that of the faux southern plantation houses that filled the development. Cookie-cutter Taras built for wealthy, retired golfers, I'd told myself by the time we'd passed a dozen or so of them.

It was really beginning to rain, and the wind had picked up a bit from the stillness we'd experienced for the last several hours. The leaves on the oak trees were starting to rustle. So Sybil and I hurried up the crushed oyster shell drive and climbed the steps to the building's veranda.

"Oh my God!" Sybil exclaimed as, standing on the veranda, we looked more carefully at the house. "All the windows are boarded up." She hurried to the massive front door and attempted to open it by pulling on the large colonial brass handle. "It's locked."

"It's the clubhouse for the golf course," I informed her pointing to a glass-encased bulletin board mounted beside the front door. Under the Palmetto Crown Golf Course letterhead of the sheet of paper that was posted on the other side of the glass we read: CLOSED DUE TO HURRICANE WARNING.

"Hurricane!" I heard myself exclaiming.

"Yes, hurricane," Sybil was reacting more calmly than I was. "It must mean that Hurricane Marcus is going to make landfall somewhere around here. That's why the place is empty. I noticed all the fancy shutters over the doors and windows of the houses when we passed by. I thought they were just for decoration but I bet they're hurricane shutters."

"But why didn't the lady at the motel say something about the hurricane. And what about the guy at the gas station?" I asked heatedly.

"I don't know why the motel lady didn't mention the weather," Sybil answered wryly, "As for the gas station Adonis, he had just about enough brain cells to run the gas pump, period! If we'd just listened to the radio on our way here, or called the Red Hats…"

"I hate listening to the radio," my voice was surly.

It was true. I did dislike radios, in general. Every time Bud and I got into the car he turned on a sports talk show. Yuck! The host seemed to always be shouting at the callers-in and denigrating them. The confrontation reminded me too much of years spent in the classroom. Like those shows, I considered so much of radio's programming to be nothing but noise, inane chatter, and defending my stance on radio listening always put me on the defensive.

But, now, I felt responsible for our not knowing that we were possibly in danger because we hadn't turned on the radio and listened to the news. And I was the one who had left the cell phone back in the van so we couldn't even call anyone right this minute to find out just how much danger we really were in.

"Let's get out of here," Sybil started down the steps. "Let's find the front gate and just walk right out. The guards there should know all about the weather and how much danger from the storm there really is. I don't care if we get in trouble for sneaking in here. I want out!"

I started to join Sybil in flight from the Palmetto Crown Golf Club veranda. The only thought in my head was to escape the weather, which was becoming more threatening with every minute. Then, suddenly, my eye settled upon the nearest street corner on our left. The now familiar palm tree bedecked street sign had just caught my eye. "Look!" I shouted, "Windsor Way!"

Chapter Thirteen

"I don't know how I let you talk me into these things!" Sybil was shaking water from her hair and mumbling a few minutes later, as we stood on the Palladian porch of number 65 Windsor Way. Despite her protests, once I had spotted the street sign I had dragged her down the Windsor Way through pelting rain.

Luckily there were only four houses on either side of the block. Like the first house we had encountered, when we struggled out of the mud and water into Palmetto Crown Plantation, Larry's property ended at the waterline of the inlet. Through sheets of rain I could just make out a landscaped yard behind the house, leading down to a dock where two boats were tied up.

As we took refuge on Larry's front porch from the gathering storm, rain growing ever heavier, trees beginning to sway and creak, I was relieved to see that the hurricane shutters were not drawn across the windows and front door of this house.

"I'm going to knock," I announced reaching for the heavy

brass knocker on the front door. "It isn't closed up like the rest of the houses. Someone must be home. If it's Larry, I'll have my say and we'll leave. If he isn't here we'll just leave and hotfoot it back to the gate and the van."

"That's the first sensible thing you've said since we started on this trip," Sybil's voice was filled with relief. "Go ahead."

I raised the arm of the knocker and banged it against its backplate as hard as I could. I felt a sense of urgency as the rain and wind, which had only started up about fifteen minutes before, seemed to be intensifying with every second that passed. There was no response from within to my first knock, and so I raised the knocker's arm again and gave the backplate four or five whacks, using all the strength I could muster.

The wind had really picked up. It was positively howling. What was worse, it was blowing the rain sideways from the inlet, across the yard, to the porch, drenching our already damp bodies. Sybil huddled close to me. We were both soaked with rain.

"Oh, for God's sake!" I could hear my disgusted voice above the noise of the wind. I grabbed the door handle and, in desperation, pushed it and the door inward, with both hands. To my amazement, it swung open! Sybil and I turned and stared at each other.

"Come on!" I pulled her over the threshold and into the house. When we turned back to the door it took both our efforts to close it .We leaned hard against it and pushed with all our might. At last we overcame the intensity of the wind and the door closed with a genteel whoosh.

"Wow!" as we turned back to the room, Sybil's exclamation expressed both our reactions. She and I stood, dripping, on the largest oriental rug I'd seen outside a museum, in a dazzling white foyer that featured a winding staircase that went up two stories. On each side of the hall, which was wide enough to be a room in itself, there was a mahogany Sheridan table. On one table was a silver vase, polished within an inch of its life, filled with a lovely bouquet of fresh flowers. On the other table rested a statue; it was a marble Pieta with a lavabo mounted above it.

"Wow," I echoed Sybil. "I knew that Larry's wife was rich but I didn't expect this. Maybe we'd better see if they're here." I took a few steps forward, down the foyer and called, "Hello! Anybody home?"

Despite the howling of the wind outside, the house was quiet as a church.

"Hello!" I called again.

No answer.

"Let's look around," Sybil ventured and reached for the knob of a door to our right leading from the hall. I followed directly behind her and we found the room on the other side of the door to be a large, tastefully appointed powder room, complete with colonial wallpaper, a window swag of matching fabric, and a customized, hand painted vanity bowl.

"Hm-m-m," we both murmured, as she closed the door and we continued our foray into Larry's house.

At the end of the foyer, steps led down into what I imagined was a sitting room. It would have been called the living room at my house but, with nothing that looked to be out of place, it didn't appear that much living went on in this room. It, too, sported a large oriental rug and it had a white marble fireplace. The furniture looked uncomfortable and expensive. It featured lots of burnished wooden surfaces and was upholstered in pale yellow and blue watered silk. Scattered around the room, framed in lovely silver, were pictures of all sizes of children and adults. Topping it all off, tastefully arranged on the mantelpiece of the fireplace was a large, ornately framed photograph of Larry and a slender blonde woman who I assumed was Martie.

"They certainly live well," Sybil commented, fingering a silver snuffbox that was part of a group resting upon a piecrust table.

"Oh, who knows whether those are family heirlooms or just things that their decorator provided to create ambience?" I answered waspishly. The opulence in which my ex-husband now lived was adding, moment by moment, to my anger over the annulment that he thought he deserved and the child support he'd never sent to Maggie and Anne when they were young. The smiling picture of him and his second wife made me want to gag.

"I wish the Red Hats were here to see this," Sybil whistled as she spotted a Sheridan sideboard set up as an elaborate bar. Every bottle of liquor had its own silver stopper and nameplate.

"Oh, please!" I pleaded. "I just wish the Red Hats were here, period!"

"Are you kidding?" Sybil turned to me with her eyebrows raised. "For one thing, Harriet never would have agreed to sneak in here with us, and Jaye would already be back in the van with her lips turning blue at just the thought of a hurricane approaching."

"Sally would think what we're doing was an adventure," I lamely reminded her.

"One out of three. Great odds!" Sybil made her point.

"I know," I agreed wretchedly, "But I miss them, and I'm scared, and I wish Bud were here, too."

"That's rich!" Sybil gave a laugh that was a half snort. "He's going to kill you when he finds out what we've done."

"Let's not think about that now," I pulled my wet self together. "Let's look through the rest of the house for any signs of life."

I strode from the sitting room through an archway to the right. We were in a dining room that had wide bow windows, a pastel mural covering one wall, and more burnished wooden surfaces, this time a long, glossy cherry table with twelve Windsor chairs.

"Of course, Windsor chairs," I muttered to myself, "This is Windsor Way. Larry and Martie would definitely have a Windsor table and Windsor chairs."

"Say again?" Sybil asked.

Not bothering to answer I continued through another archway and had to choose between a hallway leading to the right and one that led to the left.

At first I thought it was my imagination but then I was sure that I heard the sound of a telephone ringing in a nearby room. Neither of us made a move to find out where it was or to answer it. It rang only twice, as my friend and I stared at each other, and then it stopped as suddenly as it had begun. While we stood completely still, I slightly ahead of Sybil at the convergence of the two halls, I also thought I heard a door closing softly in the distance. I've always had an acute sense of hearing but, still, I couldn't be sure from where the sounds of first the ringing telephone and then the closing door came. I started to ask Sybil if she'd heard the same sounds I had heard but didn't bother when I saw that she was as confused as I was.

"I wonder who that was?" I lowered my voice to a whisper, which seemed totally silly since we'd yet to find anyone in the house.

Sybil impatiently shook her head, "Well, it 'ain't hants', Honey. Even if we are in the South and Charleston is known for its ghosts." Changing the subject she asked, "Okay, what now?" She'd caught up with me and was peering over my shoulder.

"To the left," I answered trying to make my voice sound firm.

Our turn to the left rewarded us with a restaurant-sized kitchen and an adjoining laundry room. Both rooms looked as if they'd never been used. In the kitchen marble counter tops gleamed and stainless steel major appliances blended into Italian tiles which seemed to be everywhere; on walls, splashguards, even the floor.

"Think of the feasts we could prepare in here," Sybil sounded wistful. "I'm getting awfully hungry."

"Me, too," I admitted. "Let's try the hall to the right, and if we can't unearth anyone we'll leave. I don't relish touring the bedrooms upstairs."

The last thing I wanted to see was where Larry and his fourth wife made love. Probably soon with the complete blessing of the Catholic Church.

The blast of rain we'd received while trying to get into number 65 Windsor Way had washed away much of the mud that had caked our legs and feet, but, still, Sybil and I were leaving dirty puddles of water and dark footprints on tile and hardwood floors, as we made our way throughout the house. Too bad, I thought sardonically, eyeing framed hunting prints on walls and tastefully placed accent chairs with petit point seats as we continued down the second hall.

The door at the end of the hall was open, and, as we approached it, we heard the first sounds of voices that we'd encountered since we'd entered Palmetto Crown Plantation. Sybil and I stopped in our tracks. People, at last! Perhaps they were the ones who'd opened and closed the door I thought I'd heard, and answered the telephone. I held my finger to my lips and moved forward on my tiptoes. She followed.

Cautiously we peeked around the corner and into what we saw immediately was a den or office. It had a huge desk facing a large window that must have afforded a gorgeous view of the inlet, when sheets of rain weren't obscuring everything outside, as they were now. To our surprise the voices we'd heard were coming from a television set that was nestled between books and objects d'art on wooden shelves that reached from the floor to the ceiling of two walls. The television program which had produced the voices was a re-run of *Law and Order*, one that I recognized at once. Bud and I had seen them all. It was one of our favorite TV shows. On the screen, Sam Waterston and Angie Harmon were arguing loudly about a legal case. The room appeared as deserted as the rest of the house.

"That's it?" Sybil let our her breath, which apparently she'd been holding, and asked. "Those are the voices we heard?"

"I guess so," I stepped into the room and walked around the desk to see if I could get a better view of the late afternoon outside, which was darkening rapidly. We'd have to brave the elements and leave soon if we hoped to get back to the van before dark.

As I stepped around the desk I almost stumbled over something lying on the floor. I stopped, abruptly, and looked down to see what it was. There, lying face down in a pool of blood, on another exquisite oriental rug, lay the vaguely familiar body of a man. Even seen from behind, with two bullet holes in his head, it couldn't have been anyone other than my ex-husband Larry O' Brian.

Chapter Fourteen

It would not be a cliché to say that Sybil and I stood, rooted to the spot, staring at the body for what seemed like minutes, but must have been only seconds. I had begun to shake all over, and my friend grabbed me and held me close.

"It's. It's. Is it?" I was finding it impossible to put my thoughts together in intelligible words, as my brain reeled, and I found my face buried in her shoulder. "I think it's Lar – Larry!"

"Yeah. I figured as much," I heard Sybil saying from what seemed like a long distance away. I was aware that she was leading me very slowly out of the room and back into the hall.

"Do you think he's dead?" I asked when I could speak again, raising my head from her shoulder and gazing confusedly into her eyes.

"I think there's a good chance," she answered a bit dryly, shaking her head, "And I think we need to get out of here right now!"

"We can't!" I wailed, feeling as if I were going to be violently sick, and very soon. "We have to do something!"

"Like what? We aren't even supposed to be here. Remember?" she was continuing to lead me down the hall. "This is something we don't want to get mixed up in."

"I think it's a bit too late for y'all to avoid that," an unfamiliar voice wafted over Sybil's shoulder.

Startled, I let out a small shriek, and we both turned to find a rather tall, thin, man of about forty standing behind us in the hall. He was dressed in khaki oilskins that sported an official looking badge on the left shoulder, and he was dripping water into a pool that was forming at his feet on the hardwood floor.

"Would it be presumin' too much to ask who y'all ladies are and what y'all're doing here?" our wet visitor inquired, removing his hat and shaking drops of water from it, showing no apparent regard for the highly polished floor.

I moved away from Sybil, hesitantly, and blinked my eyes several times, as if I thought that would bring the man and the situation into clearer focus.

"I, I beg your pardon..." I attempted to speak but my voice sounded muffled and far away to me. I wondered, vaguely, if I were in shock.

"My name is Sybil Curtis and this is Sukie Davis," Sybil spoke up in her authoritative teacher voice. Hearing it seemed to help me stabilize my thoughts.

"I'm Larry O'Brian's first wife," I offered, speaking slowly and softly, as if that were a complete explanation as to what Sybil and I were doing, standing wet and dirty, in a house we'd never seen before today, in a state so far away from the one in which we lived.

"That takes care of who y'all are," the man's voice was as authoritative as my friend's had been. "Now, why are y'all here?"

"We're just visiting," Sybil shot back. Her next sentence was spoken almost as a challenge. "May I ask why you're here, Mr., Mr.?"

"I'm Russ Guthrie. Lieutenant Russ Gutherie of the

Hollywood Sheriff's Office, and someone called in a B and E at this address. Was it either of you ladies who called it in, or are y'all the B and E?"

"What's a B and E?" I asked, again my voice sounding strange to me.

"Breaking and Entering," Russ Guthrie answered in a voice that implied he did not appreciate explaining police jargon to members of the lay community. "Two strange women are reported to have entered number 65 Windsor Way. This is number 65, and this is Windsor Way, and you ladies don't look as if y'all're here as invited guests."

By now the tone of his voice and the questions he was asking, on top of the knowledge that there was a dead body in the next room, probably that of my ex-husband, had set me to shaking again.

"Lt. Guthrie, we, we…" I attempted to explain God-knows-what through my chattering teeth, and then the hunting prints on the walls began to whirl, and the hardwood floor appeared to rise up to meet me. My last thoughts were that it was growing very late in the day, indeed, because everything had become very, very dark. And my last words, heard from very far away, as if they were being spoken under water, were, "There seems to be a dead body in the den."

*   *   *

When I opened my eyes again I was lying on the floor of the hall with something soft pillowing my head. It turned out to be Sybil's lap, which I discovered as I attempted to sit up and fell back again.

"Take it easy, there, Little Lady," Russ Guthrie's voice penetrated the fog around me that was slowly lifting.

"I told you it was quite a shock for her, finding that body," Sybil's tone was accusatory. "Is it Larry O'Brian?"

"I really can't say, but we'll know for sure as soon as my

deputies and the M.E. get here," he was sliding a two-way radio back into a pocket hidden beneath his poncho. "Can't move the body, turn it over, yet," he informed her and leaned down to speak to me face to face. "My boys're mostly out evacuatin' people who live up and down the coast. Hurricane coming, as y'all must know. Now, Miz Davis, tell me, again, what y'all and your friend are doing here, in Miss Martha's house."

"Miss Martha?" Sybil was taken aback at his reference to Larry's wife. "Do you know Mrs. O'Brian well enough to call her Miss Martha?"

Lt. Guthrie ignored the question and continued, "You say y'all're Mr. O'Brian's FIRST wife?"

"Yes," I murmured, adding inanely, "He's had four wives."

"Larry O'Brian's had four wives!" the policeman seemed shocked.

"You know Larry well, too?" Sybil continued her line of questioning and was again ignored.

I tried a second time to sit up, and this time was successful.

"Lieutenant Guthrie," I felt much better, although still a bit queasy, and my mind seemed to have cleared a bit. "How do you know my ex-husband?"

"I think the question of major importance, here, Miz Davis, is still what are y'all doing in this house?" the tone of his answer was cool and official.

"I came down, that is my friend and I came down here to speak to my ex-husband on a personal matter. I haven't seen him in years. And when we got here we found his body, or whoever it is, in there," I gestured toward the room at the end of the hall. The Lieutenant had not touched a thing. He had not even closed the door to the room. I dragged my mind away from the memory of the body lying in that room.

"How did y'all get into the Plantation?" he asked, "I checked with Marv and Charlie at the gate, when the B and E came in, and they told me that since everyone left last night and early this mornin' no one had come onto the premises."

"We didn't use the gate," Sybil spoke up, as she reached out to help me rise to my feet. Russ Guthrie beat her to it and taking both my hands pulled me up expertly.

"Y'all came by boat?" He sounded surprised.

"No, we didn't come by boat," I was becoming fatigued by this line of questioning and decided to tell him the whole story, which I did.

Ignoring my now almost dry, dirty jeans, I settled upon the petit point seat of one of the hall chairs and launched into the tale of our trip from Pennsylvania to Palmetto Crown Plantation and why we'd come.

"We didn't really B and E," I finished my explanation. "The front door wasn't locked, so I pushed it open to escape the storm. We were frightened. We didn't know the hurricane was coming."

"How could y'all not know?" Guthrie's retort was incredulous. "It's been all over the radio and television since Marcus changed course yesterday."

"We don't listen to the radio," Sybil told him acerbically. "It's just a bunch of noise."

I cringed.

Chapter Fifteen

I don't know how long it was until more policemen and a man dressed as a civilian carrying a black case came noisily into the hall. After our short explanation of how we'd gotten into Larry's gated community and why we'd come, I'd continued to sit on the petit point chair, with Sybil sitting on one she'd pulled up next to me. We'd held onto each other's hands and kept our silence. So had Russ Guthrie who had stood leaning against the wall, facing us and writing in a small notebook he'd pulled from his pocket.

From time to time he'd shaken his head and muttered things like, "Didn't listen to the radio...just noise. Waded around the fence..."

The policemen and medical examiner had disappeared into the study. The sound of their voices now joined the dialogue from *Law and Order* since no one had turned off the television set.

When I glanced toward the open door I saw occasional flashes of light which I assumed were coming from a camera, as one of the policemen photographed the body and took shots of the room. I heard Larry's name mentioned once or twice, confirming that the body on the oriental rug was, as I had suspected, his.

"Larry's dead, Larry's dead." The words kept going around inside my head like the turntable of an old stereo set. I kept hearing them, internally, but the concept just didn't seem to sink in. Everything seemed so unreal, almost surreal.

Finally the mantra "Larry's dead," turned into "Ding, dong the Wicked Witch is dead!" And it was all I could do to keep from laughing out loud. The situation was so absurd. It was enough to make anyone laugh, even someone who was not slightly in a state of shock as I felt sure I must be. I mean, consider the situation. I don't have any communication with my ex-husband for years, and then I discover his dead body under circumstances that are unusual, to say the least? The scenario was straight out of a 1940s, B-grade movie.

I'd been furious with Larry. I'd even told myself that I hated him and wished him dead. But when confronted with the actual fact of his death all I felt was an overwhelming sadness. That body on the oriental rug seemed so foreign, so alien a thing.

And my daughters! How was I going to break the news to Maggie and Anne that their biological father had been murdered, and that it was I who had found his body by almost tripping over it? What would their reaction be? There was no love lost among them but his death and my being present at the murder scene would be a shock to them, to say the least. Last but not least, how would my present husband take the news; what would Bud say and do when he found out?

All of these thoughts tripped through my slightly hazy mind as my friend and I sat quietly. I held on to her hands as if they were a lifeline that kept me from being dragged under the surface of a murky pool of unreality.

"We'd like to call someone," Sybil broke the silence that had fallen in the hall after Lt. Gutherie had finished musing to himself and put his notebook away. "Mrs. Davis needs to call her husband and I need to contact our friends."

"Do the friends live hereabouts, in Charleston?" Russ Guthrie asked, preparing to join the others in the study.

"No," Sybil answered him, "They're all in Pennsylvania, where we live."

"Do y'all have a cell phone?"

"Yes, er no," Sybil admitted. 'Not with us, at the moment."

At that point we heard an outside door, close by, open and shut and a booming voice called out, "Russell, Russell! Did you find those women I called y'all about?"

A large man, who appeared to be about seventy, wrapped in a flowing Burberry raincoat, rushed into the hall. He had a full head of silver hair, from which he was shaking drops of water, and he had removed his streaming glasses and was swinging them in the air, apparently in an effort to dry them. His attitude when he saw us seemed adversarial, to say the least.

"Is this them?" he sputtered after catching his breath.

Lt. Guthrie turned first to face the new arrival and then back to us as he made rudimentary introductions, "Plushy, this is Miz Davis and Miss Curtis. They're from Pennsylvania. Miz Davis says she used to be married to Larry O'Brian. There's a body in the library and I'm just goin' to check on my boys to see if they know whose it is. I'd appreciate if y'all'd stay with the ladies until I return. Ladies, this is Col. Plushmill. He lives across the street. I'll get back to y'all later about that phone call."

And with that Russ Guthrie left us and entered the room I'd called the den but he'd referred to as the library. Sybil and I were left facing the scrutiny of the newcomer.

I stared down at my hands, which were clasped in my lap, but Sybil met his gaze boldly. I guess she and I appeared harmless because Col. Plushmill's attitude and body language softened perceptibly.

"Hello, Ladies," he removed his dripping coat, folded it, and laid it on one of the side chairs. "I'm the O'Brian's neighbor from across the street, as Russell told you. The name's Col. Barton

Townsend Plushmill, retired. Citadel class of '52. Just call me Plushy. Everybody hereabouts does."

He whipped out a handkerchief, wiped his glasses well, sank down on the chair next to his coat and leaned forward studying us. "What on earth're you Yankee ladies doin' down here?"

My heart sank in despair. Were we going to have to tell our story endlessly, to every stranger who came along?

We were saved by the return of Lt. Guthrie who informed all three of us very professionally, "The body is that of Lawrence O'Brian. He appears to have been shot in the back of the head and has been dead for only a short while. Ladies, I'm goin' to ask y'all to come down to headquarters with me to give your statements and be fingerprinted."

"You think we did it?" Sybil jumped to her feet in astonishment. "We just got here. We never saw this place before in our lives. We'd only been here about five minutes before Sukie found the body."

"I need statements from both of y'all and fingerprints," Russ Guthrie was adamant. "As of right now we don't seem to have a weapon, but we'll be searchin' the house and both y'all, Ladies."

"Searching us?" Sybil all but screeched. "Can't you tell just by looking at us that we're not concealing any weapons?" This was a valid point since she and I wore only damp jeans and shirts, both of which were clinging most uncomfortably to our bodies.

"They do have a point, Russell," the Colonel chuckled, seeming to rise to our defense.

"And we need to make phone calls," Sybil insisted. "I've seen enough police programs on TV to know that we're allowed to make a phone call."

"Come, come," Col. Plushmill spoke up. "Now that I've met them, Russell, these ladies don't seem very dangerous, and I think we can clear them of carryin' any weapons."

"Well," Lt.Guthrie admitted, eyeing us. "They don't seem to be concealing any guns. They also don't have any identification to prove they're who they say they are."

"It's in our van back at the mill," I spoke up, coming out of the fog I'd been in ever since I'd almost tripped over Larry's body. "Our purses and our cell phone are in the van. I parked it there earlier this afternoon."

"Why don't you take Miz. Davis and Miss Curtis's fingerprints and their statements right here?" Col. Plushmill asked, leaning back in his chair and staring very hard at Lt. Guthrie. "I know your boys carry a fingerprint kit with them when they come to the scene of a crime. Once they've done that, the boys can go get the ladies' van and check out their identification. If it turns out that they're tellin' the truth, I'd hate to see you drag them into the police station."

"Now just a minute, Plushy," Guthrie returned Col. Plushmill's concentrated stare. "Let me get this straight. Y'all propose that I don't take them down to the station? With all due respect, I don't see how I can avoid takin' them in. They're suspects in a murder investigation."

"That's nasty weather out there, Russell," the Colonel rose to his feet and walked slowly toward Gutherie. "I have a better idea...just come to me. What I propose is that once y'all've fingerprinted Miz Davis and Miss Curtis and verified their identities y'all let them come on over to my house for some good, strong drinks. Y'all can come over there to take their statements once y'all finish up here.

These ladies are from Yankee territory and they need to see that all of us Good Ol' Boys aren't rebels and barbarians. Miss Millie and I have no intention of evacuatin' The Plantation. The ladies're welcome to stay a spell with us. We'd be happy to show them some good old Suth'n Hospitality. Y'all and the boys sure as shootin haven't."

We could see the police lieutenant bristle as Col. Plushmill stood nose to nose with him.

"Oh, we couldn't possibly do that," I put in hastily, also rising to my feet. "Once we've shown you our identification, we just need to call my husband and our friends. They must be worried to death about us, by now, and we need to get started home."

"Y'all can be fingerprinted here, like Col. Plushmill says," Guthrie broke his gaze with the Col. and turned to us, "And y'all can go over to his house where I'll take your statements, but y'all aren't going anywhere near the Mason Dixon Line. So set still." Guthrie was all business but he also seemed a bit subdued after having had his nose-to-nose conversation with the Colonel. He stuck his head into the now fairly silent library, "Harold, bring the fingerprint kit out here and take these ladies prints. Now."

"Maybe y'all might ought to get Miz. Davis's car keys, send some of the boys to the mill to get her van, and bring it here. Then these ladies can get their handbags and show us who they are," the balance of power between the two men seemed to have completely shifted since his arrival, and Col. Plushmill now appeared to be, surprisingly, in charge of the situation.

"Here," I fished my keys out of my stiff jeans pocket and proffered them to Lt. Guthrie, "Here are the keys. The van is parked right behind where the grist wheel used to be."

Guthrie took them and tossed them to a deputy whom he'd summoned from the library. He also gave the man instructions as to where our van was parked.

"Take Phil with you so y'all can drive the van back here. No need to let it sink into that marshy ground at the mill," he instructed. "Park it out front and bring in the ladies handbags when y'all get back."

"When you bring back the van may we use our cell phone, so we can call home?" Sybil inquired almost wistfully. Turning to me she said softly, "You call Bud. I'll call Jaye and have her contact the rest of the Red Hats."

Col. Plushmill returned to us, "Excuse me ladies. What did I just hear y'all say about red hats?"

"We belong to a Red Hat Society at home," Sybil explained quickly. "Sometimes we just refer to ourselves as the Red Hats. It's another name for our group of friends. You wouldn't understand."

"Not understand? Red Hat Society! Of course I know what a Red Hat Society is," Col. Plushmill boomed. "My wife Millie and half of her friends here in The Plantation and in Charleston belong to one. Your mother belongs to one, too, doesn't she, Russell?"

Lt. Guthrie gave the Colonel a look that became more poisonous the longer it lasted and which was returned by the man at whom he stared. He didn't bother to answer the question but took the medium-sized black box handed to him by one of his deputies. As soon as Guthrie grasped the fingerprint kit the two deputies turned and left the hall. To get the van and our belongings, I assumed.

"From what my darlin' Millie tells me, Susan Fairchild Guthrie, your mama, Russell, is the Queen Mother of the Greater Charleston Chapter of the Red Hat Society. Just as my Miss Millie was the first Queen Mother of the Hollywood Chapter," Col. Plushmill finally broke his eye contact with Lt. Gutherie and resumed his seat, musing, "Lovely ladies, those Red Hat Society ladies."

Again the Lieutenant ignored the Colonel's comments.

It only took a short time to fingerprint Sybil and me, using the portable fingerprint kit in Russ Guthrie'a possession. We moved into the dining room where inkpad and forms were spread out on the table and the process was carried out silently. By the time we'd wiped ink from our fingers the deputies who had gone to retrieve our van had returned.

"It's powerful wet out there, I reckon," the deputy named Phil reported to his superior as he handed him Sybil's Vera Bradley purse, my striped canvas bag, and my keys. Guthrie returned the keys to me and I dropped them into my purse.

A quick survey of our drivers' licenses and other cards in our wallets confirmed that Sybil and I were who we had said we were. Lt. Guthrie shuffled through them as one would a deck of cards. He even perused the pictures of my daughters that I always carried with me. When he came to Anne's college yearbook photo he stopped.

"That's a picture of my younger daughter Anne," I informed him as he gazed at the picture, "Larry O'Brian's daughter and mine."

"She sure does favor her daddy," he commented, and it was true.

While Maggie was the image of me with curly dark hair and a tendency toward plumpness, Anne was a female Larry O'Brian. They shared pale blue, almost translucent, eyes and wavy blonde hair. She even had the O'Brian nose, which had prompted my disgruntled mother, who had always hated Larry, to exclaim when she saw the newborn Anne, "My gift to her for her eighteenth birthday will be a nose job!"

As time went by Anne had grown into her nose and my mother forgot the subject completely, which was good because Anne, in her teens, had been a radical feminist. She was still political and a firm proponent of women's' rights to this day.

"Okay, Ladies," Lt. Guthrie almost sighed as he returned our belongings to us. "Y'all seem to be who y'all say you are. My boys and I need to clear the area and tape it off. We have your prints and know where y'all're goin' to be," he inclined his head, "Over to Plushy and Miss Millie's place. I'll come over and take your statements there."

As Sybil and I gathered up our purses, and I checked to make sure that the cell phone was still in mine, a thought crossed my mind like a bolt of lightning. I couldn't believe that I hadn't inquired into the subject of it before.

Turning to Lt. Guthrie, who had never explained to us how he knew Larry and Martie O'Brian so well, I looked straight into his eyes for the first time and asked, "Lieutenant, it just occurred to me that the present Mrs. O'Brian isn't here. Do you suppose that 'Miss Martha' evacuated with the rest of the residents when she learned about the storm? Shouldn't you try to inform her about her husband's death?"

"Oh, Miz Davis," Col. Plushmill interjected before Guthrie could answer my question. "Miss Martha hasn't been here, in this house, for a long time. She's over to the hospital in Charleston. Been there for several months. It's so sad. She's dyin' from cancer."

Chapter Sixteen

The sixty-mile-an-hour wind-driven rain that assaulted us as we left the O'Brian house couldn't have presented me with more of a shock than the news Col. Plushmill had given us concerning Martie's health. I'd had no inkling that she was ill. I rarely heard any news of Larry and his fourth wife from his family but I'd have thought that something like an impending death would have reached me via Larry's sister-in-law with whom I was still in contact.

I'd never met Martha Ryan Mayhew O'Brian. The only one of Larry's four wives I'd ever met had been his young, arrogant second wife Stephanie. She'd been twenty-two and blonde when we first met, and I'd certainly disliked her. Especially after she'd presented my ex-husband with his only son, and the two of them had named the child David, the name that Larry and I had always reserved for the son we'd never had. Like my own marriage to Larry, their union had lasted seven years.

All I'd ever felt for O'Brian wife-number-three, Sarah, had been pity. Larry had married her during his really "down-and-out" period. Those were the years when he'd sold drugs, run con artist scams, and disappeared from the United States for a year or two. He'd certainly been his family's black sheep.

Sarah had been pregnant when they married and had produced Larry's third daughter Winsome. I'd never met Sarah but had seen Winsome once when she was about three years old. The child's appearance had been a great shock to me. She looked very much like Maggie but had Anne's blonde coloring.

I'd resented Martha O'Brian because her marriage to Larry had been an embarrassment to the girls and me. Who wants to admit to people that their ex-husband or biological father has been married four times?

I don't think I'd ever considered much of anything else about Martha, usually referred to as Martie, except that she was rich and had provided Larry with a life style that I felt he didn't deserve.

I may have felt resentment toward her, and even a bit of jealousy concerning her financial status, but I certainly didn't wish her dead. Not even if it turned out that she was the one behind Larry's seeking to annul his marriage to me. Wish her dead? I didn't even know her!

Telling us that he'd be over soon for our statements, Lt. Guthrie had furnished Sybil and me each with a set of his men's official wet suits to make the short trip across the street to the Plushmill house. Sybil and I clutched our purses to our chests beneath the heavy oilskins. It was fortunate for us that the Lieutenant had been so chivalrous because the raging storm drenched us before we'd gone more than a few steps outside.

The rain was coming down so fast and at such a wind-driven angle that we could only make out our destination by the house lights which shone through the tempest. None of us attempted to talk. The force of the gale took our breaths away. However, I did manage to make out the shape of my van parked in the O'Brian driveway before we crossed Windsor Way to the other side.

Col. Plushmill's last instructions to Lt. Guthrie before the Colonel herded us out the door had been, "It might be a good idea, Russell, for y'all to contact Young Tom."

That comment completely escaped my mind until I ran up against it later. At that moment I didn't give a thought to who Young Tom might be. I was too eager to exit the house in which the dead body of my first husband lay and to contact my dear, sweet Bud as soon as possible. All I could think about was getting to dry ground and calling Bud on my cell phone.

"Here we are, ladies." Col. Plushmill was at last able to speak after he had fished an automatic garage door opener from the pocket of his raincoat, opened the door of his two-car garage, which trembled in the wind as it ascended. He escorted us inside his dimly lighted but beautifully dry garage. "I'll go ahead and tell Miss Millie that y'all are here."

He disappeared through a door, which obviously led into the house, calling out, "Millie, darlin', I have some Red Hat Ladies for y'all to meet," and closing it behind him.

This left Sybil and me alone for the first time in hours. She turned to me, quick as a cat and asked, sotto voce, "What do you think is going on, here?"

"What do you mean?" I answered looking around the garage and sighting, through the gloom, what appeared to be a Lincoln Town Car and a huge SUV of some sort.

"For starters, I think the relationship between Lt. Guthrie and 'Plushy" is extremely strange," she hissed back at me.

"I don't care what it is," I pushed the hood of the Hollywood Police wet jacket back off my head. "I just want to call Bud, tell him where we are, beg his forgiveness for lying to him, and throw myself on his mercy to come get us."

"Coward," Sybil accused me half seriously, half jokingly. "You got us into this mess and now you want Bud to rescue us?"

Yes, oh yes," I could tell I was on the verge of tears, and I was hungry. I always become either emotional or cranky when my blood sugar drops.

"It's a good thing that you aren't single like the rest of us Red Hats. We have to rely on ourselves to get out of messes."

"I wish I'd stayed single until I met Bud. Then we wouldn't be in this mess," I responded beginning to feel very sorry for myself.

"If you hadn't married Larry and then left him you'd never have come back to Martin's Field when you did and met Bud," Sybil reminded me, giving me a small poke in the arm that always meant "get over it, girl." She'd been doing this almost automatically to all her friends for years, and it usually worked. It worked now.

The door to the house opened suddenly and light streamed out into the garage. A woman's figure appeared in the doorway, and a soft, southern voice called out to us, "Ladies, y'all come right in here and let Plushy mix you some of his famous Planter's Punches. They'll fix y'all up right quick."

Sybil and I moved forward into the light and entered the house. We blinked as our eyes became accustomed to brightness after the gloom of the garage.

"And let's get y'all out of those wet things. Plushy, where are your manners?"

Before us stood Miss Millie Plushmill, all spun cotton candy, silver-highlighted hair and smiling, carefully-painted, magenta mouth. She was about five feet three inches tall, swathed in a royal purple chiffon peignoir, and she'd maintained the girlish figure she'd probably had when she'd met the Colonel years before at a Citadel cotillion.

"I do declare. Y'all're as wet as peahens caught in a crick flood," her voice carried the hue of amber honey pouring from a sweet hive. Putting her arm around my wet shoulders she added, "My husband tells me that y'all was once married to our friend Larry O'Brian. And now he's dead and y'all found his body. It must have been a terrible shock. I know it has been for us. Come right in and rest yourself."

Both Plushmills divested us of our wet suits and ushered us, clutching our purses, into what appeared to be the Colonel's study or library, as Lt. Gutherie had called the room where I'd found Larry's body. This one was paneled in glowing cherry wood and furnished much as the O'Brian's had been, except for one feature. An entire wall of the room was devoted to an elaborate wet bar.

"Sit down. Sit down," Col. Plushmill instructed us as he moved behind the bar.

Sybil and I gazed down at our less than immaculate lower bodies and then around the room trying to decide where we could place ourselves without ruining any furniture.

"Oh, come here," Miss Millie indicated a dark green leather loveseat. "Y'all can't get it any dirtier than our dogs do, when they're here, and it's real simple to wipe off. Isobel can worry about cleanin' up the dirt when the storm ends and she comes back to us."

Sybil and I settled into the soft comfort of the loveseat, laying our purses in our laps, sighs escaping both of us as our bodies relaxed for the first time in what seemed like many hours.

"Plushy tells me that y'all belong to a Yankee Red Hat Society," Miss Millie continued beaming at us. "Aren't they just the best? My red hat friends and I have such good times goin' out to tea and wearin' our beautiful, big red hats. Y'all must tell me about yours when we get a chance. Isn't this fun? We're just like sisters, bein' Red Hat members, and all!"

"Thank you so much," I managed to say before a tall glass of amber liquid, barely diluted with fruit juice, and sporting a slice of orange and a maraschino cherry was placed into my hand.

Sybil nodded and added her thank you, also, as she received her Planter's Punch.

"I'll bet y'all are just starvin'," Miss Millie prattled on. "When's the last time y'all had anything to eat?"

"Noon," Sybil, who had voiced her hunger before we'd found Larry's body, answered decisively.

"Good heavens! It's goin' on seven o'clock. I'll find somethin' in the fridge for y'all. I think I told y'all our girl Isobel's gone. Evacuated with the rest. Took our darlin' dogs Sweetie and Smarty with her. So there's nothin' hot. She does all the cookin'. But I'm sure she's left us things in the fridge to nibble on." Miss Millie headed toward the door. "Now don't y'all touch a drop of that punch on empty stomachs. We don't want y'all to be tiddly when Russell comes over to take your statements. I'll be right back!"

"Oh, go on," the Colonel drawled when his wife had left the room, "Miss Millie worries too much. A big swig of that punch is just what y'all need to perk right up."

Starved and thirsty, Sybil and I followed his advice. As the fruit juice and alcohol slid down my throat and into my stomach I could feel tension draining from my body. My mood began to rise, as my blood sugar climbed.

"Now tell me, Miz Davis," Col. Plushmill seated himself in a leather armchair across from us and, leaning forward, addressed me. "Y'all came all the way down to Dixie from Pennsylvania. That's a long trip. Why'd y'all do it? Make the trip with a hurricane coming? Was it to try to convince Larry not to annul your marriage to him?" He saw the surprise in my reaction to his question.

"H-How did you know about the annulment?" I stammered. "You weren't there when I told Lt. Guthrie about it."

"Larry and I are, er, a, we were, friends. He told me about his seeking an annulment." The Colonel answered, leaning back in his chair and swirling the drink in his glass.

"Col. Plushmill, I wonder if I could excuse myself for a minute to use my cell phone?" I responded to his straightforwardness, "I really need to call my husband and tell him what's happened."

I put my drink down on a brass coaster that rested on the table next to my end of the loveseat.

"Of course, of course," he responded heartily. "Y'all can take it right on into the next room, or into the powder room down the hall, if y'all want, and make your call there. Come to think of it, y'all may want to freshen up a bit before Miss Millie brings the food. But y'all're welcome to use our phone. It's right here," he gestured to a desk, much smaller than Larry's had been, probably due to the space in the room taken up by the bar.

"I'd really rather use my own phone," I demurred. "I'll have to ring his beeper and the number's in the address book in my phone. He's probably out dealing with storm preparations and sending crews down this way. Maybe bad weather has already reached our area. He works for our utility company."

"Surely, surely," the Colonel responded nodding his head, "But there's an extension in the sitting room if y'all change your mind. And, Little Lady, I insist that y'all call me Plushy. Everyone does. Enough of this Col. Plushmill stuff."

Smiling wanly, I nodded at him and gestured for Sybil to accompany me. "You still want to call Jaye and maybe Harriet and Sally, too. Don't you?" I asked her, pointedly.

"Oh, yes," she responded to my gesture, putting down her drink. Picking up our purses, we both rose from the loveseat and left the library, moving down a hall toward the dining room and kitchen, where we could hear Miss Millie bustling about.

The house was laid out with a floorplan identical to Larry's, across the street, and lights were on in every room. When we reached the powder room, on the right side of the entry hall, we entered it and closed the door behind us. For some reason I felt the need to lock it and did so.

"At last!" Sybil began to unbuckle her belt. "I've had to go for hours but that Lt. Gutherie never gave us a chance. I guess he didn't want anyone to pee at his crime scene."

I, too, felt the "call of nature" but calling Bud was uppermost in my mind. I fished my cell phone out of my bag and turned it on. As soon as it responded I tried our home number but there was no answer. I hadn't really expected Bud to be there, anyway. I didn't have a work number for him. Because he was constantly in meetings or on the phone at work, Bud preferred that I dial his beeper and leave the number at which I could be reached. Then he'd call me back. I did that now, punching in my cell phone number for his return call.

"He should call back soon," I informed Sybil as I ended the connection and handed her the phone. "I'm glad that we don't have to use the Plushmill's telephone. We're intruding upon them too much, as it is. I don't want our long distance calls on their phone bill. You can try the Red Hats but I bet all the South Carolina circuits are busy. That's usually what happens during an emergency like this." I exchanged places with her as she dialed Jaye's number.

"I can't believe Larry told good old Plushy about his trying to get an annulment," she spoke to me as she waited for her call to go through. Suddenly she switched off the cell phone and returned it to me. "I'm not getting any answer. I guess everyone down here is trying to call for help or contact relatives. But cell phones use towers not regular telephone circuits so it doesn't matter if they're all busy. The problem must be that the towers are overloaded. We'll have to try later."

"I never thought about cell phone towers. I don't use my cell phone enough to be literate about how it works," I answered, turning the phone back on so I could receive Bud's call when it came and putting it back into my striped canvas bag. "I just remember the days after 9/11. We couldn't get through to Anne and her family in Baltimore for days because of the strike on the Pentagon. I was frantic."

"Yeah, well I bet the Red Hats are frantic about us, right now. Maybe Bud called one of them, or all of them, if he's been trying to get you on your cell phone and can't. And maybe Harriet or Jaye caved in and told him where we really are. If he knows, I bet he's frantic, too."

"Thanks for sharing that. Now I feel more guilty than I did before," I told her. "As for Larry telling Plushy about the annulment, if Larry was drinking, like he was the whole time I was married to him, he'd tell anyone anything."

"I thought his fourth wife had reformed him. She's supposed to be such a good woman." Sybil's voice was sarcastic, again, as she gazed into the powder room mirror. Trying to run the comb from her purse through her unruly hair she added, "God, I'm a wreck. I look like I've 'been rode hard and put away wet' as my grandfather used to say."

"Martie," I sighed at the thought of Larry's fourth wife. "I had no idea that she was dying from cancer. What a kick in the head! Why, I wonder, did Larry want the annulment so badly when she's going to die?"

There was a soft knock on the powder room door and Miss Millie's voice called to us, "Ladies, is everythin' all right in there? Y'all've been gone such a long time Plushy's startin' to get worried."

"We're fine," Sybil called back loudly and, unlocking the door, we joined Miss Millie in the hall.

"Did y'all have any luck in reachin' your families and friends?" she asked us.

"No. I'm afraid not. The cell towers are all overloaded. I imagine that the regular circuits are, too," I answered. "But I'm sure my husband will call back as soon as he gets the message I left on his beeper."

"I've put out a tray in the library," she informed us, "And Russell Guthrie is here to take y'all's statements. I'll see to it that his boys bring y'all's luggage over here. I bet right about now a hot bath and clean clothes would feel right good."

"Thank you," we both murmured again and followed her back toward the library.

"Miss Millie," I added as we walked through the dining room. "We want to tell you how much we appreciate your opening your house to us like this. We're perfect strangers to you, and we've just come through a horrible experience, and you and Plushy are being just wonderful to us."

"It's our pleasure," she beamed at us. "And it's the least we can do for Larry and Martha, as well as for y'all. After all, Larry was our friend and y'all was once married to him. That practically makes y'all kin, as well as bein' a Red Hat Sister."

If ever there was a perfect southern lady dispensing perfect southern hospitality, it was Miss Millie Plushmill.

Chapter Seventeen

When Sybil and I were again settled on the green leather loveseat in the Plushmill's library we found ourselves facing a seated Plushy and a pacing Russ Guthrie. Miss Millie passed a tray of assorted cold cuts, cheese and crackers, small china plates and cloth napkins around the group of us. Heavy sterling silverware rested upon the coffee table in front of us and, to my delight, so did a blue cobalt bowl of what appeared to be tomato aspic, a favorite of mine. Ravenous, Sybil and I quickly piled food upon plates, spread napkins on our stiff, dirty laps, and picking up forks began to eat.

"I'll try to make this as quick as possible, Ladies," the Lieutenant cleared his throat.

I wondered if he was still technically on duty. He was holding a small crystal glass of dark amber liquid in his hand. The two men had apparently been having a conversation prior to our entering the room but both had resumed silence when we appeared and seated ourselves. Now Guthrie was forced to put down his glass so he could bring out his pen and notebook to take down our responses.

"Late this afternoon y'all entered Palmetto Crown Plantation illegally by wading around the fence at the southern border of the community. Y'all say due to having had no media contact in the last forty-eight hours y'all had no idea that Hurricane Marcus was going to strike the Charleston area. Am I right so far?"

"Yes sir," I nodded meekly after I'd swallowed a mouthful of tomato aspic.

"Y'all then proceeded to number Sixty-five Windsor Way, the home of Lawrence and Martha O'Brian, where y'all entered the house, again illegally, and found no one to home. Or at least so y'all thought."

"Right," Sybil chimed in with her mouth full of imported salami. "At first we thought the house was empty like all the other ones we'd passed."

"Until y'all found the dead body of Lawrence O'Brian in the library," Lt. Guthrie continued in a sonorous voice.

Suddenly Sybil began to choke. I leaned over and pounded her on the back. Plushy quickly poured a glass of water from an ornately cut crystal pitcher resting on the bar and thrust it into her hand. We all gathered around her.

"I'm, I'm sorry," she sputtered when she could speak again. Tears were rolling down her cheeks and amid loud wheezes she seemed to be laughing. "It just sounds so much like CLUE. You know the game. 'Col. Mustard did it with the lead pipe in the library!'"

"Miss Curtis!" angry and disgusted, Russ Guthrie backed away from her. I could tell that he was incensed by what he perceived to be Sybil's inability to grasp the seriousness of the situation.

"Now Russell," Miss Millie spoke up in her honeyed voice. "Our guests are just about completely tuckered out. In case y'all didn't know it, laughter is a perfectly natural reaction to the stress of finding a dead body in the middle of a hurricane. I suggest y'all stop being such a pompous ass and get this over as quickly as ever y'all can."

Silence fell for a second or two. Then Plushy began to laugh. Actually it was more of a bellow than a laugh. It shook his very ample body and every silver hair on his head.

Russ Guthrie ignored Plushy as his laughter sputtered out, but now the Colonel was wiping tears from both his cheeks and his glasses and gasping, "Continue, continue," He seemed to be giving the Lieutenant permission to resume his work.

"Y'all told me over to Miss Martha's house that the reason y'all wanted to see Larry O'Brian was because Miz Davis was angry about his tryin' to annul their forty year old marriage. Right?"

"Right," I answered meekly.

"Just how angry with him were y'all?" The innuendo included in his question was clear.

"I was appalled that he'd do such a thing not only to me but to our two grown daughters who have families of their own!" I told him emphatically, "But if you think I was angry enough to kill him, I wasn't. He wouldn't have been worth expending that much energy. I just wanted to tell him, face to face, what I thought of him and his annulment."

"Bravo!" Plushy applauded me on my forceful reply. Turning to Lt. Guthrie, he continued "Larry told me that he was attempting to annul his marriage to his first wife, Russell. I think Miss Martha had requested it."

The police lieutenant seemed surprised by Plushy's comment. He shook his head.

"Describe how y'all found the body," he instructed us.

Sybil, perhaps chastened by the Lieutenant's chiding, perhaps just biding her time, was completely quiet now, so I spoke up again. After all, the body he referred to had once been my first husband, even if I had come here, filled with anger, to confront him.

"We heard voices in the library," this time I was not going to make the mistake of calling the room a study. "They turned out to be coming from the television set which was turned on. I went over to look out the window and I stumbled over Larry's, Larry's body."

I suddenly felt so tired it was difficult to speak. My supply of nervous energy had run out and, without any warning, exhaustion hit me like a ton of bricks. I slumped back on the loveseat, Sybil grabbing the depleted plate from my lap to prevent what was left on it from spilling onto the floor.

Lt. Guthrie seemed not to notice. He continued, "And y'all didn't see or hear anyone else in the house at the time that y'all discovered the body? What about upstairs?"

"We didn't go upstairs," Sybil answered him acerbically. "Why on earth would we go upstairs? Whatever you may think of us we're not some kind of voyeurs. There were some noises in the house. Before we found Mrs. Davis's ex-husband we heard a telephone ring and a door close. We couldn't tell if someone answered the phone or it just stopped ringing on its own. That's it. You arrived just as we walked out of the library. Remember?" She was on the defensive. Perhaps because Guthrie had yelled at her, or perhaps because he didn't seem to care that I was about ready to collapse, or maybe because of both.

"It didn't appear to me so much that y'all were leaving the room as it did that y'all were trying to get out of the house as quick as y'all could," the Lieutenant shot back at her.

"Well, wouldn't you? If you'd just found a dead body in a strange house, wouldn't you try to leave that house as quickly as you could?"

"Y'all shouldn't have been in that house, in the first place. Of course it was a strange house. Y'all'd just broken into and entered it!" the tone of Guthrie's voice grew in intensity and he moved toward us. "It wasn't that difficult to sneak up on Larry O'Brian in his library, while his back was turned on y'all. Was it? It wasn't that hard to shoot him in the back of the head. Was it?"

"That's enough!" Plushy bellowed as he rose from his seat.

"These ladies are guests in our home, Russell. Miz Davis, here, can hardly sit up she's so tired. They will both be retirin' now, and if y'all have any further questions y'all can come back tomorrow mornin' to ask them." And, with that said, he took the Lieutenant by the arm and half dragged, half pushed him from the room toward the hall that led to the garage.

"Well, don't y'all try to leave here until we find the weapon and see if it belongs to y'all. Y'all're still prime suspects in this case, as far as I'm concerned," the Lieutenant shouted over his shoulder as the Colonel hustled him from the room.

The two men went on talking after they'd left us but I couldn't hear what they said. It was drowned out by Miss Millie fluttering about me, calling me "poor lamb," and helping me up from the loveseat.

She shepherded Sybil and me rapidly out of the library and down the other hall toward the sitting room and a winding staircase that led to the upstairs of the house.

"We're goin' to get the two of y'all into a warm bath and nightclothes. What y'all need is a good night's sleep and maybe a toddy to help make sure that y'all get one," Miss Millie spoke soothingly as she led us.

Sybil and she practically supported me up the thickly carpeted stairs. I was surprised at how strong she was for a small woman who appeared to be so soft and pampered.

When we'd reached the first door at the top of the second floor landing Miss Millie opened it. The light was already on inside the bedroom, and she and Sybil deposited me on a flowered upholstered bench at the foot of one of the twin beds, whose pale blue, padded moiré headboards rested against the inside wall.

Although we'd never heard an order given to deliver our luggage, there it was, resting next to the door that led to the room's accompanying bathroom.

"Now both of y'all soak in the bath, and I'll go see to the toddies," our hostess instructed and bustled out leaving us alone again for the first time since the few minutes we'd had in the garage before entering the house.

The wind was howling outside. Even though the bedroom windows were each hung with fabric paneled decorative shutters inside, the rain was hitting the outside of the windowpanes with the rat-tat-tat of a rapidly firing gun. The force of the wind was such that no amount of shutter or fabric could have muffled the sound. And, like the evening before, I was, again, too tired to even talk.

On the evening before my exhaustion had been produced by the physical exertion of driving many, many miles. This evening it was the result of a combination of shock, fluctuating blood sugar, and liberal swallows of Plushy's Planters' Punch.

We stared at each other in silence for a few seconds, then with Sybil's help I managed to stumble into the bathroom and strip off my dirty clothes. The jeans were so stiff with dried mud that they could almost have stood upright by themselves.

Sybil ran a hot bath in the over-sized dusty rose bathtub and added a healthy dose of bath salts from one of the many glass canisters that rested on a shelf above it. I settled down into warm, perfumed water and managed to soap my tired body and shampoo my hair with my own shampoo, which Sybil had retrieved from my overnight bag.

When I arose from the bath she swathed me in a rosy Egyptian cotton bath sheet and rubbed my body vigorously. This seemed to energize me a bit.

"I think I can do the rest myself," I told her, "Thanks a million, Sybby. You've saved my life."

"What are friends for?" she shot back as I used the hairdryer-in-residence to dry my curly mop and she took her turn in the tub.

Moving slowly into the bedroom, I pulled my nightgown from my suitcase and slipped it over my head.

"Russell Guthrie is a bully," Sybil called out to me from the bathroom, "I can't believe that he'd think we'd come all the way down here to commit murder on an S.O.B. like Larry."

"I suppose he's only doing his job," I answered pulling down the thick quilt on the bed closest to the bathroom and sinking into the comfort of it. I, too, was smarting at the Lieutenant's accusations. In fact I was furious. But I was just too tired to dwell upon the insult at that moment.

"I still think there's something fishy about his relationship with Plushy."

"I do, too. But maybe it's just that they're close friends. They seem to know each other very well. And don't forget the Plushmills and Larry and Martie were close friends, too," I suppressed a yawn as I answered her, and we both fell silent.

In an amazingly short amount of time we were both clean, in our nightgowns, and tucked into the blue moiré beds, each covered with its matching, flowered Laura Ashley comforter and pillow sham. Sybil let out a huge sigh, as she sank into her bed.

My eyes wandered around the room. Under other circumstances I would have felt that my friend and I had come to rest in a posh bed and breakfast. The perfection of the bedroom belonged in the glossy picture of an upscale magazine printed with interior decorators in mind.

Miss Millie knocked, opened the bedroom door, and was back in the room before Sybil and I could rally to continue a conversation. She carried a small silver tray bearing two Irish Coffee mugs made of cut crystal.

"Here we are," she trilled brightly, slightly tossing her spun sugar coiffure. "Toddies to help settle troubled minds and let y'all drift off to slumber land."

She placed a heavy mug in each of our hands. Inside the gleaming sparkle of the mugs was a lemony elixir that smelled warmly of cinnamon and nutmeg.

"Now drink up," she insisted sitting down on the upholstered bench at the bottom of Sybil's bed. "I'm going to wait right here until y'all drop off. It's just a dreadful night, out there," she gestured toward the Laura Ashley paneled windows. Then she turned back to us and patted the bottom of Sybil's bed cooing encouragingly "Come on, now. Be good girls. Drink up."

Miss Millie reminded me, oddly, of a sorority housemother from a 1940s Jeanne Craine movie I'd seen on late night TV. As I gazed back at her, she seemed totally filled with care and concern for us, as she perched on the upholstered bench. A housemother watching over her girls.

It was obvious that she wasn't going to leave us until we drank our toddies so, obligingly, we drank long and deep, emptying the mugs in only a few swallows.

"Now y'all should sleep tight," she smiled at us, rising and gathering the mugs from our hands. "I'm goin' to turn out the lights but I'll leave a night light on in the bathroom in case y'all need to get up later. And don't worry about any bumpin' noises you may hear. Some of the branches have been blowing off trees all up and down the block."

With that she switched off the lamp on the nightstand between our beds and the one on the dresser, and Sybil and I tried to settle down to sleep with Miss Millie watching over us. I closed my eyes, hoping if I appeared to be asleep she'd leave and I could talk with Sybil alone, again. I tried not to doze off but I could feel myself beginning to drift.

From far away I heard the bedroom door open and close, and then Sybil and I were left alone in the soft glow emanating from the small light in the bathroom.

Chapter Eighteen

I have no idea how much later it was when I struggled back upward from the depths of a sleep so deep that I hadn't even dreamed about the horror of finding Larry's body. It might have been a few minutes; it might have been hours.

Something was wrong. I felt terrible. I was going to be physically sick, and I knew that I needed to get myself out of bed and into the bathroom. It would never do to vomit on Miss Millie's beautiful bed. Not after all she and Plushy had done for us.

Somehow, although my arms and legs felt strangely heavy, I managed to drag myself from the bedroom into the bathroom. I'd just made it to the toilet and knelt down when I began to retch uncontrollably.

My stomach heaved painfully and my head was throbbing. I hovered there for what seemed an eternity, until my body had nothing more to spew forth, and then I flushed it all away.

I lay down on the soft, fluffy bathroom rug beneath my knees, and tried to catch my breath. What a night! Something I'd eaten or drunk had obviously not agreed with me, or maybe all the stressful events of the day before had caught up with me. I felt extremely weak.

Rising slowly, I splashed water on my face at the sink and washed out my mouth. I could see tiny red dots on my eyelids where capillaries had popped from the force of my vomiting. The same thing had happened to Maggie as an infant when she cried really hard.

I made my way gingerly back into the bedroom, listening to the silence of the house and the still howling wind outside. Every step I took jarred my aching head.

My eyes had become accustomed to the cheerful glow of the nightlight, and I was able to find my striped canvas bag with no trouble. Closing the bathroom door behind me, I carried it into the bathroom where I turned on the light over the sink and checked my cell phone.

There was no voice mail message from Bud, and I dialed his beeper again and entered my cell number. I began to fear that if he didn't call soon the battery of the phone would lose its charge. And, of course, packing in haste, I hadn't brought the recharger.

Putting the phone back in my bag I opened the bathroom door a crack, replaced my canvas bag inside the bedroom, and retrieved my overnight bag. I could hear Sybil's heavy, even breathing. She must be as exhausted as I was, and I certainly didn't want the light from the bathroom to wake her up.

Squinting in the bright light from over the sink, I went through the small zippered bag of medication that I'd packed for the trip, searching for some analgesic for my aching head. There was none. In my haste to leave for Charleston I'd forgotten to pack that, as well as my cell phone recharger.

Maybe there was something in the medicine chest behind the mirror. I felt along the side of the beveled glass above the sink only to discover that the mirror was mounted directly upon the wall, with no medicine chest behind it.

Rats! I thought. My head was pounding harder with every move I made.

Leaving my overnight bag on the bathroom floor, I turned off the bathroom light and shuffled back to my bed. Every muscle in my body ached as badly as my head, especially those in my torso and stomach.

I plopped down and glanced over at Sybil. She was sleeping more soundly than I'd ever seen her sleep before. I was glad that the aches and pains she must be feeling were not keeping her awake. She'd had both of her knees replaced several years ago and I knew that she suffered from arthritis, too, but she rarely complained.

No help for my headache from my sleeping friend, besides I didn't want to wake her up. She deserved to get a good night's sleep after what I and my scheme to confront Larry had put her through in the last two days.

It was becoming obvious that if I was going to find an analgesic for my headache I was going to have to leave our designer bedroom and go in search of one. Tylenol, Advil, Motrin, I'd even settle for aspirin, although it would be harsh on my stomach. I'd settle for anything that would take away the throbbing pain in my head.

The person who was sure to have a remedy was Miss Millie Plushmill. I just hoped that she was still up.

I remembered that I'd seen an ornate boudoir clock on the dresser across from our beds so, careful not to jar my head too much, I rose and located it in the dark. I carried the clock into the bathroom where I read its face by the nightlight.

A quarter after two. Since it was still pitch dark outside I figured it must be two in the morning.

I didn't know what my chances were of locating Miss Millie but if I couldn't find her maybe there would be something I could take for this headache in one of the other bathrooms, or in the kitchen downstairs. At home I kept all our medications in the kitchen. Most of them Bud and I had to take with food, anyway, so the kitchen was the perfect place for them.

Not wanting to lower my head to search through the clothes in my suitcase I decided to forgo finding my slippers or robe.

I carefully opened the bedroom door leading into the upstairs hall, which was dim but not pitch black. There were nightlights burning in several places along the wall as I made my way to the stairs. If Miss Millie had gone to bed, which seemed quite likely at this hour, I'd try the kitchen and powder room downstairs before I attempted to wake anyone upstairs for help.

My footsteps were totally silent on the thick carpeting as I descended the winding staircase. It was darker on the first floor, almost no light at all except for tiny, lighted green and red bulbs that indicated smoke and carbon monoxide detectors mounted near the ceilings of the rooms.

Remembering the floor plan of the house, I managed to feel my way through the sitting room and dining room without bumping into anything or making any noise. Unlike the hardwood floors and oriental rugs in Larry's house, this house had wall to wall carpeting everywhere except the kitchen, library and bathrooms. So I moved quite silently.

When I reached the kitchen I ran my hands over tiled walls searching for a light switch. There didn't seem to be any. Suddenly I heard a loud cracking noise and the tiny bulbs on the smoke and carbon monoxide detectors in the kitchen blinked out.

I'd been a utility man's wife long enough to know, from the noise and complete darkness that followed, it probably meant that a windblown, falling tree had taken down power lines. Most likely a pole with a transformer on it. Trees and tree branches were always a threat to power lines during summer or winter storms. With the hurricane winds that were still howling outside, most trees in this neighborhood didn't stand a chance.

Now how would I find anything for my headache? I rested my elbows on the counter in the dark kitchen and, putting my head in my hands, almost wept from pain and frustration.

It was at that point that I heard voices. They were accompanied by the sounds of people thudding their way into the house, via the door from the garage.

I slipped through the dark kitchen to the door that led to the hall and saw the thin threads of flashlight beams making their way toward the library. Someone, more than one someone, had been out and about in this terrible weather!

Chapter Nineteen

"I tell y'all the stuff is over there somewhere!" I heard Plushy's voice suddenly devoid of southern lilt if not his lazy syntax. He sounded angry as he spoke to whomever was with him. His words were accompanied by the sound of wet oilskins being shaken.

"And where would you suggest we look?" Miss Millie's usually honey-toned voice was rough with sarcasm. She, too had lost her southern accent. Her voice had developed a Midwestern twang "We've been all over that house."

"I was sure we'd find it someplace upstairs," Russ Guthrie added, his voice becoming harder to hear as the three of them moved into the library and shut the door.

I froze where I stood in the dark kitchen. My first reaction to our hosts and the police lieutenant being out in this weather, at this time of night, was that they'd been checking the Plushmill property for damage.

Considering the gist of their conversation, I'd been dead wrong. What were these people looking for, and where had they been looking for it on a night like this?

And what had become of the southern "Y'all" that Miss Millie had sprinkled so liberally into her speech up until now? The English teacher in me picked right up on that omission. I'd taught enough Faulkner and Flannery O'Connor literature to notice quickly the change in the Plushmills' speech patterns. I hadn't heard enough of Guthrie's voice to tell whether he'd dropped his southern accent, or not. But the change in their voices and what they'd said, on top of their being out at this time of night in this weather seemed more than suspicious to me.

The confusion that filled me, after what I'd just overheard, combined with the embarrassment of being discovered eavesdropping seemed to have lessened my headache. My head still throbbed but not as painfully. My main concern, now, was how to get back upstairs unobserved. Or, at least, I thought that should be my main concern. In the back of my mind, however, I felt curiosity growing ever stronger. Bud always said that I could never take things at face value. That I always questioned things, and could never leave well enough alone. He reminded me constantly that curiosity killed the you-know-what.

Again, maybe I'd been conditioned by all my years of teaching. In school if something seemed out of the ordinary, not what it should be, a teacher investigated the situation. Usually finding that there was an unpleasant reason for why things seemed curious. But the responsibility for setting things right was one that was ingrained in all teachers, at all levels of education.

Therefore, it did not seem unusual to me to find myself gliding quietly forward, out of the kitchen, toward the library door. This time I was moving in pitch-darkness. Thank goodness the Plushmill house did not have any petit point side chairs placed along the walls of the hall that led to the back of the house, as the O'Brian house had. I probably would have fallen over one of them, broken my neck, and alerted Guthrie and the Plushmills of my presence.

I crept silently, thanks to the thick wall to wall carpeting, toward the library door. Crouching beside it I could make out the movement of dim lights beneath the door's bottom and the uncarpeted floor of the room. Flashlights, again. Pressing my ear to the door I could hear Plushy's voice and the sound of movement in the library as if someone was pacing.

"You think those two upstairs had time to find it?"

"Nah," Guthrie answered. "I got to the house as soon as I could, after y'all called me. They didn't have time to search anywhere. I think they were really shook up at findin' O'Brian's body. After checkin' their drivers licenses and Social Security cards, I think they're really who they say they are."

"How can y'all tell their ID's aren't fake?" Plushy seemed unsure. "How do we even know they're still in bed upstairs. Have y'all checked lately? We have to make sure we keep them out of our way."

His question must have been directed to Miss Millie because she chortled in response to the question and answered, "After the number of prescription sleeping pills I emptied into their bedtime drinks, those two will be lucky to wake up in the morning. They're not going anywhere. They're out like lights, believe me. I stayed to make sure they drank it all."

Her words hit me like a ton of bricks. Sybby and I had been drugged! No wonder I'd felt so sick. No wonder my head hurt! No wonder I felt as if the falling tree that had taken out power to the house had hit me, too.

Thank God I'd gotten sick and woken up when I had! I might never have known about the drugs. Even worse, Sybby and I could have been made very sick from ingesting an unknown amount of sleeping pills. I felt a wave of nausea rush through my body at that thought. And my friend was still upstairs under the influence of the pills, still asleep!

I half turned to retrace my steps in concern for her. I'd shake her awake and get her across the street into my van. We'd head for home immediately. Then reality set in. There was a hurricane blowing outside the house. Even if I could get Sybby safely out of the Plushmill's house into our vehicle what kind of condition were the roads in? Would we be able to drive out of the low-lying, perhaps flooded area around Palmetto Crown Plantation? What should I do?

"Well we can't afford to have them wanderin' all over the place," Plushy continued. "Bad luck that they showed up right when they did. Before we could find the stuff. I still think it's in the house, somewhere. Damn that power company. Lights out all over the place just when we need them most."

"Since tonight's search was a bust what are the plans for tomorrow?" Russ Guthrie's voice, now that I'd heard him speak for a longer time, still retained its southern accent.

"We should really be back over there, still lookin'," Miss Millie answered. "By tomorrow the weather may clear and we'll be expected to deliver as usual. Young Tom is bound to come by the house tomorrow. There's another complication."

"When I called him he sounded more glad than shocked that his stepfather was dead," Guthrie commented. "Y'all know how much those Mayhew kids hated O'Brian. He didn't even ask questions about the cause of death. I bet he's at the hospital with his mama tonight, and will be so tired tomorrow he won't bother to come by. Y'all saw how much tape my boys put up around the house after they removed the body. And I replaced the tape on the back door when we left just now. That tape'll keep everyone else away for a while."

"Yeah. It's a good thing your boys didn't know about the entrance to the main house through the boat house, so we can still get in and out when we want." All three murmured assent to Plushy's matter-of-fact comment.

Understanding rushed in on me. So that's who Young Tom was. Martie's son from her first marriage. I'd heard the name earlier that evening, when Plushy had suggested to Guthrie that he contact Young Tom. I'd also known that Larry had several stepchildren by his marriage to Martie, but I'd had no idea how many or what their names were.

"I'm still concerned about those two upstairs," Plushy grumbled.

"Okay, okay!" Miss Millie's chair creaked as she got out of it. "I'll go upstairs and check on them, if that will shut you up."

My heart skipped a beat. I stood up quickly, not bothering to rub away the arthritic pain in my knees, the result of having been in a crouching position for so long.

Turning, I fled back up the dark hall as fast as I could go without falling. I had to get back upstairs before I was discovered! I had to get back to Sybil.

By the time I reached the dining room I was in a full run, praying that I wouldn't smash into anything in the dark. I was still running when I reached the sitting room. The toes of my right foot hit the riser of the bottom step when I reached the staircase. It was so dark, I had no way of judging exactly where the stairs were.

Now my head throbbed, my knees ached, and the pain in my toes was so sharp I'm sure I would have cried out when I stubbed them if I hadn't been so terrified of discovery.

Holding my hands out before me to catch myself, in case I fell forward, I took the steps two at a time in pitch darkness. My breath was coming in quick gasps that I was sure Miss Millie would be able to hear as she followed behind me with her flashlight.

Somehow I found the knob of the door to our bedroom, opened it, and slipped inside. I closed the door as quietly as I could, behind me, and headed toward where I vaguely remembered my bed had been. The bedclothes tangled around my legs as I jumped into it and tried to pull them up to my chin.

I had just barely enough time to settle myself before the bedroom door opened and Miss Millie and her flashlight beam entered the room.

I made sure that my back was turned to the door and Miss Millie, and I willed my heart to stop pounding and my breath to become more even.

I guess all seemed normal to Miss Millie, as she ran her flashlight beam over the two beds, because she stayed only a few seconds and then left, closing the door behind her. I let my breath out in a long but soft "whoosh" and lay there trying to collect my thoughts.

As I listened in the dark to Sybil's soft, even breathing I was overcome with guilt. What had I done to my loyal friend? I'd dragged her to Charleston when all she'd wanted to do was go on our traditional, every few years, shopping trip to Williamsburg. I'd forced her to sneak into the Palmetto Crown Plantation and Larry's house, where we'd stumbled across his dead body. And now, thanks to my selfish impulse, she lay drugged in the bed next to me, in the home of people who did not appear to be who or what they'd presented themselves to be.

I could feel hot tears welling up behind my eyes. Stop it, I told myself! I felt like I needed a good shaking, as if I were a willful child. I didn't have time for crying! I'd gotten us into this situation and it was up to me to figure a way out of it. As Sybil had pointed out to me earlier in the evening, that's what the other Red Hats would have had to do in my position. Now, even though I was used to years of Bud taking care of me and solving my problems, I had to do it, too.

I tried to sit up to go to Sybil in the adjacent bed. As I did the darkness seemed to tilt and I was forced to lay my head down again. Apparently all the effects of the sleeping pills I had ingested had not worn off yet, because the thought, that it was up to me to find a way out of the mess I'd created, was the last one I had before I abruptly lost consciousness.

Chapter Twenty

"I swear, I don't know why I'm doing this. I must be crazy," I muttered to myself, several hours later, as I braved the dark, wet, and wild early South Carolina morning.

I couldn't have been unconscious for more than about three hours, after I'd fallen into bed for the second time, in the Plushmill's guest bedroom. Waking slowly in the dark room I could still hearing Sybil's slow, even breathing coming from the next bed. The fact that she was breathing at all reassured me. I felt my curiosity and desire to clean up the "mess" I'd gotten us into both increasing at a lightening rate, as I tried to gather the strength to sit up.

Curiosity peaked by the strange and unsettling conversations I'd overheard a few hours before burned in me. It was accompanied by deep senses of anger and shame. Who was Russ Guthrie to accuse me of being a murderer when he seemed, himself, to be involved in something questionable? What could possibly justify the Plushmills' secret drugging of two defenseless women? Strangers to them? How could I have gotten Sybil and myself into such a bizarre situation, in the first place? There were too many questions and, so far, in my mind, no answers.

How I missed the Red Hats and their supportive words of wisdom as I faced this ugly, confusing situation! How I longed for Bud's quiet strength and the warmth of his arms around me!

Moving quietly to Sybil's bedside, I grasped her wrist and took her pulse. I was deeply worried about her. She still had the full amount of sleeping pills administered to us by Miss Millie in her system. She moved and uttered a small sigh as I touched her wrist and began to count her heartbeats. To my relief, her pulse was strong and even. Next, I checked my cell phone, again, for any sign of a message from Bud. There was none but the phone's lighted face had begun flashing the "low battery" signal. Not wanting it to go dead before my husband and I made some kind of contact, I turned it off and replaced it in my purse, noting that my van keys were still tucked safely beside it.

The only way I could think of to find the answers that I needed to all the questions running through my head at breakneck speed was to return to Larry and Martha's house. Something strange was going on, there was no denying it. And after overhearing the Plushmill/Guthrie conversation earlier I knew it seemed to center around "stuff" that was in that house.

If I could discover what that "stuff" was, I bet myself, I could solve the situation I'd created for Sybil and me. I could end Guthrie's innuendoes that she and I had anything to do with Larry's murder. I might even be able to discover how Larry, the Plushmills and Guthrie were really connected. There was something more than just the close friendship that Miss Millie had alluded to going on there. Even if this theory might not have made a lot of sense to someone else, I planned to give it a try. I didn't know what else to do.

I figured that Sybil would be safe as long as she still slept. And I planned to be back long before she awoke. Guthrie and the Plushmills expected both of us to sleep for a long time. I carefully arranged pillows in my empty bed to make it appear that I still lay there.

Dressing in the murky darkness of the bedroom, I put on clean clothes from my suitcase. Then, carrying my shoes, I prepared to creep downstairs a second time. The boudoir clock, which thank goodness was not an electric one, had indicated that the time was slightly after 5:00 A.M. This time, as I descended the steps, there were no friendly nightlights in the upstairs hall to guide me. The first floor was hardly less forbidding at five than it had been at two in the morning but there was a sickly, gray light discernable around the edges of some of the windows, even though they were covered with storm shutters.

It's not that I'm a stealthy person by nature, or even one who is good at sneaking around places. I'm not. I think it was just pure, dumb luck that allowed me to locate one of the flashlights the trio had left behind in the library, struggle into a set of still-damp oilskins hanging from a peg inside the door to the garage, and exit the house by the kitchen door without alerting anyone. All was quiet. I figured, after their frustrating early morning foray to Larry's house, Plushy, Miss Millie, and Lt. Guthrie must be somewhere else, catching up on their sleep.

If the Plushmill house had an alarm system the power outage must have disarmed it. With no interference from anyone or anything, I found myself picking my way, once again, through raging wind and horizontal rain. I had no idea whether Marcus was a level one, two, or three hurricane. However, at five o'clock in the morning, its rain and wind seemed just as strong to me as they had at seven the evening before, when we'd struggled through them to reach the house across the street from the one in which my ex-husband lay dead.

Once I reached the sidewalk in front of 65 Windsor Way, I stood in the gloomy early morning light, shielding my face from the lashing of the rain, and surveyed my destination. True to his word Lt. Guthrie's men had surrounded the O'Brian house with many loops of yellow crime tape. It fluttered in the heavy wind that blew from the East. The front door was tightly closed but didn't sport a large "X" of tape across it's breadth, as I had expected. Tape lay scattered on the porch beneath the door. I figured that it must have been blown off by the whipping of the wind.

Climbing the porch, I tried the door's brass handle. This time it was securely locked. All the windows on that level were closed and covered with tape. No access to the house from this direction.

Passing my van, still parked in the O'Brian driveway, I tried one of the doors. It was locked. I skirted the property, slogging through mud and water in some places up to my shins.

Avoiding huge tree limbs that lay all over the back yard I approached the house from the North. The doors and windows at the back of the house were all covered with tape. I tried them but to no avail.

Maybe I was able to hear the banging of a screen door, above the roar of the wind, as a result of my acute sense of hearing. Or maybe it was a fluke caused by a pocket of air in which I unknowingly stood. Whatever the reason, the banging brought to my attention a door on a small balcony jutting out from the third level of the house.

Not having explored the back of Larry's house, before, I hadn't known that it had a third story. No third story was visible from the front of the house. The banging door must lead to an attic. I imagined that it also afforded a lovely place to sit on a warm evening to gaze out at the water to the right of it and the sunset on its left.

Now, in the storm, the door leading into the house was whipping back and forth in the frenzy of the wind. The police must have overlooked taping it, or figured no one was crazy enough to try entering the house from the third floor in the middle of a hurricane. I knew I certainly wasn't crazy enough to try.

How would anybody get up there even if they didn't have to battle gale force winds to do so? That door might have been overlooked when the taping occurred but it wasn't going to be my entrance to Larry's house.

A door. An untaped door. Wait a minute! When I was eavesdropping on the conversation in the library a few hours earlier, hadn't I heard the Plushmills and Lt. Guthrie mention an untaped entrance to the house through the property's boathouse? Turning my head I could just make out the shape of the boathouse in question.

It was situated at the foot of the sloping yard, about a hundred yards from the main house. If there'd been any boats tied up there earlier the wind and high level of thrashing water had either destroyed them or sent them careening out to sea. There were signs that there had been a dock at the edge of the boathouse but that, too, had disappeared. Only a wooden pole sticking out of the water marked the place where it must have stood.

I fixed the pale ray of my flashlight on the boathouse and made my way down the precariously slick slope of the yard. My New Balance walking shoes would never be the same, I mourned. I winced with each muddy step I took, praying that I wouldn't lose my footing and go tumbling headfirst to the bottom.

When I was finally able to locate a door to the boathouse I discovered that there were actually two. There was a wide garage door, probably for the moving of boats into and out of the boathouse, and there was a regular-sized personnel door located just to the left of that. I could understand why it had been easy for the police to overlook taping them both. They were on the inlet side of the building, and since the water level had risen and the dock was gone water was now lapping against them.

Putting my flashlight into the pocket of my dripping oilskin jacket, I made a leap of faith for the second time in twenty-four hours. Grasping the remains of the departed dock with my right hand, I stepped into the water at the edge of Palmetto Crown Plantation. It seemed to be the only way possible to reach the knob of the smaller boathouse door. I was determined to find the mysterious entrance to the main house that lay inside its dark, waterlogged exterior.

How different the water felt this time. When Sybil and I had sneaked into the development the day before the smooth water of the inlet had been cool and refreshing, a welcome change from the hot sticky conditions of the underbrush outside the property's fence line. Now the water was icy cold and thrashing as if an ancient sea monster lay beneath its surface.

I could feel my feet sinking quickly into the muck and mire below the waterline as I grasped the doorknob with my left hand and put my shoulder against the door. I pushed with all my strength, praying that I would not be sucked down into the pulsating water before I could open it. Unlike the front door of the O'Brian house the day before this door did not yield easily.

I began to panic as I felt water rising up my legs to my knees. The force of the heavy current kept pushing me toward the door as the water tried to encroach even farther onto the land. This steadied me, somewhat, and I gave the door another shove with all my might.

As the thrashing water rose around me, I was really beginning to lose hope of not only opening the door but of surviving my efforts to do so. What had ever possessed me to risk my life like this? I was sure that I'd never see Bud or my children and grandchildren ever again. Their sweet faces sprang into my mind, making me feel guilty as well as frightened. I was nauseated with fear, sobbing uncontrollably, and breathing in short gasps as I fought against the wind and water.

What would become of my family if I drowned in this foolish manner? If I were dead how could I make them understand why I'd done what I'd done?

What would become of Sybil, sleeping soundly across the street in the Plushmill house, unaware of what her hosts were really like? How would she fare if she woke to find me not only gone from my bed but dead, as well?

And what about the Red Hats, my loyal friends? What if I never saw them again? If only I had taken their sound advice and ignored the annulment letter. If only I'd never come here!

Wonder of wonders! Just as I was about to give up and turn back in an attempt to reestablish a footing on dry land I felt the door begin to yield. I continued pushing and between my feeble attempts and the force of the water behind me the door gradually opened far enough for me to squeeze inside. It took every ounce of effort that I could muster to lift first one leg and then the other out of the mud and water. Each time I wrenched a leg free and lurched forward it made a loud sucking noise.

I struggled inside the boathouse, the wooden floor of which quickly flooded behind me. Turning, I tried to shut the door but the force of the invading water was too strong. As soon as I was steady on my feet, I pulled the flashlight out of my pocket and turned it on.

I found that I was standing in water up to my shins inside a room that was empty of anything except one small rowboat hanging from heavy hooks embedded in the rafters. I was wet and I was traumatized by the watery danger I'd just escaped but, at least, beneath the water I was standing on a solid wooden floor. This was the first reassuring thing that I'd encountered in the last several harrowing minutes.

I drew in a deep breath of damp, musty air and let it out in a momentary sigh of relief. I hadn't been sucked down into the stormy vortex of the water outside. I was still alive! Now I had to find the entrance that ran from the boathouse to the main house and find it quickly. Before the small building was flooded completely by the encroaching water. Where could it be? Oh, where could it be?

I ran the flashlight beam from wall to wall of the boathouse. I even explored the rafters above my head. I couldn't see anything. No door, no opening of any kind. The water level inside the boathouse and my panic had both begun increasing at an alarming rate. Then, as if in a dream, a small, square opening, up high, near the peak of the boathouse roof swung slowly open and a male voice called out, "Who's there. What do y'all want?

At this point in time I didn't care if it was the voice of Devil himself that I heard. The light that streamed from the opening portal looked like heaven to me.

Chapter Twenty-one

Standing almost directly beneath what I now saw was a wooden door, much like those situated in the haylofts of Central Pennsylvania barns, I held the beam of my flashlight aloft and called out to the stranger above me, "Oh, thank God you've come! I'm stranded here, and the water is getting higher every minute. How do I get up there?"

"Wait just a doggoned minute, Lady. Who in the hell are y'all, and what are y'all doin' here?" an indignant voice drifted down to me.

"My name's Susannah Davis. I used to be married to the man who owns this boathouse, and if you don't help me I'm afraid I'll drown. I have a family back in Pennsylvania where I live. Please, please help me!"

"Well, I'll be damned. I'll be double-dog damned," the voice continued. "There's a ladder up here. I'm goin' to lower it to y'all. Do y'all think you can wedge it against the iron bar under the water and climb up? That's what the bar is there for. To steady the ladder. Try to find it. If y'all just try to stand the ladder on the floor the current will push it away."

"I don't know if I can. Oh, I don't know. I'll try," I called back to him in a voice made hoarse by the dampness and my shouting to be heard above the roar of the wind and water.

An iron bar to wedge the ladder against was down there, somewhere under the water. I tried reaching down into the rising water, searching for the bar with my hand. Nothing. Standing upright, again, I tried to judge where the bar would be in relationship to where I stood. A little more to the right? Farther to the left?

I began moving my feet back and forth through the now knee-high water, trying to kick out with first one foot and then the other, searching for the bar. I was doing a good deal of splashing.

"A little farther to your right and closer to the back wall," the young man above me shouted instructions over the splashing I was creating. I followed his directions and almost immediately my right foot struck something very solid.

"I think I've found it. Yes it's an iron bar," I called up to him.

"Good. I'm lowering the ladder. When y'all can reach it, try to guide it so the bottoms of the legs are tucked behind the bar."

I focused the flashlight and my gaze upon the dark shape that began to descend from the dim opening above me. As it drew closer I could see that it was an extremely long and heavy wooden ladder.

"Put your flashlight away and take hold of it with both hands," instructions accompanied the ladder's slow descent. "I have a lantern. As soon as y'all have hold of the ladder I'll hold it on the rungs so y'all can see to climb."

I obeyed, turning off my flashlight and again putting it into my pocket. I missed the pale cheer its beam had afforded me, as I held out both my hands waiting to touch the ladder approaching me.

Time seemed to crawl by as I waited for the ladder to come

within my grasp. My arms ached from holding them above my head in anticipation. Finally I felt the feet of the ladder touch my hands and I grabbed them as if they were a lifeline. I steadied the ladder as it continued its journey downward, in front of me, and finally felt it thump against the wooden floor.

Reaching down into the dark water with both hands and trying not to topple over, I attempted to push the ladder behind the iron bar. The weight of the ladder made this difficult, but not as difficult as moving it would have been had there not been so much water present to make the floor slippery. Of course, the current of that water fought against my efforts as it pushed with all its might from behind both the ladder and me. Wrestling with the ladder and the current, it took several minutes for me to secure it behind the bar.

When I looked up again I could see the light from a powerful battery-operated lantern focusing upon the ladder from above. Because of its brightness and the fact that its light was between my rescuer and me I still could not see his face.

"I've got it wedged behind the bar," I called up to him.

"Good," he answered. "Now start to climb. Hold on tight and take your time. Do y'all think you can make it?"

"Oh, sure," I spoke up bravely. "I'm not very strong but I have enough adrenaline in me to make it up there." I spoke bravely and only hoped that what I told him was true.

Grasping the sides of the ladder and lifting my right foot upward in the water and onto the first rung took a great effort. A tremor of fear ran through me at the thought of placing my left foot upon the second rung and thereby forsaking the solidity of the wooden floor. Stop thinking about it and just do it, I told myself. And, grasping the ladder even tighter, I did.

Hampered by the weight of wet clothes and arthritic knees that screamed with pain from the cold and damp, I pulled my body upward along the ladder. Each time I placed a foot upon a ladder rung I prayed that the sole of my muddy shoe would not slip and send me plummeting to the floor.

Hand over hand, one foot after the other I moved slowly upward.

"That's it. Keep on coming. Just a little farther," my rescuer's voice encouraged me from above.

Looking back on that climb up that ladder in the dark of early morning, with the wind howling outside the boathouse and the water of the inlet swirling just a few feet beneath me, I know I thought, at the time, that it was probably the most frightening experience I'd ever had. As fate would have it, the climb was not to be the most frightening of my experiences in Charleston but it was certainly the most surreal one I've experienced in my lifetime.

I am able to philosophize about it, now, so long after I reached the safety of the open window. But back then I'd had to stay completely focused on what I was doing in order to reach my goal. Surprisingly, my fear receded toward the end of my climb and was replaced with determination. I would make it to the top. I would!

Suddenly the bright light of the lantern was no longer in my eyes and I felt strong arms wrapping themselves around me. I was pulled off the ladder and onto a firm surface above me as if I were no heavier or bulkier than a bundle of laundry.

"Oh, thank God. Thank God, " I'd heard myself murmuring softly, over and over again, just as I remembered I'd done in the delivery room after the births of each of my babies.

I lay in a fetal position. Tears of relief streaming down my face. In a way my climb up the ladder had been like being in labor. Great physical exertion, mental and physical stress, followed by a safe delivery. The euphoria I felt was akin to that I'd felt following Maggie and Anne's births. As I lay there, the first normal thought I'd had in an hour occurred to me. I was very, very hungry!

"I'm Tom Mayhew," the young man who sat next to me introduced himself. I'd pulled myself up and we were sitting side by side in a circle of lantern-light on the wooden floor of a small room. He'd retrieved the ladder, as I had gathered enough strength and composure to sit up, and it now lay on the floor beside us.

Our backs rested against a wall of the room. The place smelled musty, as had the boathouse below when I'd first entered it. I'd finally stopped shaking from the chills that had replaced my euphoria a few minutes earlier.

"I told you that my name was Susannah Davis but everyone calls me Sukie," I found myself smiling timidly. "And I'm oh so very glad to meet you."

"I haven't got any idea why y'all're here," Tom faced me squarely. He was a very handsome young man who appeared to be in his mid to late thirties, about the same age as my daughter Anne. "Y'all said you used to be married to Larry O'Brian? Are y'all the lady he and my mother talked about? The one who was his first wife?"

"Guilty," I nodded. "He wanted to annul our marriage. I got a letter from the Charleston Archdiocese, and it made me angry. So I came down here to speak to him about it face-to-face. I don't know for sure but I think maybe your mother wanted him to get the annulment for her."

Tom ran his hand through his curly, dark hair as he digested what I'd said.

"She surely did. She surely did," he murmured to himself, under his breath." Then he addressed me, "Let's go up to the house." And, standing up, he held out his hands to help me in joining him. It was the second time in less than a day that I'd been pulled to my feet by a young, southern male.

Chapter Twenty-two

As I followed him from the room and up a sloping hallway, I realized that Tom Mayhew was not only handsome he was also very tall. He had to lean forward so as not to bump his head against the low ceiling above us. He held the lantern out ahead of us and, holding my hand in his led me behind him.

"This hallway is actually a tunnel that runs underground for a couple hundred feet and comes out in the basement of the house," he enlightened me as we made our way. "It wasn't in the original plans of the house because of the high water table this close to the inlet. Larry had it built despite the architect's objections. The guy didn't think it was a safe way to reach the boathouse. Building it didn't make sense to me, either."

"Thank goodness, for me, you just happened to use it to come down to the boathouse. I probably would have drowned without you."

"I didn't just happen to be at the boathouse. I went down there purposely to check on the boats. We usually have two tied up at the dock, and I couldn't see them from the house," he informed me as we reached the end of the tunnel. "In case you're wondering, I got into the house by tearing the tape off the front door and using my key."

"I'm afraid your dock and your boats are gone," I told him as we stepped through a door into the basement of the house. "I saw them earlier this afternoon but, just now, I held onto a post to reach the boathouse door, and I think it was the only part of the dock that was left. There were no boats at all."

"It figures," I could hear the disgust in his voice as he led me up the basement stairs to the first floor. "Larry knew the hurricane was coming. Talk about lazy! He couldn't be bothered to pull the boats out of the water and into the boathouse. Pah! Typical."

We stood in a small mudroom, off the kitchen, at the back of the O'Brian house. Sybil and I hadn't gone far enough into that part of the house the evening before to notice that it was there. Turning off the lantern and putting it down, Tom divested me of my dripping oilskins. Together we hung the pants and the hooded jacket on pegs placed in the walls for that purpose.

"Maybe he got killed before he had a chance to move the boats," I suggested finding it hard to believe that I was defending the non-actions of a man I had so despised.

"I doubt it."

"Look, Tom," I turned to him, "I hardly know you, and you have just saved my life. But I have to tell you something. I'm feeling very weak from low blood sugar. I have absolutely nothing in my stomach. The last meal I had that stayed down was peanut butter crackers and a coke around noon yesterday. Do you suppose there is anything in this kitchen that I could eat?"

He looked at me incredulously. I'm sure he wondered how anyone so recently snatched from the jaws of disaster could be hungry. I bet myself that if he was married his wife must be a thin woman who hardly ever ate. Maybe his mother was one, too. She'd certainly appeared to be slim in the picture I'd seen of her and Larry on the sitting room mantel.

"Sure," he mumbled opening the refrigerator door. "There must be something."

The "something" turned out to be a ham sandwich already prepared and resting in a plastic bag on the second shelf. He handed it to me and no food had ever looked so inviting, either before that minute or since. I pulled it out of the bag and took a large bite while he retrieved two sodas and closed the door. Since the refrigerator light had not come on when he opened the door I assumed that power had not yet been restored to Palmetto Crown Plantation.

It occurred to me that the sandwich that I was eating had probably been made by or was, at the very least, intended for Larry O'Brian. I was too hungry to care. He certainly wouldn't need it anymore. Providing it for me to eat was, in my opinion, the very least he could do to make up for my being in the mess in which I found myself. I never would have come here in the first place and discovered his body, been accused of his murder, any of it, if he hadn't tried to annul our marriage.

Pulling out kitchen chairs Tom gestured for me to join him at the table. We drank our sodas and I ate Larry's sandwich in silence for a minute or so before he spoke.

"So, I'll ask y'all again, what are y'all doing here? Y'all live in Pennsylvania where my mother came from. Don't y'all? And does that van parked in the driveway out front belong to y'all?"

I knew Tom was a southern boy, born and raised in Charleston, but I was amazed that he could get five "y'all's" into four sentences, which he'd asked while taking only two or three breaths.

I swallowed the last of the sandwich and answered, "It's my van. I live in Pennsylvania but not the same part that your mother and Larry came from. My husband and I live pretty far northwest of Philadelphia. It's a small town called Martin's Field. You've probably never heard of it. I came down here to ask Larry face-to-face why he wanted to annul our marriage. I mean, it took place over forty years ago and we are already divorced. I felt that an annulment was a slap in the face to both me and my daughters. You knew that he and I had children, didn't you? Maggie and Anne?"

"I guess I knew," he answered. Then he turned full face to me and almost spat the words, "That annulment! Like getting the annulment and marrying Larry in the Church was going to wash the slate clean. Make that son-of-a-bitch a decent human being! My mother was obsessed with the annulment once she got sick."

"I, I didn't know your mother was sick when I came down here," I told him hesitantly.

"I hated Larry O'Brian. I've hated him for so long that I can't remember a time when I didn't hate him," Tom told me emphatically. "He was a leech and a skirt chaser. I'll never know why my mother married him, or why she stayed married to him. I'm glad he's dead."

His words and the tone of his voice took me by surprise. But, then, I remembered overhearing Lt. Guthrie remind the Plushmills, the night before, that the Mayhew children had heartily disliked their stepfather.

"I left him for just exactly those reasons," I told Tom. "Larry cheated on me from the time we'd been married only a couple months. If we hadn't had children I probably would have left him sooner than I did."

"Y'all were smart," his voice drifted off as, resting an elbow on the table, he ran a hand through his hair again.

"I just found out that your mother has cancer. I'm so sorry. I can very well imagine what life has been like for her, married to my ex-husband. There were two other wives between her marriage to Larry and mine, you know, and two other children."

"My sisters and brother and I had heard rumors about that. Mother wouldn't discuss it with us. She wouldn't hear anything bad said about Larry, so we didn't talk about him much. If we did talk about him there was always a huge argument."

"How many sisters do you have and how old are all of you?" my curiosity had got the better of me again.

"I'm the oldest, named for my dad. Thomas Hunt Mayhew the third. I'll be thirty-six my next birthday. Then there's my sister Bitsy; her real name's Tabitha. She's thirty-three, married, and has three kids. She lives in Charleston. The twins Bella and Mandy, that's Arabella and Amanda, are thirty. Bella's married and has two boys. Lives near Atlanta. Mandy isn't married. Neither is Joe. He's the youngest. Only twenty-one. I think my parents felt that having Joe might save their marriage. My father was an alcoholic. He and my mother were having a rough time of it. Then Joe was born and things got better for a while."

Tom hesitated trying to maintain his composure. "My dad may have been a drunk but he was a gentleman, just like his father before him who drank too much, too. Those men put away bourbon like it was going out of style but they were cultured, and kind, and boy could they make money!"

"What happened to your father?" I asked quietly, leaning back in my chair.

"He died ten and a half years ago. His heart and liver gave out. He was only fifty-two."

"I'm sorry," I said softly thinking what a sad, tragic life Martha Mayhew O'Brian had led. She may have been left a wealthy widow but there had been no wonderful Bud Davis awaiting her at the end of her first, unhappy marriage as there had been for me.

"Yeah. Mother jumped right out of the fryin' pan into the fire. She was a widow for less than a year when she heard that her old high school sweetheart, Larry, was available. She actually went looking for him. Nothing any of us could say would stop her. She found him, all right. He was a bum. Totally destitute. And she brought him home to our house in Charleston. Paid for his divorce from whoever he was married to then..."

"Sarah was his third wife," I supplied softly.

"I never knew if the second wife was real or a rumor, and I never heard Sarah's name until now," Tom continued. "I've heard y'all's name before, though. Larry was never very complimentary when he spoke about y'all."

"I'll bet he wasn't!" I found myself laughing. "Did he say that everything that went wrong with our marriage was my fault?"

"Yeah. He did, kind of," Tom admitted.

"Pah. Typical!" I told him with a wry smile.

Chapter Twenty-three

"I wish I hadn't come here," I told Tom Mayhew wistfully as we continued to sit at the kitchen table in his mother's home in the gray light of early morning. "The last time I came to Charleston I was on vacation with my husband Bud. He's my second husband, and he's a wonderful man. Not at all like Larry. We've been married for almost thirty years. We loved seeing Charleston and The Isle of Palms. I wish Bud were here now. If I'd stayed home with him I wouldn't have been the one to find Larry's body and Lt. Guthrie wouldn't suspect me of killing him."

"Y'all found the body? Russ Guthrie thinks y'all killed Larry?" Tom seemed amazed at the thought. "That's crazy!"

"Yes, it is, and yes, I did. And yes, I think he does," I answered. "How well do you know Lt. Guthrie? And the Plushmills?"

Since I'd overheard the police officer's conversation with the Plushmills, a few hours earlier, I wanted to find out as much information about the three of them as I could.

"Russ Guthrie and Bart and Millie Plushmill were Larry's friends," Tom answered slowly. "My family's known the Guthries for a long time, and the Mayhews have known the Fairchilds all their lives. The Fairchilds are Russ's grandparents on his mother's side. Russ's mother and father, Susan and Big Russ grew up with my father. The families go back a long ways together.

Russ is about my age. We were at school around the same time, and for a while we were friends. But we went to different colleges. I went to Ole Miss and Russ went to S.C. State. We lost touch. Someone told me he got kicked out of State and later ended up at the Police Academy." He ran his hand through his hair as he spoke. It was a gesture of his that I'd become accustomed to.

"What about the Plushmills? They more or less told me that they were close friends of your mother and Larry."

"Friends! Close? My mother couldn't stand Bart and Millie Plushmill. Mother and Larry sold my family's house in Charleston a couple years ago and moved here, to The Plantation. When my mother found out that Bart and Millie were buying the house across the street she and Larry had a huge fight.

Mother wanted to have nothing to do with the Plushmills. Threatened to sell this house and move. She thought they were common and pushy. I think there was something else that she knew or suspected about them, too, but she never came right out and said anything."

"The Plushmills act as though the four of them were bosom buddies," I continued. "And Lt. Guthrie calls your mother Miss Martha."

"That's just an old southern custom. People in these parts who have known ladies for a long time call most of them 'Miss'. Russ grew up knowing my mother as 'Miss Martha'."

"So, if I lived in the Charleston area my friends would call me 'Miss Sukie'?" I asked, half jokingly. "Like Col. Plushmill calls his wife 'Miss Millie'?"

"Most likely. But the Plushmills aren't from Charleston, originally. I don't know where they're from."

"Plushy told me he was a graduate of the Citadel," I informed Tom.

"Pah! That doesn't mean he's from Charleston. Everyone gets all dewy-eyed whenever the Citadel is mentioned. Let me tell you, it can be a nasty place. Did y'all ever see the movie "Brother Rat"? It isn't too far off the mark when it shows how the cadets are treated there."

I was quiet for a minute. I had seen the movie "Brother Rat" and I'd read Pat Conroy's novel about attending the Citadel, too. Plus, I remembered several years before when women had attempted to enroll at the Citadel as cadets. It had been a nightmare situation, a travesty. I pondered these things.

When I spoke again I told Tom, "The Plushmills were all *southern hospitality* when my friend and I first met them last evening. They were 'you alling' us all over the place. They even invited us to spend the night at their house. Later on they drugged us when we went to bed, and I overheard them having a conversation with Russ Gutherie that was really strange. They'd lost their southern accents, too."

"I think Bart Plushmill's from somewhere in the South. I don't know about her. They haven't been in Charleston for that long, and they haven't been married very long, either. Y'all say they drugged you? Are y'all sure? Whatever for?"

The rosy assumptions I'd made earlier about Col. Plushmill and Miss Millie meeting while he was a dashing young cadet at The Citadel and she a blushing Southern Belle fell flat and died. The two of them were certainly not turning out to be at all like the warm, long-married couple Sybil and I had supposed them to be.

"In the talk they had with Russ Guthrie they said it was because they were looking for something in this house, over here, and didn't want us to get in their way. The whole thing sounded really strange to me. Can you think of anything in this house that would be so important to them that they'd try to get my friend and me out of the way so they could look for it?"

"No. I can't. Mother got rid of all the antique furniture from the Charleston house. She and Larry sold it when they moved here. There used to be a lot of silver that belonged to Dad's family but I haven't seen it in this house in, oh, the last six months or so. Between y'all and me I think Larry pawned things from the house when he wanted money and Mother refused to give it to him, especially after she got sick and wasn't here anymore. All of Mother's jewelry is in her bank box in Charleston. She had me put it there when she learned how sick she really was. I don't think there's anything else of value here. Not that I remember, anyway."

After this update Tom sat quietly and seemed to be digesting what I'd told him. His hand strayed to his hair again.

I can rarely stand a pregnant pause in any conversation so I changed the subject, asking, "Are you married, Tom? I know you said two of your sisters are. Both my daughters are married, and I have four grandchildren."

"No," he answered softly. "I'm not married."

He raised his eyes to mine, "As the oldest son, I always felt I needed to stay single after Dad died. Available to look after my mother and sisters and Joe. Now it looks as if Mother won't need me to look after her much longer. She's dyin', in case y'all didn't know."

"Yes. Col. Plushmill told me she was," I answered very simply, not really knowing what to say to a young man I'd just met about the impending death of his mother, a woman I'd heartily disliked until quite recently.

"That's another reason I'm glad Larry's dead. He can't inherit any of my father's money now. If my mother had died first he'd have gotten a good chunk of it.

Once she knew how sick she was she threatened to cut Larry out of her will unless he got his marriage to you annulled.

They'd had a civil ceremony when they got married nine years ago, and Mother wanted to marry Larry in the Catholic Church before she died.

She was absolutely obsessed with the notion. She's a devout Catholic, y'all know, and there's nothing can rival the single-mindedness of a Southern Catholic Lady. Whether she was born in the South or not, makes no never-mind.

I'd have killed Larry, myself, to keep him from inheriting, if I'd had the nerve to do it. In a way, I'm a better suspect than y'all are. I had motive, means, and opportunity, since I've always had a key to this house. Something Larry wasn't very happy about.

In my opinion, this house isn't nearly as nice as the one my parents had in Charleston. That house had been in my father's family for generations. I was really glad when Mother and Larry moved, and he didn't live in my Dad's house anymore. I'm really happy that Larry isn't living at all, anymore. I need to call my sisters soon. They'll be glad to hear that Larry's dead, too."

"Does your mother know?" I asked softly.

"No. There's no need to tell her. She's in and out of a coma most of the time. The doctors don't give her much longer to live. Her cancer started in her breast and just spread like wildfire."

"I'm so sorry," I told him softly and went on, "I thought there had to be a strong reason that Larry wanted to annul our Catholic marriage, out of the blue, after we'd already been divorced for thirty-some years. Now I understand why. Your mother was pushing him to do it and threatening to take away his future comfort if he didn't. Apparently, she knew just which buttons to push to get him to do what she wanted. Money was involved. Money is all that ever meant anything to Larry."

We were both silent for a while.

"Getting back to Russ Guthrie and the Plushmills, I wonder what's in this house that they want so bad that they drugged y'all to keep y'all away?" Tom mused, at last.

"And my friend, too. She's still sleeping off the drugs over at the Plushmill's house," I reminded him.

"Something in this house. Something in this house," Tom muttered to himself turning his head from side to side as if he thought he'd find whatever it was right there with us, in the kitchen.

"The Plushmills seemed to think whatever they were looking for might be upstairs," I told him, attempting to be helpful. "They came over here around two this morning, in the storm, to search for it. I don't know where they are now. No one tried to stop me when I sneaked out of the house so I assumed they might be sleeping. But I'm beginning to get nervous about leaving my friend Sybil over there all alone. I don't think she's safe."

"I guess we shouldn't stay here, either." Tom told me. "It is a crime scene, after all, and we're probably breaking some law or other. I have an apartment in Charleston. I haven't been out here much since Mother and Larry moved in. I haven't wanted to be here."

"But it's completely your family's house, now that Larry's dead. Isn't it?" I asked him.

"Yeah. Y'all are right. It is. In fact it always was. Mother's lawyers wouldn't let her put Larry's name on the deed when they bought this house. Not that she wanted to by that time. Larry wanted Mother's power of attorney but she never gave it to him, and if she had it would have died with him," Tom rose from the table and wandered over to the kitchen windows where he gazed out. "It looks like the wind is slowing down." He told me over his shoulder. "But the rain is still fierce."

"Tom," I rose and joined him at the windows. "I came over here, originally, to try to find out what the Plushmills and Russ Guthrie are looking for. I thought that if I could find out what it is and why it is so darned important I might be able to prove to the police that I had nothing to do with killing Larry. Maybe I could even discover who really killed him.

Originally I wanted to prove my innocence to Lt. Guthrie but now he sounds to me like a cop who's gone bad. Even so, I don't think the police are going to let me go home until I can clear myself. And I want to go home in the worst way!"

"Well, let's go upstairs and see what we can find," Tom turned to me and suggested. "Like y'all said. It's my family's house, and I guess I can look for anything I want in it. Come on."

He led me out of the kitchen and back toward the dining room. Opening a door in the hall between the two rooms he announced, "We'll take the back stairs."

Back stairs. Another feature of the O'Brian house, like the mudroom, that I hadn't known existed. Barely able to see in the gloom of the stairwell I followed him up the modest steps to the second floor.

"The master suite is on the far side of the house, facing west. There are three other bedrooms, a sitting room, and two bathrooms all along this hall," Tom explained as we found ourselves on the second story of the house. "Let's start searching in the master suite."

I followed him down the hall with great reluctance. I really didn't want to view the intimacy of the room in which my dead ex-husband had slept with his fourth wife.

At the end of the hall Tom threw open large, white double doors and stepped inside. A few seconds later, as I reached the doors, I heard him exclaim, "Well, I'll be damned. I'll be double dogged damned!"

Peering around the corner of the doors into the large bedroom I could see what had provoked his response. Larry and Martie's lavish boudoir was in a state of upheaval. Drawers had been pulled out of armoires and dressers, their contents spilled over the Aubusson rug on the floor. The entire contents of the walk-in closet had been pulled from its depths and thrown around the room. The king-sized mattress from the cherry canopied bed had been dragged off the box springs and slashed in several places. Even the Williamsburg seasonal flower prints had been pulled from the walls and lay about the room, their glass smashed and their backings slashed.

"What on earth happened?" I gasped as I joined Tom in the room.

"I think y'all could say Sherman's troops have ravaged the flower of the South, again. Only this time I think the troops are named Guthrie and Plushmill!" Tom was running both hands through his hair as he spoke.

Chapter Twenty-four

If Plushy, Miss Millie and Lt. Guthrie had wreaked the havoc in the bedroom that lay before us I wondered what else they'd done in their search for the mysterious "stuff" they thought was hidden somewhere in Larry's house.

"Do, do you think we should look in the other rooms up here?" I asked Tom hesitantly. He appeared distraught at the sight of his mother and Larry's things strewn wantonly around their bedroom.

"Yeah. Sure," he answered me absently, still staring at the mess.

I backed out of the master bedroom and made my way down the hall, opening doors as I passed them. There were two feminine bedrooms done in pastel colors and one that was definitely masculine in its decoration, all hunter green and brown finished off with a border of game birds. All three of them appeared neat and undisturbed, as did the small sitting room that was furnished in what appeared to be more comfortable furniture than that in the sitting room downstairs.

The two tiled bathrooms were another story. One was attached, en suite, to the masculine bedroom and the other opened right off the hall. They were as torn apart as the master bedroom had been, with the contents of linen closets and sink vanities tossed over the floors.

Turning, I made my way back to Tom in his mother and stepfather's room to report my findings. I found him in the master bath attached to the suite, surveying the damage there. It greatly resembled the other two bathrooms I'd just seen.

"What on earth could they be looking for?" he asked me as I stood beside him. "What is missing that would make those people desperate enough to ransack the place like this? They can't think that they'll get away with doing this; that no one will notice the upstairs of the house has been trashed."

"Maybe the Plushmills and Lt. Guthrie didn't do this," I offered. "Maybe whoever killed Larry did it, either before or after they shot him."

"Oh, please!" Tom turned to me. "Hasn't it become pretty obvious to y'all that the three of them are mixed up in Larry's murder, as well as in tearing up these rooms?"

"And the other two bathrooms," I added, then enlarged, "But the three bedrooms and sitting room seem to be okay."

The thought that the Plushmills and Guthrie were involved in Larry's murder sank slowly into my brain. How could they be? Lt. Guthrie was a police officer, even if he was a crooked one. The Plushmills were wealthy, respectable residents of Palmetto Crown Plantation, even if, at the moment, they appeared to be involved in something questionable. Weren't they?

I finally brought myself to the point where I was able to ask Tom, "Do you really think they could be murderers?"

"Yes, I do," he answered me emphatically, and in my heart I knew I was beginning to agree with him. Actually it was a relief to think of Lt. Guthrie being involved in the murder. That way I wouldn't ever have to prove to him that I hadn't done it. I might have to prove it to some other police officer, but not to him!

Still I questioned, "Weren't the four of them good friends? That's what you told me."

"They were friends, all right," Tom turned to look me squarely in the eyes. "But I don't think any of them were what y'all could call "good" friends. I think they were more like four people caught up in something that forced them to be friends rather than people who chose to be friends. If that makes any sense to y'all."

It did. I remembered how easily Larry had been drawn into many shady, money-making schemes during our marriage, and how I'd agonized over his seeming lack of conscience. I remembered how much embarrassment his family had suffered when, years after he and I had been divorced, it had become known that he was dealing drugs to college kids.

He'd disappeared for a period of time and his mother had thought he was in the Cayman Islands. She'd been so concerned for his safety that she'd tried to enlist the State Department to search for him.

Larry's brother, her other son, who was an attorney had ended that by cautioning her that it was dangerous to bring in the government if Larry was in the Caymans buying drugs. Eventually, Larry had turned up and no one had ever been sure where he'd been, or so my ex-sister-in-law had told me. I'd been happily married to Bud and living quietly and sanely in Martin's Field at the time.

Wherever Larry went trouble followed, or so it seemed. It was growing easier and easier for me to believe that he, the Plushmills, and Guthrie were mixed up in something illegal. That their friendship had been one of convenience not of real camaraderie.

I put the question that had been brewing in the back of my mind to Tom, "Do you think they could be involved in a drug ring? The four of them? Do you think the 'stuff' that Col., Plushmill was talking about is drugs?"

"There's been some talk, of late, about drugs being dealt in this area. When I first heard about it I thought it was just a rumor. Who'd need to sell or buy drugs around here? Everybody in Hollywood's gated communities is well off and most of the folks are retirement age," Tom acknowledged. "But if it's true I could believe that Larry was involved. I wouldn't've put anything past Larry. He was the most cold, selfish bastard I've ever met. I could see him bringing drugs ashore right at this house and selling them. He wouldn't care if it put my mother or anybody else in danger."

"I don't think there's any age limit involved in being a drug dealer. Larry's dealt drugs before," I admitted. "It was after I was divorced from him. I'm afraid that he had no scruples. He'd do anything to get his hands on money."

"My mother had him on a pretty tight leash as far as money was concerned," Tom enlightened me. "When they were first married and he was so sickeningly attentive to her that it made me want to puke she gave him full run of her bank accounts. Then there were discrepancies at the bank and she took back control of their finances. He must have spent a bundle because after that she put him on an allowance. A generous one, but still an allowance."

"Did Larry have a job?" I inquired out of curiosity.

"He jumped from one sales job to another," Tom told me, confirming my suspicions. "He never lasted long with any of them. If they didn't make him a vice president after six months he just quit, cold. And, as he got older, it became harder and harder for him to find a job. So he just hung out around the house, watched TV, and played golf."

"Too bad that old alligator on the golf course didn't make a meal of him," I answered waspishly. "Then he'd have been good for something."

"Ol' Mose!" Tom laughed. "How'd y'all know about Ol' Mose? Have y'all seen him?"

"If that's his name. Yes, my friend and I have met him. Down by the creek on the golf course when we were sneaking into The

Plantation, trying to find this house."

"That old gator wouldn't harm a soul. I doubt he's got but two, three teeth," Tom laughed for the first time since he and I had met. "But I guess it would have made things a lot simpler, in the long run, for Mother if Larry'd been a meal for Ol' Mose. I never could figure out whether she really loved Larry or wasn't about to admit she'd made a mistake in marrying him."

"In my opinion, your mother 'paid too much for her whistle' as Ben Franklin put it. It seems your mother's threat to cut Larry out of her will unless he got an annulment from me was a serious one," I commented and then asked. "She controlled the purse strings completely?"

"Completely." He answered.

I sank down on a chair covered with clothes ripped from an armoire or closet. I was suddenly very tired. I could feel the adrenaline in my body that had kept me going since Tom had rescued me from the boathouse draining away. My mind ricocheted back to Sybil again.

"I really should go back to the Plushmill's house and get my friend. I never should have left her there. Especially if the Plushmills are really involved in Larry's murder."

"How about I go with y'all?" Tom offered. "We could bring her over here. If we run into the Plushmills or Russ Guthrie I'll just tell them that the two of y'all are now my guests in my mother's house. I doubt if they'd give you a hard time if I'm with you. Too many witnesses."

"Oh, yes!" I answered. "It's so kind of you. Could we go right away?"

"Yes Ma'am," he answered reaching out for my hand to draw me to my feet.

It didn't take us long to make our way downstairs, don oilskins in the mudroom, and leave the house by the front door. The wind was still whipping in from the water but not at such great speed that we had to fight against it to make our way across the street, as Sybil and I had the night before. Rain lashed us but Tom held tightly to my hand. All the streetlights were still dark and there was no evidence of electric light anywhere on the block.

My van was still in the driveway, all by itself, which made me wonder how Tom had arrived at his mother's house earlier this morning. There wasn't another car in sight on the whole block. I asked him about this, over the roar of the wind, as we carefully made our way through the storm.

"I took a taxi from the hospital," he shouted to me as we neared the Plushmill house. "And, believe me, it wasn't easy finding one in the middle of the night in a hurricane in Charleston. I have the keys to Mother's Mercedes, which I assume is still in the garage. I wanted to get it off the property, now that Larry's dead, and figured I'd drive it back to my apartment once I'd checked out the house. Then I found y'all."

I squeezed his hand in further gratitude as we reached the other side of the street.

"When I left this house it was by the back door, and I didn't have any problem," I raised my voice to be heard above the whining wind, "So let's try to get into the house that way."

Tom nodded assent.

When we reached the back door to the Plushmill house it appeared that we would, indeed, have no problem entering the house. The door stood wide open.

Tom and I looked at each other, quizzically, and he entered the kitchen ahead of me. The silence of the house was welcome after the moments we'd spent in the maelstrom outside. Everything in the kitchen was dark and appeared undisturbed, just as I'd left it and I pulled the back door shut since the wild wind outside was blowing in behind us. It had disturbed the curtains at the windows and even blown place mats around on the kitchen table.

Silently, I took the lead and we moved quietly through the downstairs rooms of the Plushmill house to the staircase, leaving wet footprints behind us. Tom and I climbed the stairs in

192

single file and I motioned for him to follow me along the hall to the guest bedroom from which I'd sneaked only a few hours earlier.

The door to the bedroom was open, too, and I felt a rush of panic. What if Sybil had awakened found me gone, and set out to look for me in the storm? I hurried inside, Tom right behind me.

The bed I'd slept in had been hastily disturbed. The pillows I'd placed under the comforter to make it appear that I still slept there lay on the floor. I rushed to the second bed where Sybil had lain, sleeping peacefully, only a short time ago.

It was empty. My friend was gone!

Chapter Twenty-five

A quick check of the bathroom produced no trace of Sybil. By now I was close to panic.

"Where could she be?" I almost sobbed to Tom as I gestured toward the second twin bed. "I left her sleeping right here."

"How long ago?" he asked logically.

Checking the hands of the boudoir clock I answered, "A little over two hours ago, I guess."

My eyes strayed over the room, which was filled with much more light than it had been when I'd left. To my horror I discovered that not only was Sybil missing but so were our luggage and handbags. Now I'd never get a call from Bud on my cell phone. It was in my striped canvas bag and both were missing!

"Everything's gone!" I wailed, not bothering to keep my voice down.

"Let's check all the rooms in the house." Tom spoke grimly, "And we'll stick together, since we don't know what we're likely to find."

I followed Tom out of the guestroom and into the upstairs hall. Methodically he led me along it, opening doors as we came to them. The floor plan was identical to his mother's house across the street: master suite and bath, four additional rooms and two baths.

The master suite, when Tom bravely threw open the white double doors, was lavishly decorated with maroon brocade upholstered furniture and window hangings. There was gold fringe and gold braided rope everywhere, including the canopy on the king-sized mahogany bed. It reminded me of a room right out of Scarlett O'Hara and Rhett Butler's ostentatious mansion in the movie *Gone With The Wind*. The accompanying bathroom carried through the décor. There were gold plated fixtures and marble surfaces everywhere.

The only thing that wasn't in either room was any sign of the Plushmills. There were no pictures of them resting on either of the bedside tables or on the very ruffled vanity in the bedroom. None of their clothes were in sight. Not even a pair of shoes. There were no toilet articles like toothbrushes or a razor in evidence in the bathroom.

Now that I thought about it, there hadn't been any pictures of Plushy and Miss Millie in any of the downstairs rooms, either. At least none that I'd seen. Unlike the house across the street, there were no framed family pictures anywhere.

Leaving the master suite, Tom and I started out together exploring the rest of the upstairs. The other three rooms, which I assumed could be used as bedrooms or, as in Tom's mother's house a sitting room, were, to both our amazements, totally unfurnished. There was not a stick of furniture nor was there so much as a curtain at any of the windows. The bathrooms were sterile and deserted. It appeared that Plushy and Miss Millie used only the master suite and the guestroom, in which Sybil and I had stayed. This was quite a surprise.

"What do y'all make of it?" Tom asked, as we found

ourselves back at the head of the spiral staircase again. "They've certainly lived here long enough to furnish these rooms."

"I have no idea. The Plushmills are an enigma to me. But, more importantly, where is everybody? Where's Sybil?!"

"Let's check the garage, and then the basement. If there is one. Most of the houses on this side of Windsor Way are built on slabs because they're so close to the water. The water table's too high over here to dig basements. The houses on our side are exceptions. The lots over there are higher than those over here," Tom started down the stairs.

"Do they have attics?" I called after him. "I think your mother's house has a third floor. I saw a door and a balcony above the second story at the back of her house. Maybe this house has a third floor, too."

"That's just a little room with a porch on the third floor, over to Mother's house. She used to joke and call it a 'widow's walk'," Tom called over his shoulder. "It's not really an attic and it was built special, to Mother and Larry's specifications. I didn't notice anything like that on this house when we came in here the back way."

"Traditional 'widow's walks' were built on top of the roofs of New England houses," the teacher in me explained to Tom as I followed him down the stairs. "In New England, so many of the men in the seventeen and eighteen hundreds made a living from whaling and sailing on merchant ships that they were at sea most of the time. The women they left behind used to climb up to the little platforms enclosed with railings on the top of the houses to wave goodbye to the ships as they put out to sea, or to look for their return."

"Yes, ma'am," Tom answered politely, heading toward the back of the house. "I guess if the men never came back and their wives were widows that gave those platforms their name. But Mother didn't use her porch to look for ships. She used to sometimes sit up there of an evening and watch the sunsets."

"Yes. I thought she, or someone, might have," I told him,

196

smiling a little, as we reached the door to the garage, "But I bet, if Larry was involved in drug dealing again, he used it to look for planes or boats coming into the inlet."

"Y'all could be right," Tom stopped short and turned to me. "Larry did spend an awful lot of time sitting up there, all year round. Even when the weather was bad."

Turning the knob of the door to the garage Tom swung it open. Everything inside was quiet. Standing behind him and peering into the garage, I could make out the outline of the Lincoln Town Car. The SUV I'd seen parked in there the evening before was missing. A fact I quickly pointed out to Tom.

"So, it looks like the Plushmills are long gone. They probably drove right out of here while y'all were over to my house," Tom closed the door and the two of us wandered down the hall to the library.

"And they probably took Sybby with them," tears began to course down my face as I spoke. "Heaven only knows what they'll do to her. And it's all my fault. I never should have made her come to The Plantation, and once we were in this house I never should have left her alone."

I sank down on the green leather loveseat, sobbing. Physical and emotional exhaustion had caught up with me.

"We're getting out of here," Tom informed me, taking hold of my arm and pulling me to my feet. "Come on. We'll be safer at my house."

I followed him with a heavy heart. We closed the kitchen door behind us and traipsed across the yard to the street. Turning, I looked upward toward the roofline of the Plushmill house.

Tom was right. There was no third story or balcony in evidence. I don't know if it was my imagination or not but the amount of rain and wind seemed to be lessening in intensity. The sky was brighter and I could see things much more clearly.

"I want to check on my van," I told him as we approached the sidewalk in front of 65 Windsor Way. I'd stopped crying and was beginning to calm down and to feel less sorry for myself. Although my nose was still running and my head ached fiercely. The waning storm was raising my spirits to a certain degree. "My keys were in my purse which is gone, but Bud always tapes a key to the underside of the license plate in case one of us locks ourselves out of the car. If you can find a screwdriver we can get to the key and I can get inside."

I stopped beside the van, peering into it's interior for the first time since I'd left it behind the mill the day before. To my amazement it wasn't empty. Piled on the front seat was my luggage and Sybil's.

Even more amazing, on the backseat, wrapped in a blanket, there lay a body! A woman's body. A familiar woman's body.

"Sybby!" I screamed at the top of my lungs, tugging in vain upon the van's locked front door. Giving that up I began to smack the flats of both my hands on the window by her head. I'd found my friend, but was she alive?

Chapter Twenty-six

Tom had joined me beside the van and while I yelled at the top of my lungs we both beat upon the window. Anyone watching us would have thought we were two lunatics trying to break into a vehicle in the middle of a storm.

"She has to wake up," I moaned. "She just has to!"

Tom had moved to the other side of the van. He grasped the handle of the front door on that side. "Miz Davis," he called to me, "This door is open!"

I was beside him in a flash. He'd already opened the door and hit the button to unlock the rest of the van. Sliding open the back door I clambered into the back seat of the van, practically falling on top of my friend.

I grabbed Sybil by her shoulders and shook her. Her body was soft and warm, which encouraged me and I shouted again, this time close to her ear.

"Sybby, wake up!"

"Mnnn," she responded, her head flopping back and forth.

"She's alive!" I crowed and turned my head to look over my

shoulder at Tom. "Help me get her out of here. Oh, thank God, thank God!"

Between the two of us, Tom and I managed to drag Sybil out of the van into the pouring rain. She was wrapped in one of the Laura Ashley comforters from the Plushmill's guestroom, not a blanket as I'd first thought. It fell onto the muddy ground as we carried her upright, dangling over our shoulders, toward the house.

Somehow Tom managed to open the front door and we deposited Sybil onto the oriental rug inside the foyer. I knelt beside her, chafing her hands, still calling out to her to wake up, while Tom went back to close the door to the van. She had never looked so good to me, drenched pajamas, hair plastered to her face, and all.

"I brought in both purses," Tom told me as he came back inside and closed the front door. "I didn't know which one was yours. And I locked your van since now you have the keys." He placed my striped bag and Sybil's Vera Bradley beside me on the floor.

"Thank you. Oh thank you," I murmured distractedly, raising Sybil's head and cradling it in my lap, as she had held my head the evening before.

"There are smelling salts in the powder room," Tom moved quickly down the hall and returned with a small bottle in his hand. Smelling salts. I hadn't heard anyone mention those in years. I hadn't used them since I'd been pregnant with Maggie in the 1960s and prone to fainting. It seemed fitting that there'd be some in the home of a southern lady, even one transplanted from Philadelphia. Traditionally the ladies of the Old South had always kept them close at hand. Those women had been cinched into corsets so tightly they'd passed out all the time.

Unscrewing the top of the bottle, Tom bent down and waved it under Sybil's nose. The bottle was packed with purple crystals that smelled really strong. The scent of ammonia and lavender wafted upward and made my eyes water.

"Mnnnh!" Sybil began to move her head back and forth, trying to escape the stinging scent beneath her nose. Her eyes flew open, closed again for a few seconds, and then opened slowly.

"Where? Where?" she tried to speak.

Tom recapped the smelling salts and moved backward.

"Oh, Sybby," I clutched her to me, gasping with relief. "Oh, Sybby, I thought you were dead!"

"Sukie? For God's sake stop choking me!" Sybil brought both of her hands up slowly to cover her face. "Whew," she attempted to sit up. Tom and I came to her aid.

Once she was in a sitting position a look of horror crossed her face.

"Oh, no. I'm going to be sick!"

I remembered how I'd retched for what had seemed close to half and hour when I'd awakened from my drugged state earlier that morning. Apparently Sybil was at that point right now. Giving Tom a furtive look I tried to lift my friend up off the floor.

"Quick," I yelled to him. "Help me get her to the powder room!"

Again supporting her with our shoulders, we dragged poor Sybil, none too gently, down the hall.

Once we'd deposited her beside the toilet, Tom withdrew discreetly from the room, closing the door behind him. I stayed with Sybil, holding her head while she was sick. When she was finished I ran one of the beautifully matched guest towels that hung from a brass rack under cold water. After wiping her face with it I held it tightly to Sybil's forehead.

She leaned back against me and asked thickly, "What the hell happened to me?"

"It's a long story. I'll tell you the whole thing in a few minutes. But first, do you remember being carried out of the Plushmill's house and being put into our van? Do you know who carried you?"

"What are you talking about?!" Sybil turned and looked at

me as if I was crazy, as the two of us sat there on the powder room floor.

"That's where you were just now. In the van. The Plushmills drugged us with those bedtime toddies and somehow you ended up in the van."

"You're kidding!"

"I only wish I were. We're in big trouble. A lot's happened since you fell asleep last night. Can you stand up? I can get Tom to help us if you can't."

"Who in blazes is Tom?" Sybil struggled to her feet with my support. She leaned against the wall looking very pale and unsteady.

"Believe it or not, Tom is Martie's son. He's a wonderful young man, and he saved my life when I almost drowned in the boathouse earlier," I held onto her and opened the powder room door at the same time.

Once we were out in the hall I led her to a chair in the sitting room. She sank into it with a dazed look. I pulled up a stool close to her, sat down on it, and began to bring her up to date on all that had happened since I'd awakened in the Plushmill guestroom the evening before.

She didn't speak until I'd finished my lengthy narration. Then she shook her head, gingerly, and looking into my eyes said, "This is crazy. It's all crazy."

Chapter Twenty-seven

Sybil, Tom and I sat at the kitchen table drinking cokes that were rapidly growing tepid. There was still no power so we couldn't use the stove to boil water for tea or plug in the automatic coffee maker.

I'd introduced Martie's son to my friend, who was now wrapped in a terrycloth robe that Tom had retrieved from his mother's room upstairs. As soon as she'd recovered enough to understand who he was and where we were, Sybil had taken to Tom as swiftly as I had.

He and I had gone over and over the happenings of the night before with Sybil. I'd emphatically ticked the occurrences of the evening off on my fingers right under her nose.

First, she and I'd been drugged by the Plushmills. Following that, I'd overheard their conversation with Lt. Guthrie when I'd awakened and gone downstairs. None of them were who or what they appeared to be.

Then, I'd left their house and attempted to re-enter the O'Brian house through the boathouse, almost drowning in the process. Tom had rescued me.

I'd gone on to explain how he and I had searched through the upstairs of this house looking for whatever it was that Plushy, Miss Millie, and Guthrie were seeking, perhaps drugs, and, in the process, found the upstairs ransacked.

Sybil seemed to understand what I was telling her, however, her eyes were not yet completely clear and she kept shaking her head as if to get her thoughts straight. I knew it was a lot of information for her to comprehend, especially when she wasn't feeling particularly well.

I thought a lot of it must have sounded unbelievable to her. I knew it sounded that way to me when I itemized what had happened to us, so far.

"I honest to God don't know how I got from the Plushmill's house into the van," Sybil admitted emphatically to us when I finished my resume. "I don't remember a thing. I went to sleep in the guestroom and woke up, soaking wet, on the rug, here in the hall. Who could have moved me? Who would have moved me?"

None of us could answer her question. I reached over and reassuringly patted her hand.

Tom had tried to call his sisters on his cell phone to tell them about Larry's death but could get no reception at all. We assumed that due to the power outage the cell phone towers weren't receiving power. The fact that all the other telephones in the house were dead told us that the telephone lines were down, as well.

"With no power, we're cut off from everything," he moaned after he'd returned from trying the telephones. "There isn't even any way we can turn on a TV or radio to find out what's going on and how much longer this damned storm's going to last."

"We could try the radio in the van," Sybil spoke up for the first time in a long while. Her voice sounded small and tentative. "Sukie never uses the radio but if there's any news to be had I bet that's where you're going to find it."

Of course! Why hadn't I thought of that? I can't begin to tell you how chagrined I felt that my prejudice about listening to the car radio had kept me from coming up with the idea, myself.

"Sybby, you're a genius!" I leaned over and kissed her forehead. "We'll be right back."

Tom was already heading for the front door, oilskins in hand and, grabbing mine, I was right behind him. I retrieved my car keys from my purse and we again braved the storm. Once we were in the van I turned the key in the ignition. Heaven be praised, it turned over with no hesitation, and I switched on the van's radio.

There was much crackling and sputtering as Tom, who knew the local stations, attempted to raise something intelligible. At last a voice recognizable as that of a newscaster came across the wires.

"…with winds diminishing to seventy miles an hour by early afternoon. Rain continuing for another twenty-four hours as Hurricane Marcus moves up the coast. There is no estimation as to how long it will take to restore power to Charleston's outlying districts.

Again, if you're injured or in need of assistance try to contact your local police. There is still room in most shelters although driving is hazardous on most roads.

At this point officials have no idea how long it will take to restore telephone service. All lines and cell phone towers in the immediate area have been damaged or are not functioning…" the voice faded away.

"Pah! We know about as much now as we did before we turned the radio on!" Tom was clearly disappointed at the information we'd been able to hear. He spent another minute or so twirling the dial on the radio and pushing the scan button. Finding no other stations, he turned it off.

"Well, we know that the winds are diminishing and that the rain is going to stop in a day or so," I tried to sound optimistic.

We left the van and returned to the house where we once more hung our wet oilskins in the mud room. I carried my suitcase with me and Tom brought Sybil's.

Sybil was looking brighter as we shared the sparse information we'd gleaned from the van's radio with her and put her Vera Bradley case at her feet.

"Some news is better than no news," she chirped slyly looking at me out of the corner of her eye. "Don't you feel better knowing that the hurricane is moving away?"

"I'd feel a whole lot better if we had found what Larry's friends are looking for," Tom, who'd been fairly quiet since we'd re-entered the house shared his thoughts with us.

"You and Sukie looked absolutely everywhere? And you think its drugs you're looking for?" Sybil asked.

"We're fairly sure it's drugs," I answered and then turned to Tom. "I don't know. Have we looked absolutely everywhere in the house there is to look?"

"We really haven't searched down here, or in the basement, or the garage," Tom mused. "I didn't see anything suspicious in the basement when we came up from the boathouse, Sukie. Did y'all?"

I shook my head. He and I hadn't spent much time in the basement but I remembered thinking how clean and empty it appeared when we came through it. So unlike the basement in my house at home, which had become a storage place for the whole family's castoffs over the years.

Tom continued, "I don't think Mother and Larry had much to store once they moved in here. Certainly nothing they'd put in the basement. Larry didn't bring anything with him when Mother took him in. He didn't have anything.

Their two cars are in the garage but no tools or lawnmowers, or anything like that. They didn't have to worry about cutting the grass or any house maintenance. The community association hired people to do that. Larry would have been too lazy to do anything that required tools, anyway."

"The boy certainly knew his stepfather well," Sybil commented wryly.

"I guess the downstairs is the only place left to look," I sighed. "Shall we each take a room or two?"

"Sounds like a plan," Sybil rose from the table. "That's if it's all right with you, Tom."

"Fine. Fine," Tom answered. "I think the police did a job on the library. I'll take the sitting room. Y'all can search the dining room and in here."

And so we continued the quest Guthrie and the Plushmills had begun upstairs. I sent Sybil into the dining room to look, which I thought would be a less strenuous task, and I began opening cupboards and drawers in the kitchen. I could hear Tom working in the sitting room and Sybil right next door as I emptied out the contents of boxes of food that were already opened into bowls I'd taken from shelves in the cabinets.

There weren't many food items in the kitchen. Larry had been living alone in the house for quite a while and had not replaced supplies as they had run out. I searched through drawers filled with placemats and towels, twirled mostly empty lazy susans in the pantry closet, and even went through the refrigerator. It seemed to hold mostly soda and gourmet cheeses, all still sealed.

"Well, that was a useless exercise," Tom commented when we'd all finished our searches and regrouped at the kitchen table. "There's nothing in the sitting room that shouldn't be there and only the smelling salts and band aids in the powder room. Y'all find anything interesting in here?"

"I don't know what Larry lived on after your mother went into the hospital," I informed him. There isn't a speck of meat in the freezer. No vegetables in the refrigerator bin, no eggs, butter. Nothing."

"I reckon he sent out for pizza or ate out most of the time."

"The dining room's lovely. All that china and crystal in the credenza, or hutch, or whatever it's called. But nothing that even smacks of drugs," Sybil added. "I hate to say it," she turned to me, "But I'm getting hungry."

"About the only things I found that don't need to be cooked are a couple boxes of crackers in the pantry and some cheeses in the refrigerator. We could make a meal out of those."

"Let's," Tom nodded assent. "It must be about lunch time, by now."

I'd lost all sense of time but my stomach agreed with him.

As we sat eating our cheese and cracker meal something kept pulling at my subconscious. I had the feeling that I'd forgotten something very important. I hate that feeling! How many times had I experienced it when I'd been teaching? At least once a week, when I'd been writing lesson plans or correcting papers. We've overlooked something my mind kept telling me. There's somewhere else to look for the drugs. What are we missing?

"You're awfully quiet, for you," Sybil commented as she chewed.

"I know," I answered looking up from my plate, slowly realizing that I'd been staring at it. Trying to come up with an answer.

"Uh oh! Sukie's been thinking. We're in trouble," she joked.

"Let's look up on the third floor!" I jumped up quickly as what my mind had been searching for suddenly became a full-blown idea. "Come on, Tom. It's the only place we haven't considered. How do we get up there?"

Chapter Twenty-eight

"I've never been up there before," Tom explained as he led Sybil and me down the upstairs hall toward the door to the third floor of the house.

On the way we'd stopped and shown Sybil the ransacked master suite and bathrooms. She'd reacted to the mess the same way Tom and I had, agreeing that it was a terrible shame for someone to create such havoc. At least, this time, we understood possibly why it had been done. What the searchers had been looking for.

"The only people who ever came up to that little porch were Larry and my mother, as far, as I know. And I don't remember them ever being up there together. She watched sunsets by herself when she needed to escape problems," Tom pulled open a very ordinary looking door at the end of the hall.

"And we all know why he probably went up there," I added. "To watch for drug deliveries from the inlet."

The door looked so much like the others that it might have belonged to a closet or another bedroom. I'd overlooked it in my search, earlier, because I'd headed back to Tom in the master suite as soon as I'd encountered the two torn-apart bathrooms.

Behind the door everything was very dark. There was probably a light switch on the wall close by but without power there was no way to illuminate the flight of stairs that lay behind the door and which led directly upward.

Tom had fished out a flashlight from one of the kitchen drawers before we'd begun our trip upstairs. He pulled it from his pocket now and flicked it on. A narrow beam of light sprang forth and he placed his foot on the first step.

"I'll go first. Y'all follow me," he instructed us.

"That's fine with me," Sybil murmured to me in a soft voice as Tom began to climb the stairs. Grasping my arm, once he'd disappeared from view, she spoke urgently, "I don't see why you and I can't just get in the van and drive home. Personally, I don't care where any drugs, if there are any, are hidden in this house. I just want to get out of here safely."

"I know how you feel," I answered, turning to face her, "I'd like to get out of here, too. But before we do I want to clear both of us of Larry's murder so the police don't go on suspecting us. Just because Lt. Guthrie's probably mixed up in it doesn't mean the other police officers don't already think I'm guilty of killing Larry. After all, I found him and you were with me. If we find a stash of drugs it will prove that Larry may have had other enemies."

"Yeah. You're right," Sybil conceded reluctantly, as I began to mount the stairs. She followed close behind me. "I just don't know why we have to be the ones to search for it."

"Because we're the ones who are here," I answered her.

At the top of the stairs was a small room, made even smaller by the gloom that pervaded it. We couldn't see past the circle of light thrown by Tom's flashlight. The room's corners remained dark. There were no windows anywhere to let in the feeble light from outside.

As before, the screen door I'd seen on the other side of the solid one leading to the balcony was still thrashing in the wind. We could hear its demonic banging as we huddled in the dark. I began to feel claustrophobic as well as nervous. I could feel the hair beginning to rise along my arms and at the back of my neck.

"This place is really creepy," Sybil spoke for both of us as she moved as close to me as she could.

"I'll open the door and let in some light," Tom left our little group and moved forward, following his flashlight beam toward the outside door.

Suddenly he let out a grunt and toppled over, his flashlight going out as he hit the floor and it rolled from his hand. We were plunged into complete darkness. The suddenness of this event produced a shock in me as physical as if someone had thrown a bucket of cold water over my head.

Sybil let out a piercing shriek and grabbed me by the shoulders. Hardly aware that I had shaken her off I took a step forward.

"Tom! Tom! Are you all right?" I cried out frantically. "Tom, answer me!"

"I'm fine. I just tripped over something," Tom's muffled answer came from the darkness. "See if you can find the flashlight."

I immediately knelt where I was and began to sweep the floor around me with my hands. I was aware that Tom was beside me on the floor doing the same thing. Behind us I could hear Sybil moaning softly in fear.

"Sit down where you are, Sybby. Take a deep breath," I commanded her. "As soon as we find the flashlight we'll get out of here. I promise."

I could hear her following my instructions. Her moaning stopped and was replaced by soft hiccups.

"Double dog damn it!" Tom was swearing under his breath. "There's something here that just won't move. It's what I fell over. Where the devil is that flashlight?"

I was suddenly aware that my hands felt wet and sticky and

wondered if the roof of the little room were leaking. I couldn't feel any water dripping on us. I looked upward but could see nothing in the complete darkness.

I continued to sweep the floor with my hands but was now aware that every surface of the floor around me that I touched felt wet.

"Ah," Tom let out an appreciative sound. "I've found it."

A beam of light sprang into being in the darkness as Tom turned on the lost flashlight.

That was when I screamed involuntarily! As we both rose to our feet we saw what it was that Tom had fallen over. Lying on the floorboards of the small third floor room, his vacant eyes staring up at us, was Colonel Barton Plushmill, retired, Citadel class of 1952.

Chapter Twenty-nine

I remember backing slowly away from Plushy's body in the gloom of the small room, holding my gory hands out before me like Lady MacBeth in her sleepwalking scene. And my hands were gory. They dripped with the blood that had covered the floor around the body. My knees were also wet with blood from the pool in which I'd knelt trying to help Tom find the flashlight.

Sybil was behind me calling softly, "What's wrong, Sukie. What's happened?"

Tom still stood beside the body holding the flashlight beam on it.

Turning, I tried to remain calm even though I was quivering inside as I told her, "It's another body, Sybby,"

"Oh, my God! Another one? Who this time?" Her voice sounded more intensely interested than frightened by the news I'd just given her. With the flashlight behind me it was almost impossible to see her face.

"It's Plushy. Now, turn around and let's go back downstairs," I instructed her as I continued to move toward the back of the room. "And don't touch me. I'm covered with blood."

Sybil let out a small squeal as she heard this news, and I could hear her moving quickly back to the stairs. I followed her, my hands still held out in front of me.

I didn't want to leave bloody handprints on the walls on either side of the staircase, as I descended to the second floor, but it was difficult to make my way downward in the gloom. I was tempted to support myself by holding onto the walls but, somehow, I managed to avoid doing it. Maybe it was because I was afraid Lt. Guthrie or the police would come to the house and accuse me of killing yet another resident of Palmetto Crown Plantation if he found bloody handprints that were mine.

Sybil was waiting for me when I finally emerged from the staircase door. In spite of the frightening sight I must have made she threw her arms around my neck.

"We've got to get out of here. We've just got to, before someone else gets killed!"

I couldn't have agreed with her more.

"Shot through the heart." Tom's matter-of-fact comment as he joined us from behind made both of us jump. His hands and knees were bloody too. The three of us just stood there, two of us dripping blood on the carpeted floor.

"Come on. Let's clean up. We can't notify the police 'til the storm lets up some," Tom led the way to the nearest bathroom. Sybil and I followed. Inside the pristine, tiled room he and I washed the blood from our hands and arms and wiped them with soft, fluffy towels.

"I'm going to find a pair of Larry's jeans and dump these slacks," he informed us. "Y'all come along and use some jeans or sweatpants of Mother's."

I leapt at his suggestion.

Later, dressed in a pair of powder blue, monogrammed French terrycloth sweatpants belonging to Martha O'Brian, I joined Tom and Sybil in the upstairs sitting room. The sweatpants had been the only garment from Martha's closet or armoire drawers into which I could fit my body. She was one slim lady, even though I knew she was a year older than I was. I had deposited my bloody jeans in the bathtub of the master bathroom where Tom had discarded his slacks while I searched in the master bedroom for something to wear.

"Well, that's two pairs of jeans I've managed to ruin in less than forty-eight hours," I spoke acerbically as I plopped myself onto a couch beside Sybil. Tom sat facing us in a deeply upholstered chair. Neither of them spoke. No one seemed to want to discuss the body upstairs.

Finally Sybil found her voice, "All that blood. I don't know how either of you could stand to be covered in all that blood!"

"Blood, rootbeer. There really isn't very much difference," I shot back at her rather flippantly, maybe because it had been such a horror to have been soaked Col. Plushmill's blood. When she and Tom both stared at me in disbelief I continued, "When I was in second grade my family moved into a post war apartment in Arlington, Virginia. The rooms were all the size of a postage stamp. My parents bought a set of narrow, wooden bunk beds from the Army Navy store for me to sleep in. Nothing else would fit into my bedroom, and they figured they could use the top bunk for storage.

My father decided to make homemade rootbeer that summer. It was the worst stuff you ever tasted but he'd grown up watching his father make it, and so he whipped up a batch. Capped all the bottles, himself, and stored them on the top bunk in my room.

One hot night most of the bottle tops popped and the sticky rootbeer came right through the mattress of the top bunk down on me. I woke up in a puddle of the stuff.

I used to joke about it when I got older, saying it was my second baptism. The first was by water the second by rootbeer. Maybe the third would take and make a good Christian of me. Searching around in the dark, up there, in that pool of blood, felt to me exactly like waking up in the night, in a pool of rootbeer, when I was a kid."

This story had brought smiles to people's faces, even a few guffaws, as I'd told it over the years, but neither Tom nor Sybil responded to it. It fell flat and just lay there, between Tom and us two women.

When I finished speaking Sybil shuddered, "I may never drink another rootbeer!"

Finally Tom spoke, "When do y'all think he got shot? How long do y'all think he's been up there?"

Sybil and I just looked at him, trying to remember when each of us had last seen Col. Plushmill alive.

"The blood was pretty sticky. I don't think it just happened," I spoke up tentatively.

"Blood, again. Yuck!" Sybil shook her head. "I'm afraid I can't help you with a timeline. Whatever drug Miss Millie put in our drinks last night has wiped out most of what I remember. Except for finding Larry's body, of course."

"Sybby and I seem to be getting pretty good at finding dead bodies," I told Tom dryly. "I'm surprised you're not afraid to spend time with us. It looks like we have a deadly effect upon men."

Tom grinned at this then began to speak, "Miz Davis, you told me you left the Plushmill's house around four or five this morning, and there was no one over there when you left."

"Oh, please!" I interjected. "After all we've been through you have to call me Sukie. And not 'Miss Sukie', either."

"Yes Ma'am, Sukie." The young man agreed rather sheepishly.

"You're right. When I woke up the second time it was around five this morning. I didn't search the house but it was completely quiet and no one seemed to be around. I assumed they were all sleeping."

"You just up and left me," Sybil assumed an accusing little girl's voice.

"I thought you'd be fine until I got back," I reminded her. "I didn't have any idea that I'd be gone so long or that you'd disappear before I could come back for you."

"Ladies, work with me here, please, y'all. Now, Miz Davis, I mean Sukie, you and I were in the boathouse for what, half an hour?"

"I guess. About that. I'm not a very good judge of time," I admitted.

"Then we came up to the house. Y'all had a sandwich, and we came up here to the second floor to search for whatever the Plushmills and Russ were looking for."

"A sandwich!" Sybil screeched. "Now that you bring up food, I'm starving! I was across the street, drugged out of my mind, or being stuffed into the van, and you stopped for a sandwich?"

"Sybby, hush! We'll get some more cheese and crackers in a few minutes. I didn't plan on eating a sandwich. It was just there, downstairs in the refrigerator."

"We found the upstairs trashed, and then went back to the Plushmill's to get Miss Curtis. I mean just plain Sybil," Tom continued, ignoring our comments.

"You forgot to figure out what time you arrived at the house before you found me in the boathouse," I reminded him. "There was probably a period of time between when I fell asleep for the second time at the Plushmill's and when you arrived here. The Plushmills and Guthrie and who knows who else could have come back over here before you and I arrived."

"True," Tom agreed leaning forward, resting his elbow on one knee, and running his hand through his hair. "You fell asleep the second time around two-thirty, three o'clock?"

"Around then."

"I left Mother at the hospital and by the time I found a taxi and got dropped off here it must have been close to five. So anyone could have been in the house, if they had a key to one of the doors, or could get past the tape, or they brought a ladder and came up thorough the boathouse between let's say three and five this morning. And anyone including Russ or Millie Plushmill could have shot Bart."

"They mentioned having to make a delivery as usual," I reminded Tom. "That means someone or more than one someone else could have been involved."

"I have a feeling he was killed while you were sleeping and before I got here," Tom concluded. "Not long after you overheard them all talking."

"Hey, you guys," Sybil interrupted the scenario that Tom and I were laying out. "In case you're interested, I just looked outside and it has practically stopped raining. I think the hurricane's almost over."

Chapter Thirty

As far as I could see this bit of information was both good and bad news. Good news because who wants to be trapped by wind and rain in a house with a dead body? And bad news because improving weather could mean that the murderer might find it easier to return at any time to the scene of the crime.

I don't know what we should do next," I admitted to Tom and Sybil. "What if Lt. Guthrie didn't run off, like we thought the Plushmills did? What if when we get through to the police he's the one they send here? I don't think I can stand him yelling at me and accusing me of killing someone else. It was bad enough the first time."

"He can't accuse you," Sybil reassured me. "All three of us found Plushy's body at the same time."

"But I was here, in the house, before you were, Sybby. For all Lt. Guthrie knows I woke up earlier than I said I did the second time and came over here and killed the Colonel before Tom got here."

"Now that would be a neat trick, considering that I found

y'all half-drowned in the boathouse and hauled y'all out of the water. I'm y'all's alibi, if y'all need one," Tom reassured me.

Sybil, who'd been picking at the border of one of the couch's throw pillows, raised her head and asked slowly, "Here's something we haven't considered. How do we know that Lt. Guthrie isn't the murderer?"

"Oh, my God!" I leaped out of my seat on the couch. "She's right. How do we know?"

"We don't," Tom admitted.

As I began to pace the floor in front of the window he continued, "It could very easily have been a falling out among thieves. Russ or either one of the Plushmills could have killed Larry over stolen drugs or drugs hidden in this house, and Russ or Millie Plushmill could have killed Bart."

"But why?" I asked, fighting the urge to wring my hands as I paced.

"Another falling out?" Sybil suggested. "In my experience it's hard to get three people to agree about anything, anytime."

"There are three of us, and we agree," I reminded her.

"Yeah. We agree that we're all in a lot of trouble," she observed acerbically.

"Since it isn't raining as hard as it was do y'all want to accompany me to the police station to report Bart's death, or would y'all rather wait here? I have no idea what shape we'll find the roads in but it will probably be a long time before the phones work again and we can call them," Tom asked rising from his chair.

"Ooh. I don't want to go driving in this rain on those narrow roads we took to get here," Sybil moaned standing up also, "But I don't want to stay here with a dead body upstairs, either."

"Should we take my van or your mother's Mercedes?" I asked logically.

"Probably your van," Tom decided as the three of us moved to leave the room.

"Y'all won't have to make that trip to the police station," a by now familiar voice reached us from the upstairs hall. There, in the doorway, looking as ethereal and ladylike as ever but with gun drawn and pointed at us, stood Miss Millie Plushmill. "Y'all won't be going anywhere."

Chapter Thirty-one

"Miss Millie!" Sybil and I cried out at the same time.

"We thought you'd gone. What are you doing here?" I asked in great agitation.

"I think y'all better just sit down, right now," Miss Millie instructed us in a very cool voice, motioning at us with the gun she held in her right hand.

"Just what the hell are y'all doin' in my house?" Tom's face grew red and the cords in his neck began to stick out as he stared at her.

"I said sit!" Miss Millie bellowed in a very unladylike voice, sounding nothing like the way she had when she'd spoken to us before.

Sybil and I sat down immediately. Tom took a seat with great reluctance.

"Why can't the two of y'all stay out of my business?" the small lady with spun sugar hair hissed at Sybil and me. "Everytime I turn around there y'all are."

"B-but Miss Millie," I attempted to appease her, "we didn't

know what was going on. We didn't mean to barge in here and find Larry's body."

"Or your husband's," Sybil added.

The displeasure on Miss Millie's face intensified as she heard Sybil's words.

"Y'all found Barton?"

"He's right where you left him, I assume," Tom addressed her harshly, "And you can drop the southern accent, Millie. Miz Davis heard you talking with Russ and Bart, last night and she says you can speak Yankee as well as she does."

Millie Plushmill's face grew as red with anger as Tom's had been a few minutes before. "Don't you throw it up to me that I don't belong at Azalea Hall, or I'll make you wish you hadn't. I'll make all of you so sorry!"

The three of us who were seated looked quickly at each other in great puzzlement.

"What are y'all talking about?" Tom demanded.

"Oh, I know what all the girls are saying about me. Just because my father's the gardener, and I don't wear cashmere twin-sets and pearls to class, and I don't go off in red sports cars with boys from the Citadel or Pender Academy, you all think I'm trash. Well, I'll show you!

I may be from Peoria and dirt poor but someday I'm going to have more money than all of you put together. Right now I'm already smarter than any of you. I'll get even. You'll see. No one is ever going to make fun of Mildred Breakbone again!"

By now Miss Millie was brandishing her gun so wildly that Sybil and I yelped with fear every time it was pointed at us. A mad woman was confronting us, and I was sure that she'd shoot all of us at any time.

"Who the devil is Mildred Breakbone?" Tom demanded. He wasn't calm but he was certainly more in control of his demeanor than Sybil and I were of ours. "I thought y'all were Millicent Plushmill."

"Don't play games with me, little rich boy. I'm Mildred

Breakbone, and well you know it. You and all the other rich boys who think they can get into my pants just because I'm a scholarship student, here, at Azalea Hall, are going to learn real fast who's in control.

I spread my legs for all of you so I can blackmail you into taking me places I want to go. That's all right for now but someday I'll be where I want to be and that's when you'll all pay. All of you! When Mildred Breakbone becomes Millicent Bradley, you'll see!"

"What about y'all's husband? What about Col. Plushmill?" Tom was egging her on while Sybil and I hugged each other as close as we could, shaking with fear.

"Barton Plushmill? He's a Mama's Boy, just like the rest of you southern dandies. I can get him to do anything I want him to. He got rid of his first wife, didn't he? She didn't last long once he met me, and I introduced him to my friends. It's amazing what seeing how much money a good ole boy can make running drugs can persuade him to do."

"Is that what Larry O'Brian did? Become y'all's friend so he could run drugs and make money?" Tom continued.

"You bet your southern-fried ass!" Miss Millie leaned against the doorframe as she began to smile. "Larry and I hit it off as soon as we met. One con-artist can spot another a mile away. The only problem with Larry was he was stupid. He'd done the drug scene before, when he lived up north, but he didn't know how to make the big bucks.

Like Bart, he'd do anything for money but he didn't know squat about keeping his mouth shut or handling that mealy-mouthed, bead-rattling wife of his. It was a happy day for Bart and me when she was out of the picture. Your Mama's a real drag, Honey. In case you didn't know it."

Tom made a move to get out of his chair. I thought for a second that he was going to hit Millie Plushmill.

"Easy, Mama's boy," she stuck the gun near his ribs. "It was real easy to kill Larry and not that hard to shoot Bart. I wouldn't mind at all sending you along with them."

"B-but why?" I found my voice, trying to distract her, now that Tom was in trouble.

"Why what?" Miss Millie spoke to me without taking her eyes off Tom.

"Why did you kill Larry and Plushy?"

"Plushy. What a ridiculous name! How he liked to pretend that he'd really been somebody when he was at the Citadel. All that old-boy military talk. He barely graduated and never made a dime off the connections he claimed he made there.

Do you know what most Citadel graduates are doing today? They're selling insurance, or used cars. Bart wasn't doing much better. That is until he met me. Millie Bradley, the gay divorcee with a hefty settlement and connections of my own." She preened as she spoke, pushing back a lock of her frothy hair and running her hand over the jacket of the purple velour running suit she wore.

"So he was a disappointment to you. Why kill him?" Sybil had stopped shaking and entered the fact-finding conversation that Tom and I were having with Miss Millie.

"For the same reason I had to 'off' Larry O'Brian. Bart began to think he was smarter than I was. He wanted to be in charge. When Larry tried to cheat me by hogging a drug drop I had to shoot him.

It's your fault that I killed him before he told me where he hid it. He would have told me but you two showed up at just the wrong time. I had to get out of there quick. Thinking back on it, now that I had to kill Bart too, I should just have stuck around and shot both of you then."

"You, you were here when we found Larry?" I gasped.

"Nah. Bart called me from our house and told me you two were coming. I got out through the garage before you found your dearly-departed ex-husband."

"So you're the one who answered the phone we heard ringing," Sybil mused.

"And the one we heard closing the door," I added.

"Bright ladies," Millie laughed. "I always said a Yankee had twice the smarts of any Rebel. And give me a woman, anytime. We're much smarter than the stronger but dumber sex." She leered at Tom.

"What about Russ Guthrie?" Tom responded to her taunting. "How does Russ fit into the picture?"

"Ah, yes. The not-as-respectable-as-he-seems-to-be police lieutenant. The I'm-from-a-good-old-Charleston-family, mama's boy, Russell Guthrie. He's in this, with us, up to his eyebrows. Even though he can be awfully squeamish for a cop. He loves easy money as much as the next guy, family connections or not. What about him?"

"Where is he now?" Tom continued.

"He has to keep up his credibility as a cop or he wouldn't be any use to us. He's out taking care of the fools who didn't make it to high ground before Marcus hit, or some such police work. He should be along any time, now." Millie motioned toward the window. "He should be here real soon, now that the rain's letting up."

She turned her attention back to us. "I may as well take care of the three of you before Russell comes back. Like I said. He can be awfully squeamish at times. His old family values might make it hard for him to shoot women or someone he's known all his life, like you, Tom."

I gasped and I could feel Sybil shudder as Millie spoke.

"On your feet ladies and gentleman!" The small woman who only hours before had convinced us that she was our friend and a southern lady-of-the-old-school ordered. "Get ready to meet your maker, if you believe in that nonsense."

Chapter Thirty-two

The three of us had no choice but to move single file out of the upstairs sitting room into the hall. As soon as we could, Sybil and I paired up and held on to each other for comfort and support. Tom was behind us, and Miss Millie brought up the rear.

"No sudden moves, now," our captor warned us as she herded us toward the door to the stairs leading to the third floor. "I'm a crack shot. My daddy taught me all about guns and how to use them. I've never missed a target in my life, not even a moving one."

"You plan to take us upstairs and shoot us like you did Bart?" Tom's voice sounded very calm as he asked the question. Sybil and I were shaking so hard we found it hard to walk.

"He and I were up there, searching for the drop, and he gave me a hard time. I don't like a mouthy man," was Millie Plushmill's answer. "Now open the door, ladies."

Sybil put out a shaking hand to turn the knob. I was so petrified with fear I couldn't have moved my hand for a million dollars.

"It's pitch dark up there, you know," Tom reminded the little woman with the gun.

"You have a flashlight, unless that bulge in your pocket just means you're glad to see me," she shot back at him, bawdily. "Move your ass up front, turn it on, and open the damned door!"

Tom slowly followed her directions, and then she continued, "Up we go, my pretties, and no funny business. I'd just as soon shoot you on the stairs as up there."

I had fainted the day before, after we'd found Larry's body, and I could feel the same numbness and sensation of darkness beginning to creep over me again.

"I, I think I'm going to pass out," I gasped as I clung to Sybil.

"All the easier to shoot you, my dear," Miss Millie cackled, paraphrasing the wolf in "Little Red Riding Hood."

"Go ahead. Be my guest."

"Get hold of yourself, "Sybil shook me none too gently and, still clinging to my friend, I meekly followed her up the gloomy stairs behind Tom, who had turned on the flashlight and was leading the way. I could feel Miss Millie's warm breath on the back of my neck and the end of her gun barrel in my back as she prompted me to move faster.

When we reached the top of the stairs Tom shone the flashlight beam into the center of the room illuminating Barton Plushmill's remains. Sybil and I both cringed. I turned my head away; unable to look at Plushy lying in the dark pool of his own blood, but Miss Millie laughed again.

"Isn't he the perfect booby?" she crowed. "Thought he was going to take over the operation, become the brains of the outfit. Look at him now. Some big military man he turned out to be. Colonel Dead-on-the-Floor. That's Bart."

Millie's demented laughter echoing in the close darkness of the room removed any doubts Tom, Sybil, and I might have had concerning the state of her mind. I was wondering how long

Millie Plushmill had been insane, and I knew that my two friends must have been thinking the same thing.

"Okay," she began to give us further instructions. "Over to the outside door. The three of you are going to walk right off that little porch out there with some help from the hot lead in your backs."

"Oh, Miss Millie," I pleaded. "Please don't! We'll go away and never come back. We won't ever tell a living soul what went on here. Please, please don't kill us!"

"Oh, shut up, you sniveling coward," she answered me. "Tom, open that door. Both doors. The screen door, too."

Tom moved forward but he didn't open the door. The feeble beam of his flashlight went out suddenly as he turned and yelled to us in the dark, "Jump to the side, ladies!"

And then, in the pitch dark, I threw myself to the floor, away from Plushy's body. I could see the flashes and hear the reports of gunshots. Someone, Miss Millie, I assumed, kept firing into the dark even though there was no way she could have seen her targets. Close by me, someone cried out in pain and before I could call out Tom or Sybil's names, to see if either of them had been hurt, to my amazement my eyes were dazzled by a number of brilliant lights. They banished the thick darkness and made the little room as bright as day.

Chapter thirty-three

There was scuffling and confusion as three policemen, led by Russ Guthrie, squeezed themselves into the small space of the third floor room. All of them held heavy-duty, battery-powered lanterns and had their guns drawn. Lying in a corner, I covered my head with my arms, expecting that at any moment the Lieutenant would begin shooting at us. Finishing off what his partner-in-crime Millie Plushmill had started.

When that didn't happen immediately, I raised my head. I couldn't believe my eyes! Col. Plushmill's wife lay on the floor beside him, moaning loudly. Blood was quickly covering the shoulder of her purple velour jacket. I couldn't tell whether it was her own or her husband's.

"Russ! What are y'all doing here?" Tom, who'd been squatting near the bloody couple on the floor, asked in amazement as he rose to his feet.

"What every good under-cover cop does," Russ Guthrie grinned at his boyhood friend. "Taking a criminal into custody."

It was then that I noticed that the policemen, who had holstered their guns and were lifting Millie Plushmill to her feet, were not any of the ones who had been at the scene of Larry's death. They wore different uniforms and seemed much more professional in their movements. I got the feeling that they were not from the local constabulary.

"Take her in and book her. Then send the M.E. back here with the van from the morgue. I'll be right down to the station to complete the paperwork we've got going on her," Russ called over the officers' shoulders.

Millie, although wounded, was screaming and screeching at the top of her lungs, "What the hell do you think you're doing, Russell Guthrie? Take your hands off me, all of you! I'll have you know that you're dealing with the first Queen Mother of the Hollywood Red Hat Society. How dare you treat a lady this way? I'm going to make you so sorry. Sorry you were ever born. All of you!"

Never mind that she was grasped tightly in the custody of the officers who were now moving her down the steps. We could still hear her threats ringing in our ears for several minutes before she exited the house.

Sybil came crawling out of the corner of the room directly opposite mine.

"Are you really an under-cover cop? Are you really not one of the drug ring?" she asked shakily.

"Yes, Ma'am," Russ Guthrie raised her to her feet, took her arm, and led her toward the stairs, as Tom helped me up and guided me around Plushy's body. To my surprise, I was too dazed and amazed by what had happened to feel even the least bit faint.

When we'd reached the second-floor hall Lt. Guthrie turned to us and said very apologetically, "Ladies, I'm afraid, this time y'all're going to have to come down to the station. Y'all, too, Tom. I'm wrapping up a case that has been ongoing for two years and I need y'all's statements. Then, ladies, I'd like to take y'all into Charleston and have y'all meet my mama. She's a Red Hat Society Lady, like y'all, and I know she'd love to meet y'all and make y'all welcome to our fair city."

"It was all an act, then?" I asked Russ Guthrie, reaching out to grasp his forearm in an effort to reassure myself. "You weren't serious when you accused me of killing my ex-husband?"

"Yes Ma'am, it was an act, and, no Ma'am, I did not think for a minute that you murdered Larry O'Brian. I knew it had to be one of the Plushmills who killed him. Probably Millie. She's always been the ringleader. I've been working under cover as a member of their drug ring for two years, now. In cooperation with the FBI"

"Well, I'll be double dogged damned," Tom said softly, a grin creeping across his face. "You sly devil, you."

"And another thing, Miss Curtis," Russ spoke to Sybil.

"Call me Sybil," she smiled at him, "Or, better yet, call me Miss Sybil."

"What ever y'all prefer," he grinned. "I sure hope I didn't bang y'all's head too badly when I laid y'all on the back seat of Miz Davis's van."

"You!" Sybil and I exclaimed, practically in chorus.

"Yes, Ma'am," he addressed my friend. "I came back for both y'all, once I knew Bart and Millie were out of the way. They told me they were going to palaver with the guys who were expecting us to turn over the drop to them, but I didn't trust what they planned to do with y'all once y'all woke up.

Imagine my surprise, Miz Davis," he turned to me, "When Miss Sybil was the only one I could find. I didn't have the faintest idea where y'all had disappeared to, and I figured I didn't have but only a few minutes to get anyone safely out of the house.

So I grabbed Miss Sybil and the keys from your purse, Miz Davis, and," he continued, turning to Sybby, "Carried y'all through the rain to the van. I had y'all wrapped in a bed cover, and I made a second trip with both y'all's luggage, but I didn't have time to search for Miz Davis. I was mortally afraid that I hit y'all's head on the van door when I shoved y'all in."

"I'm fine," Sybil smiled at him. "And ever so grateful that you saved me from the Plushmills and stashed me safely in the van. Now, if a certain person had been patient and had stayed loyally with her friend you could have saved both of us, and one of us could have avoided almost drowning." She gave me an arched look as she spoke.

The four of us laughed heartily in response to her criticism. It felt wonderful to release the tension of the last half-hour in peals of laughter.

"But then," Tom spoke up, his eyes shining as he looked at me. "Sukie and I would never have gotten to know each other as well as we have. I'd fish y'all out of the boathouse again, anytime, Ma'am."

"That's true," I admitted raising my eyes to his, "And, after all we've been through, I think you can start calling me Miss Sukie now, Tom." Then, turning to Russ Guthrie and revisiting one of the immediate problems still facing us, I asked, "Is the power on anywhere? Is there any way I can call my husband or we can call our friends?"

"The best way of finding that answer is by getting out of here and going down to the station," Russ Guthrie smiled at Sybil and me and held out his arm as if to usher us down the hall. "Ladies?"

Chapter Thirty-four

Susan Fairchild Guthrie, Queen Mother of the Greater Charleston Red Hat Society, was the loveliest, most charming lady of the Old South that I have ever met or, probably, will ever hope to meet. Unlike the false, stereotypical Miss Millie Plushmill, who'd been all candy floss hair and fluttering, ruffled peignoir, Mrs. Guthrie was in her early sixties, had wavy gray hair, with a hint of the auburn it had once been, and the biggest, bluest eyes I'd ever seen. Dressed in sage green linen slacks and a blouse that matched, she came down the front porch steps of the Guthrie family home on Radcliffe Street to greet us with both of her arms spread wide.

"Ladies, y'all come right on in. Tom, Honey, it's been too long since we've seen y'all," she greeted us as if she'd known Sybil and me all her life. Turning to her son, who was escorting us up the walk, she never skipped a beat as she instructed, "Russell, darlin', seein' y'all just warms my heart. Come give your mama a kiss."

Blushing, Lt. Guthrie complied.

It was late in the afternoon and the rain had stopped. The sky had lightened to the point that Charlestonians might hope to see a ray of sun before evening fell. Hurricane Marcus had definitely moved off shore and up the South Carolina coast.

Earlier, Sybil, Tom, and I had given our depositions to the police and FBI agents at the Hollywood Police Station. After that Lt. Guthrie had called his mother on a broadband radio to alert her to our arrival and driven Sybil and me to his parents' house in an unmarked car, with Tom following us in my van.

We hadn't seen Millie Plushmill at the station, although we'd heard her voice echoing from another part of the building. She appeared to be a lady who had much to say about her incarceration. To our disappointment the regular telephones at the Hollywood Police Station were still not working so we would have to continue waiting to talk with our loved ones.

"I'd love to stop a while, Miss Susan," Tom smiled and kissed her cheek, also, "But my sisters and Joe don't know yet what's happened, and I'm plumb tuckered out. I've been up all night."

"All right, darlin'," Susan Guthrie acquiesced. "Y'all go on home to bed. Y'all do look like y'all're all in. But come back and see us soon, hear?"

"Yes, Ma'am," Tom nodded his head. "Russ, can you carry me over to Concord Street to my apartment? I'll have to go back to The Plantation to get my mama's car tomorrow."

"I'll be right back, Mama," Russ and Tom headed back down the walk toward the police car.

"Wait, Tom. Oh, wait," I called after them and quickly ran to where they'd stopped in the middle of the brick walkway. Throwing my arms around Tom's neck I hugged him hard. My throat was thick with tears. "If I'd ever had a son I wish he'd been just like you," I whispered in his ear. "Your mother can be very proud of you. I'm sure she always has been, and I'll pray for her just as hard as I can."

"I thank y'all for that, and I'll surely miss y'all, Miss Sukie," he whispered back then held me by my shoulders, at arm's length, and looked deeply into my eyes. "I don't guess I'll ever meet a Yankee lady like y'all again."

"Let's hope not! At least not under the same circumstances," I gave a little laugh to cover the strong emotion that I felt, and then I begged, "Please stay in touch with me. I'd like my daughters to meet you, someday."

"That I will do," he smiled. "I'd like my sisters and brother to meet all of y'all, too."

With an extra pat and a hug we parted before I could shed any tears, and I joined Sybil and Mrs. Guthrie on the porch.

"I'm just going to make a few phone calls to some Red Hat Ladies who are special friends of mine who I'd like y'all to meet," she told us as we entered the house. "Thank goodness only part of Charleston lost phone service and only for a few hours. And, lucky for us, it never affected this neighborhood. The only problem is we can't call long-distance, yet. The local circuits are all busy. Why don't y'all freshen up while we wait for them to come on over? I've given you the guest room at he back of the upstairs hall."

As we made out way through the warm and welcoming home we'd just entered, Sybil and I could hear Susan Guthrie's soft voice behind us speaking into the phone, "Emmy Lee? It's Susan. Honey, I sure would appreciate it if y'all could come over here right away. And bring Sissy and Anita-Claire with y'all. We've got a bit of a Red Hat Society emergency…"

"Sounds like something one of us would say to the rest of our Red Hats, only without the southern drawl," Sybil murmured in my ear. "I guess Red Hat societies aren't very different no matter what part of the country they're in."

"Hm-m-m. I think you're right," I answered, a wisp of an idea beginning to form in the back of my mind. "I hope we can use the Guthries' telephone to call home soon. My cell phone's dead as a doornail."

Sybil and I retired to the guest bedroom Susan Guthrie had kindly designated as ours for the duration of our stay. Like the rest of the house, it was filled with graceful antique furniture, and we badly needed to use it and the adjoining bathroom to bathe and change our grubby clothes. I was still wearing Martie O'Brian's ill-fitting terry cloth running pants and although Sybil had changed from Tom's mother's bathrobe at the police station she'd put on the clothes she'd worn the day before.

I would gladly have collapsed onto the antique four poster bed and taken a long nap but my friend and Red Hat sister wanted to talk. Russ had delivered our luggage and we couldn't wait to change our clothes.

"I'm glad that Millie Plushmill is in jail awaiting arraignment. Just thinking how we blindly trusted her and what she had planned for us makes my blood run cold," Sybil announced as she plopped herself down on the bed after indulging in a sponge bath and changing into the last clean outfit she'd brought with her.

"It's disappointing that neither Russ, nor the police, nor the FBI could find the drugs Larry hid," I answered her sleepily. Bathing and changing my clothes had sapped what little energy I'd had left.

"Do you know what I think?" Sybil asked excitedly and continued before I could answer her. "I think Millie and Bart found the drugs and fought over them, and that's why Millie killed him. I think she's faking insanity and she probably stashed them somewhere while we were in the attic finding Bart's body."

Borrowing Rhett Butler's famous line from the most famous movie ever made about the South I answered sleepily, "Frankly, my dear, I don't give a damn!" I'd had enough of my ex-husband, his friends the Plushmills, and the drug trafficking they'd all done to last my entire life, however long that might be.

Later we went downstairs where Susan Guthrie's friends arrived and hugged us, murmuring how delighted they were to meet two Red Hat Society members from the North. We all sat drinking reviving cups of tea and nibbling on cheese straws and bourbon balls, which our hostess assured us she always kept on hand for just such emergencies as our unexpected arrival.

I'd given Susan the jars of preserves that I'd purchased at Mrs. Taylor's Restaurant in Virginia as soon as we'd arrived at the Guthrie home. They were the only articles that Sybil and I had with us that in my estimation could pass as a hostess gift. Susan had thanked us and assured us that we'd sample them at breakfast the following day. With any luck Sybil and I would be able to stop at the restaurant on our trip home and pick up a new supply of Mrs. Taylor's goodies, as well as enjoy a home cooked meal.

Within a few short minutes all five of us Red Hat Society Ladies were on a first name basis with each other. Susan explained how Sybil and I had come to be her guests and that my husband worked for a Pennsylvania power company. She went on to explain that we two Northern Red Hat Ladies hadn't spoken to our families in two days and that they must be worried sick about us.

"The reason I wanted y'all to meet Anita-Claire, Sukie," Susan spoke, putting down her cup, "Is because her husband is the president of our Charleston Power and Light Company. If anyone can reach your darlin' Bud for you I'm sure Tyrone Kincaid can. What do you think, Anita-Claire? Can y'all get hold of Ty and explain our situation, here?"

"Sweetheart! Of course," Anita Claire Kincaid, a still-lovely blonde who must surely have been Miss South Carolina at some point earlier in her life, whipped her cell phone out of her Coach bag and dialed quickly as it lighted up.

"Annette? Can y'all put me through to Mr. Kincaid, Honey? I know he's busier than a long-tailed cat in a room full of rockin' chairs but just tell him it's his wife, and I have an emergency."

I sat in total amazement. I would never be able to reach Bud and enlist his help for a situation that wasn't truly a major emergency. But, then, Bud wasn't the president of his power company, either.

Tyrone Kincaid must have been one very loving, caring man, or at least one who adored his wife. Smack dab in the middle of all the wind damage Hurricane Marcus had caused in the Charleston area Mr. Kincaid put through an emergency call to Bud at PPL.

"Your husband should call back here, for y'all, as soon as he can be located, Sukie," Anita-Claire smiled at me beatifically.

"It's so kind of you and your husband to do this for me. I'm overwhelmed. I don't know what to say," I responded, close to tears. "You ladies must have a very special Red Hat Society to show such kindness to total strangers."

"There are over a hundred of us in the Greater Charleston Chapter, and I wouldn't give up even one of our members," Sissy smiled broadly. "I can't tell you how satisfying it is to catch up on everyone's gossip and be there for each other in good and bad times. It's like having a second family."

"And when we say the ritual," Emmy Lee rhapsodized, "It just gives me goose bumps!"

"We don't say a ritual," I admitted softly. "Our club isn't registered."

"It isn't registered!" Emmy Lee gasped. "Why ever not?"

"There's nothing we wouldn't do for a Red Hat Society Sister," Anita-Claire told me very seriously. "It's like being in a sorority in college. Helping each other is a solemn duty, and one we are so glad to carry out. If y'all were you in a Greek organization when y'all were at school y'all know what I mean."

"Oh, yes," I replied, shaking my head in the affirmative. "I was a Pi Beta Phi at Bucknell University and have kept in close contact with several of my sorority sisters for years."

"I was a Delta Gamma at Penn State," Sybil put in hastily.

"After we left Azalea Hall all of us were Chi Omegas at Ole Miss," Susan added. "Now that we've joined our Red Hat Society we're double sisters." Susan, Sissy, Emmy Lee and Anita-Claire all took each other's hands and squeezed them in friendship and sisterhood.

"My daughter Maggie is a Chi Omega," I told the ladies before me. "She went to Penn State, and there's a Chi Omega chapter at Bucknell, too."

Susan laughed, "Chi Omega was started in Arkansas, which considers itself to be a southern state. Sounds like our good old southern sorority has invaded the North!"

"And there's lots of Pi Phi chapters in the South," Emmy Lee smiled at me. "I know that it started in Illinois but two of our members, Suellen McClellen and Nancigale Warren, were Pi Phi's at William and Mary. It is very strong chapter there."

"You didn't happen to be at Azalea Hall when Millie Plushmill was there? Did you?" Sybil asked, changing the subject. "I'd never heard of the school until she started ranting and raving about it this afternoon."

"Azalea Hall is the oldest, most prestigious private girls' school in Charleston," Susan told us. "All of the daughters of good old Charleston families go there. I know Tom's sisters Bitsy, Bella and Mandy did, as my daughter Charlotte did, too. However, none of us were there when Millie was. She's a tad bit older than we are. But her reputation lingered on long after she left the school."

"My older sister Madge was a freshman at The Hall when Millie was a senior," Emmy Lee commented. "She said all anyone ever talked about was Millie's wild behavior. Her name was Mildred Breakbone than. I guess she changed Mildred to Millicent after she left school."

"She married a man named Bradley from out of town and just sort of disappeared from Charleston for many years," Susan picked up the story. "Her father was the gardener at Azalea Hall, y'all know. He seemed to be a very nice man, and he knew God-All about raisin' flowers."

"Just not about raisin' daughters," Sissy spoke in a wry voice. "Course her mother runnin' off when Millie was so young probably left a mark on her. I know it would have on me if I'd been in her position."

"Yes. And it would have been hard to be a scholarship girl at The Hall," Anita-Claire agreed. "She was real active in the

Hollywood Red Hat Society. Friends of mine there tell me she had real good ideas. Makes y'all wonder how she could be so bad and do good at the same time."

The arrival of Russell Guthrie, Sr. and his son Russell Guthrie, Jr. ended our discussion of Millie Plushmill's past. Our new friends and Red Hat Society sisters rose to leave in a flurry of welcoming hugs and kisses for the men and farewell hugs and kisses for Susan, Sybil and me. At the same time our hostess attempted to introduce her husband to his new guests. The mood was quite party-like.

"Let us know if there is anything else we can do to help y'all," Anita-Claire called back merrily as they left.

Once the ladies' silvery laughter had died away Susan Guthrie's husband turned to those of us who remained and spoke in a very subdued voice, "Sad news, ladies. Russ and I have just heard that Martie Mayhew has passed."

Chapter Thirty-five

It seemed that none of Martha Ryan Mayhew O'Brian's friends ever referred to her as Martie O'Brian. I learned very quickly that, to them, she would always be Tom Mayhew, Sr.'s wife. Larry O'Brian had been a crass Yankee bounder whose name didn't deserve to be linked with hers. I understood this sentiment perfectly. I didn't particularly want Larry linked to me or to any of my family either.

I was surprised at how much sadness I felt upon learning of Martha's death. After all, I'd never met her. I had resented her for giving Larry a life-style that I felt he didn't deserve. And I had certainly been angry with her for encouraging my ex-husband to annul our Catholic marriage, dredge up hurtful memories from the past, and challenge my daughters' legitimacy. It had been only after I'd gotten to know her son and heard from him the true story of her relationship with Larry that I began to feel both empathy and sympathy for her.

A somber mood pervaded the Guthrie house for the remainder of the evening. As soon as she'd shed a few tears and wiped them away, Susan made calls to friends and family. She contacted Tom to offer her assistance in making arrangements for his mother's funeral and a reception afterwards. Then she put together a quick cold supper for all of us, allowing Sybil and me to help her only to a minimal extent. After dinner Russ, Jr. left the house.

"I think I'll just stop by and check on Tom before I go back to the station," he explained. "Sleep well, ladies. I'll see y'all tomorrow."

Sybil and I offered to go to a motel for the night and were gently rebuffed by our host and hostess, "Don't be silly." Susan chided us. "Every motel room in Charleston is probably filled with people who had to flee their homes in the risin' water. And, besides, y'all are Red Hat Society Sisters! There's no question about it. Y'all are stayin' right here for as long as y'all need to. The guest room is already made up, and it's y'all's for as long as y'all need it."

Russ Guthrie, Sr. nodded his head in agreement and the decision was made. And so, while everyone else made his or her way to bed, I settled down in the parlor, next to the telephone, in the hope of hearing from Bud.

"I sure hope he calls tonight, Sukie," Sybby hugged me before she climbed the stairs. "I'd stay up with you but I can't keep my eyes open. I wonder, though, how many chickens it will take you, this time, to crawl back into his good graces?"

I knew she was joking, but, to tell the truth, I felt a terrible amount of guilt and was a bit worried about explaining the situation to Bud, when and if he called. I must have dozed as I snuggled down into a comfortable armchair, with only the light from one lamp illuminating the darkness of the room, because the next thing I knew a bell was ringing loudly in my ear. Not knowing where I was, I reached out groggily to turn off what I thought, in my sleep-dazed condition, was an alarm clock going off.

I managed to knock the telephone to the floor with a great

clatter and had to scramble to retrieve it.

"Hello? Hello?" I gasped into the receiver.

"Sukie, is that you?" Bud's worried voice sounded a long way off. "Where the hell are you? I've been going crazy not hearing from you. I got a call from headquarters saying the president of the Charleston Power and Light Company wanted me to call this number. Are you all right? I thought you were in Virginia."

"Oh, Bud," I burst into tears at the welcome sound of his voice. It didn't matter in the least whether he was angry with me or not. "I'm so sorry I worried you. So very sorry," and I began to bring him up to date on where I was and what I had done.

Bud had spent the last two days in his power company's systems room, sending out trouble trucks and crews to at least four states south of the Mason/Dixon Line. When he first heard the saga I had to tell he was incredulous and intensely angry. Not having had any contact from me in nearly three days and having worked around the clock, he was both tired and frustrated. However, once he'd calmed down, we both agreed that Sybil and I should wait until the roads north of South Carolina were safe and passable before we attempted to drive home.

I told him, over and over, how much I loved him. I promised to prepare chicken dinners for him every day once I was back in Martin's Field.

By the end of our conversation both of us were laughing, and he promised to call Sally, Jaye and Harriet to tell them that the two missing members of the Red Hats were safe. When I hung up the phone I felt happier and calmer than I had since I'd left home. As I climbed the stairs to the bedroom I was to share with Sybil there was a serene smile on my face. I did so love my husband!

I insisted to Sybil that she and I stay in Charleston for Martha Mayhew O'Brian's very Catholic funeral and requiem mass. It seemed to be the least that I could do for Tom, under the circumstances. It was, without a doubt, the last thing that I could do for him and his family.

I felt a faint stirring of wonder that I could so desire to attend a service that honored his mother; a woman who I had come south prepared to hate. Maybe it was because Martie and I had both seen something good and promising early on in our relationships with Larry O'Brian. Watched those attributes fade during our marriages to him and be replaced by betrayal. Whatever the reason, somehow, attending her funeral brought me the feeling of closure that I'd thought to find in my planned but never executed confrontation with Larry.

The Hollywood Police had contacted Charlie O'Brian, Larry's attorney brother in Philadelphia, concerning Larry's death. His instructions to them had been to send Larry's body north for burial. I wondered who would attend that funeral. Neither his family nor any of his old friends harbored kind thoughts of Larry. It would be a bleak, lonely occasion but, thank God, I would not have to worry about being there.

Sybil and I had one major problem when it came time to prepare for Martie's funeral. We hadn't brought any suitable clothes with us to Charleston. We'd packed only jeans, slacks and shirts. The sort of clothes one always packs when planning to break into one's ex-husband's gated community!

Susan Guthrie pressed another of her Red Hat Society Sisters Angelique Fontaine, who she declared was just my size, into lending me some very stylish dark clothes for the solemn event. Slender Sybil looked haute couture in a black crepe dress donated to the cause by Anita-Claire.

It was a bright, sunny day, three days after Hurricane Marcus had passed by Charleston, when Martie was laid to rest in the Mayhew family plot. The church was filled to overflowing with mourners, only some of whom Sybil and I recognized. It seemed that half of the graceful South Carolina seaport's citizens had come to wish Larry's fourth wife a fond farewell.

Bouquet upon bouquet of flowers were in evidence throughout the narthex and surrounding the altar. Tom and a group of men and women, some young some older, who I assumed were his family members, dressed in black, sat as still as statues in the front row.

"Don't you feel a little strange attending the funeral of your first husband's fourth wife?" Sybil whispered to me as we took our places in a pew at the back of the church.

"No. I feel very good about it," I informed her. "I just wish Jaye and Harriet and Sally were here to see all these old southern family members gathered in one place. It isn't often we travel in old-moneyed, refined society."

"Try never. At least not at home."

A reception for family and close friends was held at the Guthrie home, following the service. Tom introduced us to his sisters and brother, who were numb in their grief but nodded politely.

Since Martie had remained a member of the Greater Charleston Red Hat Society even after her move to Palmetto Crown Plantation, a huge number of Charleston Red Hat Society members were present to pay their respects and greeted us enthusiastically. As we spoke with them, the wisp of an idea that had begun in the back of my mind a few days before grew into one that was full-blown.

The next day, after wishing the Guthries, Emmy Lee, Sissy and Anita-Claire Kincaid a fond farewell, Sybil and I were driving through North Carolina on our way home. Taking a deep breath, I turned to her and put into words the idea that felt more right to me with every passing day, "Sybby, when we get home. After we've had a nice long lunch with the Red Hats at The Victorian Lady. Do you know what I think we should do?"

"Sleep for two days solid and then have a long lunch with the girls at the Victorian Lady?" she asked.

"No. I think we should call Helen Oberheim and Dottie Swank and see about the possibility of merging our Red Hat Society with theirs. After what you and I have been through and meeting Susan Guthrie and her friends, I think the five of us Red

Hats could use as many sisters as we can get."

I can't repeat the epithet this announcement elicited from my friend but, in the end, that's just exactly what she, Jaye, Harriet, Sally, and I did. For better or worse, the Red Hats joined the Martin's Field Red Hat Society. Helen Oberheim and Dottie Swank were very kind when I approached them about our desire to do so. So far, it has proved to be a most satisfying merger for everyone.

Once Sybil and I were safely home, my husband Bud proved that he is the most wonderful man in the entire world, something I've always known. It only cost me a token amount of roast chicken dinners and the promise to never do "anything so damned stupid again" to put a smile back on his face and find myself tucked safely into his arms. It didn't hurt, either, that Penn State beat Ohio State in their grudge match football game the following weekend.

To add to my happiness, over the next three years, Tom Mayhew and I stayed current with the events in each other's lives through letters, e-mail, and the occasional phone call. Our relationship became so relaxed and comfortable that I began to feel he was one of my daughters' cousins. Almost a son.

Our entire families have only met quite recently, however. It was at Tom's lovely wedding, which was held this spring at Charleston's historic St. Mary's Church, established in 1789. Although the animosity that I'd felt toward the Catholic Church, because of its collusion in Larry's attempt to annul our marriage, has lessened over the years imagine the irony I felt on my way to the wedding when I was informed that St. Mary's was the Mother Church of the Catholic Diocese of the Carolinas and Georgia! Never mind. What's in the past is finally in the past.

When we all met, the Mayhews and the Davises got on *like a house afire* as Susan Fairchild Guthrie pointed out during Tom and his bride Amy's reception, held after the wedding at the Mill House Hotel on Meeting Street. This was so true. The Red Hats and I have learned that life has a funny way of bringing together people who turn out to be kindred spirits.

Printed in the United States
48714LVS00004BA/142-189

9 781413 788679